75

Death of a
Voodoo Doll

MARGOT ARNOLD

Death of a Voodoo Doll

A Penny Spring and Sir Toby Glendower Mystery

Foul Play Press

The Countryman Press
Woodstock, Vermont

Copyright © 1982 by Petronelle Cook

This edition is published in 1989 by Foul Play Press, an imprint
of The Countryman Press, Inc., Woodstock, Vermont 05091.

ISBN 0-88150-132-8

Printed in the United States of America

To Nathaniel Peter Sheldon Cook
With All My Love

WHO'S WHO

GLENDOWER, TOBIAS MERLIN, archaeologist, F.B.A., F.S.A., K.B.E.; b. Swansea, Wales, Dec. 27, 1926; s. Thomas Owen and Myfanwy (Williams) G.; ed. Winchester Coll.; Magdalen Coll., Oxford, B.A., M.A., Ph.D.; fellow Magdalen Coll., 1949-; prof. Near Eastern and European Prehistoric Archaeology Oxford U., 1964-; created Knight, 1977. Participated in more than 30 major archaeological expeditions. Author publications, including: What Not to Do in Archaeology, 1960; What to Do in Archaeology, 1970; also numerous excavation and field reports. Clubs: Old Wykehamists, Athenaeum, Wine-tasters, University.

SPRING, PENELOPE ATHENE, anthropologist; b. Cambridge, Mass., May 16, 1928; d. Marcus and Muriel (Snow) Thayer; B.A., M.A., Radcliffe Coll.; Ph.D., Columbia U.; m. Arthur Upton Spring, June 24, 1953 (dec.); 1 son, Alexander Marcus. Lectr. anthropology Oxford U., 1958-68; Mathieson Reader in anthropology Oxford U., 1969-; fellow St. Anne's Coll., Oxford, 1969-. Field work in the Marquesas, East and South Africa, Uzbekistan, India, and among the Pueblo, Apache, Crow and Fox Indians. Author: Sex in the South Pacific, 1957; The Position of Women in Pastoral Societies, 1962; And Must They Die? — A Study of the American Indian, 1965; Caste and Change, 1968; Moslem Women, 1970; Crafts and Culture, 1972; The American Indian in the Twentieth Century, 1974; Hunter vs. Farmer, 1976.

CHAPTER 1

"Crews? Why, I don't know a thing about them! . . . Oh, *krewes*. Well, yes, in a general sort of way. . . . Yes, of course I know about the background of the Mardi Gras, but, John, you don't want an anthropologist for *this* sort of thing!" Penny Spring ran an anxious hand through her already tousled mouse-colored hair, so that it stood up in spikes around her head. Her small, attractively ugly face was screwed up in concentration as she listened to the disembodied voice coming over the Transatlantic phone. When she could get a word in edgeways again, she said, "What you want is a folklorist, preferably a local one. I know a very good man at Tulane. His name is——"

"Will you please shut up, Penny, and *listen* to me!" John Everett at the other end of the phone, in the Boston office of his publishing house, danced from one little round buttock to the other with impatience. "Jules Lefau, the author of this book, is very anxious for you and Toby to come over as his guests prior to the Mardi Gras to look over the final version of the book and *for* the Mardi Gras, over which he is presiding this year as King of Comus. I'll be there, too. You'll have a wonderful time!"

"But, John, I keep telling you, I'm *not* the person you want, and Toby doesn't know beans about this sort of thing. Jules What's-his-name would be spending a lot of money for nothing," she protested.

"Oh, hell, Penny, I didn't want to get into this over the phone, but the issue is not that simple. There have been threats, to the book and to us," John started to explain, when suddenly the phone gave out with a rapid succession of beeps.

Penny heard John give out a very un-Bostonian expletive, and then there was only humming silence as the connection went dead.

She put the phone down and wavered uncertainly. Should she try and call him? No, that would be silly; he'd just be trying to call her, and they'd both get a busy signal. She just would have to wait until he reconnected. "Threats?" she muttered to herself, gazing fixedly at the mute phone. "Over a book about *Mardi Gras*? How absurd!"

There was a vague shuffling and bumping at her door. "Come in!" she called.

More shuffling and bumping, and the door slowly creaked open to reveal in sequence a plume of blue smoke, a rather battered briar pipe, and finally the knoblike, silver-thatched head of Sir Tobias Glendower. He tottered in clasping a huge pile of books and folders in his long arms, his round chin firmly stuck into the outer edge of the pile to keep it from toppling. His round blue eyes behind their equally round glasses sought hers in mute appeal. "Mmph?" he inquired around the stem of the pipe clamped in his small, round mouth.

"Are those for me?" Penny cast a harassed glance around at the overflowing bookcase and the piled-up tables and chairs. "Well, put them down on the floor—there doesn't seem to be anywhere else for them. I'll deal with them later."

Sir Tobias bent down stiffly and deposited his burden on the floor, where half the pile promptly collapsed in hopeless disarray. He straightened up his tall, spindly frame, removed the pipe from his mouth, and announced with modest pride, "A few of your books and reprints I've borrowed and am returning. I'm cleaning up my office."

"Oh, good, good," she muttered absently and continued to stare with rapt attention at the mute phone.

"Hmmph," Toby commented and went out, closing the door carefully behind him. A second later it opened again, and his head reappeared. "Why," he inquired with mild curiosity, "are you contemplating the phone like that?"

"Because I'm expecting a call from John Everett. Maybe you'd better come in and sit down. It concerns you, too." The phone immediately shrilled, causing them both to jump. Toby, his round eyes growing rounder at this apparent psychic feat, cleared a small space for himself in one of the chairs and settled into it as Penny snatched up the phone. "Hello, John, is that you? . . . Yes, we got cut off. You were saying something about threats?" Toby, who had slumped into his usual scholar's slouch, sat up straighter and looked interested.

John's voice was aggrieved as he complained about the inadequacies of Ma Bell's telephone service but then returned to his main theme. "Yes, well, I don't want to say too much. I've sent you all the details in an express packet that should reach you today. I just didn't want it to arrive unheralded. But there have been threats to the book, to Lefau, and to me. Lefau is a very rich and very private man. As I stated, he would like you to come out as his guests for the Mardi Gras. He'd also like you to do a quiet bit of investigating, as well as to cast a critical eye over the book. He'd like you to come about ten days or a week before—say around March first. Mardi Gras is on the eleventh because Easter is so late this year. The book was supposed to come out to coincide with the culmination of Mardi Gras."

"Then, it's been printed already? So what good could I do?" Penny was puzzled. "And, anyway, John, isn't this sort of vanity publishing a bit out of your line?"

"This was a very special job at a very special price." He sounded faintly apologetic. "And that's rather beside the point. When it looked as if there may be something behind these threats, I immediately thought of you and Toby. Lefau also knows your reputation. He is *very* anxious to get you here. If you need a lure for Sir Tobias, you might mention that Lefau has the finest claret cellar in the U.S.A. So how about it?"

"Well, I don't know, John. It's not that easy." Penny was hesitant. "For one thing, it's smack in the middle of the Oxford Hilary term, and I'm teaching. Toby is on a sabbatical, so *he* could come easily enough. He's supposed to be writing a book, but actually he's just fiddling around doing nothing." Sir Tobias looked pained. "But he wouldn't be any good to you on this, and I'd have to get special leave of absence, which may not be possible."

"*Try*, then. Please try. Ten days or so, that's all it would be." His tone was urgent. "I just have this nasty feeling that something is building. You'll understand when you've read the contents of that packet. When you have made up your mind, would you call me here, collect? I really *need* you here.''

"All right, I can do that much," she said reluctantly and with an exasperated sigh cradled the phone. She fixed a worried glare on her unlikely partner in crime, Sir Tobias Glendower, O.M., Professor of Prehistoric Archaeology to the University of Oxford and scholar extraordinary. "Well, this is one for the books!" she gloomed. "Our presence is urgently requested again."

"So I gather," Toby said a mite testily. "Now, do you mind filling me in on what it's all about? Apart from your snide and unwarranted remarks about *me*, I couldn't make head nor tail of your conversation."

Penny settled her plump five-foot-one body back in her chair. "I've never heard John so upset," she declared, "and all on behalf of a book about the Comus krewe and Mardi Gras. It's absurd."

"The Comus crew?" Toby echoed, bewildered in his turn.

"Krewe with a *k*. It's one of those exclusive associations formed by the aristocracy of New Orleans to put everyone else in his place and to display theirs," Penny explained with a hint of acidity. "Most of them were formed *after* the Civil War to keep all the carpetbaggers and rednecks at bay, but Comus is the oldest and most prestigious of the lot and was formed pre–Civil War by the French Creole aristocracy of New Orleans to keep the Anglos out of their charmed little circle. The writer of this book and our putative host, Jules Lefau, is to be King of Comus this year and belongs to one of the oldest and richest of these families."

"King, indeed!" Toby murmured. "Good heavens! So what has this to do with the Mardi Gras?"

"Well, the heads of the various 'krewes,' and there are a lot of them—let's see, I can remember Rex, Mystick, Momus, but there are more than that—organize the entire Mardi Gras festivities. They all have their own processions—each one trying to outdo the other, of course—their own festivities, and their own balls, culminating in their Grand Ball on the night of Mardi Gras, over which the king and queen and the princesses and so on and so forth preside. I believe people would cut their own mothers' throats just to get an invitation to these affairs. They are *that* exclusive."

Toby was puffing up a minor volcanic cloud from his pipe and gazing at her with mesmerized fascination. "How perfectly extraordinary! I never knew Americans went in for that sort of thing. Opens up all sorts of fascinating vistas on the American mind, doesn't it? Do go on!"

Penny glared at him. "No more extraordinary than all the whoop-de-do that goes on over here about debutantes' coming-out balls and royal garden parties and suchlike," she snapped.

"And this chap has written a book about it all, and now somebody has threatened him," Toby said placatingly.

"Not only him, but John as well." Penny frowned again. "It really sounds ridiculous. First John got a threatening note about the book. 'Do not publish or you'll regret it' sort of thing. He ignored that. Then he got another, much more doom-laden, threatening him and his family with all sorts of disgrace and dole if he went on with it. At that juncture he told Lefau, who then admitted he'd been receiving them, too. Hence this call for help."

"Have they been to the police?"

Penny shook her head. "Not officially. When John thought there might be something in it, he unofficially took his letters to the Boston police lab, which tested them and came up with zilch; *no* fingerprints at all inside, which indicates the writer had no intention of being traced. And that's all I know. We'll have to wait for that packet to arrive. But I *am* worried about John, Toby. All this is so unlike him. I mean, he's always been such a calm and cheerful soul, and yet he sounded positively shattered on the phone. Also, I can't imagine what a publishing house like Cosby and Son, which has always had such a sound conservative reputation, is even doing putting out a vanity publication like this."

"Well, there is a recession going on, and it's affecting publishing like everything else," Toby pointed out. "If this Lefau chap is filthy rich, maybe he made them an offer they couldn't refuse."

"So what do you think we should do about it?" Penny zoomed directly to the point.

Toby puffed reflectively for a moment or two. "We certainly owe John Everett something. If it weren't for him, you'd probably still be in the local pokey on Cape Cod doing time for all that commotion you caused there." It was Penny's turn to look pained. "But why don't we wait and see what is in that packet?"

As if on cue, there came a brisk tap on the door, and Miss Ada Phipp's ample form bounced through it. "A special-delivery packet for you, Dr. Spring," she chirped. "I thought you might want to . . ." She recoiled slightly, but whether this was from the cloud of tobacco smoke now encompassing the room or from the sight of Sir Tobias, her continual nemesis, it was hard to say.

"Oh, good!" Penny pounced on the fat package like an excited terrier after a rat. "Thank you, Ada. We were waiting for this."

"*You're* very welcome," their joint secretary said and exited with a disapproving sniff in Toby's direction.

"Gets worse all the time," he observed to the ceiling as Penny tore open the package and began to scan the contents.

"Good grief, he's certainly sent enough stuff! Here, Toby—'Background Notes on the Lefaus'—that sounds like your department. You tackle that, and I'll read the rest."

Dead silence settled on the room as they both read the closely typed sheets. After a while Sir Tobias patted his pockets and, reaching into some inner recess of his sagging Harris tweed jacket, pulled out his little black notebook and began to make notes in his neat, precise handwriting. Penny, as she read, fidgeted, frowned, ran her hands through her already disheveled hair, frowned some more, and finally looked up. "Finished? Do you want to shoot first, or shall I?"

"Oh, after you, by all means," Toby replied.

"Well, I'll break it down into sections. First of all the book: a limited edition of five hundred copies, *leather-bound*, and the finest-grade paper. Phew, what a price, even by today's inflated standards! Scheduled to come out on Mardi Gras itself, with the author ceremonially presenting copies to the library of the Comus krewe, the New Orleans Public Library, the mayor of New Orleans, and sundry notables. Contains the history of the krewe, various biographical notes on the most notable families of the krewe—including, of course, his own—and a brief history of the Mardi Gras in New Orleans. Sounds perfectly innocuous! *However*, the threatening notes started when John received the manuscript about six months ago and have averaged about one a month. He's got the dates here, but I'll skip those for the moment. The last one arrived two weeks ago and was by far the most vicious. John quotes a bit of it. 'Death will surround you. Death will destroy you.' This is apparently what lit the fire under Lefau, who had been dragging his heels about the whole thing before and telling John to cool it.

"The deal as far as we are concerned is as follows: Lefau purposes to underwrite our travel and expenses, pay any fee we might consider reasonable, and entertain us as his guests during the Mardi Gras. He wants to avoid *any* publicity about the matter and, apart from John and himself, wants us to appear simply as distinguished guests. Oh, I like that part! Though, comes to think of it, it would be a bit hampering. How the hell does he think we can do any investigating without asking questions?" she demanded of Toby, who simply shrugged. "Perhaps you'd better fill me in on the domestic situation we'd be going into."

Toby took up his notebook, cleared his throat, and went into his sonorous lecturing rumble. "Jules Lefau, born 1925, only son of the elder Jules Lefau and his wife, Pernell. One older sister, Celeste, born 1915, unmarried, who apparently lives with him. He's been married twice. Wife number one was Content Cooke, a New York heiress, who died in 1960, and the present wife is an Eleanor Duchamps, also of an old New Orleans Creole family connected with the Comus krewe. By the first wife has a son, Benedict, born 1951, who is also married and lives with him; and there are two children by the second marriage: Juliette, who is nineteen—that makes her born in 1962; so he didn't remain too long *un*married, by the looks of it—and another, younger son, Vincent, born in 1968. Lefau is involved in banking, shipping, and real estate. Has a town house in the French Quarter on Royal Street, where presumably we'll be staying, and an estate just outside of New Orleans on the Mississippi River. The whole family keeps a low profile in spite of its wealth, and the older son is associated with him in business. No wild goings-on, no mavericks indicated—at least, not here."

"Sounds equally innocuous," Penny said, "and yet I'm getting the most awful vibes about this."

Sir Tobias, who did not put much stock in vibes, prudently held his peace.

"So what do you think we should do?" she asked.

He refilled his pipe with maddening slowness and lit up, apparently pondering deeply all the while. "Well, as you know, after the affair of Zadok's treasure, I pledged myself to keep on in this business," he rumbled, "and it strikes me that it would be a very nice change if we could *prevent* something from happening rather than scurry around trying to clean up the mess *after* the fact. Nothing has happened to Lefau or to Everett yet; if our presence insures nothing *does* happen, I think it would be a very worthwhile effort."

"Then, you're for going," she muttered dubiously.

"I'm *agreeable* to going," he corrected firmly, "but, after all, John Everett is your friend, not mine. I feel we owe him something, but if you don't, well, then there's nothing more to be said."

"I don't even begin to see what we can *do* under these circumstances," she fussed. "Where would we start? What would we look for? It's all so nebulous."

"Are you worried about getting leave of absence from Jessup? Because, if so, I could easily lean on him a little," Toby volunteered.

Penny looked at him with scorn. "The day I can't handle Jessup is the day I'll *know* I'm over the hill. Besides, your idea of leaning on him is always the same. You threaten to resign 'unless.' But one of these days he's going to call your bluff, and then where will you be? Out of a job, that's where."

"I would retire to All Souls. They've been after me for years to become one of their fellows," Sir Tobias said huffily.

Penny sighed with exasperation. Although Toby's great wealth, inherited from his industrialist father, always had filled him with guilt, it also provided him with an impenetrable bulwark against the machinations of lesser mortals, such as the head of their department, Jessup, and rendered Toby, in consequence, totally bloody-minded when it came to his own desires. "No, you don't have to go into your usual act," she growled. "After all, it's only for a couple of weeks. I can easily enough find someone to fill in for me. But I still wonder what good we'll do." She got up. "I suppose I might as well get it over with and go and have my row with Jessup now."

Toby rose, too, and opened the door for her. "You know, one thing has already struck me," he said as her short, dumpy figure and his long, thin one clumped incongruously down the echoing stone stairs of the Pitt Rivers Museum, side by side, heading for the office of the hapless Jessup. "It strikes me that Jules Lefau may know a lot more about all this than he is telling; so he will be the man to watch. *I* think he wants us there on the spot because he thinks it's an inside job!"

CHAPTER 2

"Will Dr. Penelope Spring, TWA passenger from London to Boston, please contact the TWA travel desk in the lobby," the P.A. system announced in a girlish voice.

"That'll be John," Penny assured Toby as they struggled with their heavy bags through the doors of customs at Logan International Airport.

But it wasn't John. A young, fair girl was standing by the desk, clutching a paper parcel. "Dr. Spring?" she asked uncertainly as Penny puffed up. Penny wheezed and nodded. "I'm Melinda Gail, from Mr. Everett's office. Mrs. Everett asked me to meet you. She has booked you overnight into the Logan Hilton and you can fly direct to New Orleans tomorrow morning. She also asked me to give you this." She handed over the package. "I believe it's a copy of the book Mr. Everett has talked to you about."

"Is Mr. Everett all right? Has anything happened to him?" Penny asked in alarm.

The girl looked startled. "Why, no! He left for New Orleans this morning—the same plane you'll be taking tomorrow. Mrs. Everett also asked if you would call her when you get to the hotel."

Penny and Toby exchanged puzzled glances but allowed themselves to be shepherded into a cab and whisked the short distance to the hotel. While the girl was checking their reservations and seeing to their luggage, they went into a quiet conference. "Something must be up," Penny grumbled. "The original plan was for us all to fly down together tomorrow— including Millicent—and to go straight to the Lefau plantation."

"Maybe John's onto something," Toby suggested. "Any-

18

way, I'll be glad to have an advance look at this." He held up the package.

Melinda Gail departed with grateful thanks and polite relief all around, and Penny swooped down on the phone while Toby stripped the wrappings from the luxuriously bound book, poured himself a brandy from his silver hip flask, settled cozily into one of the armchairs, and started to read.

"What's happened?" Penny was saying briskly into the phone. "Why the change in plans?"

Millicent Everett's cool, well-bred voice was even and unemotional. "Mr. Lefau asked if John would come on ahead—something to do with arrangements for an autograph party. John asks that you meet him at the St. Louis Hotel in the French Quarter when you get in tomorrow. Mr. Lefau took a suite for him there. John would like to have a private talk with you before going out to Lefau's."

"Aren't you coming with us, then?" Penny was blunt.

"No, I'm not." The voice took a sharper edge. "Frankly, Penny, I've been against John's involvement in all this from the beginning and have no intention of getting involved myself. I think this whole thing is completely ridiculous and potentially very unpleasant and that it is quite absurd for a man of John's age and position to get into it."

"What about the threats?" Penny demanded. "Don't those worry you?"

"Oh, the letters!" Millicent was scornful. "I think it's just one of those elaborate practical jokes the rich play on one another. I believe southerners are quite noted for such hoaxes." Her voice became warmer and more urgent. "But I am worried about John. He has not been at all himself of late. I would appreciate it if, when you get there, you can talk him into coming home. He has no business playing the fool down there when he has so much to do, so many responsibilities, up here."

"Well, when I see what the situation is, I'll do what I can," Penny assured her and cradled the phone with a frown. "Did you get all that?" she asked her partner.

Toby surfaced from his book. "No, I wasn't listening," he said cheerfully.

She was exasperated. "I do wish you'd pay attention. After all, we're supposed to be working."

"I am," he reproved, holding up the book. "On exhibit A. Why? Was it important?"

"I don't know." Penny frowned again. "I sense some very strained relations in the Everett household. She isn't coming, by the way."

"Oh?" Toby was secretly relieved; his simple philosophy was that the fewer women there were around, the easier life tended to be.

"She also does not put much stock in the threatening letters. In fact, she seems more than a little miffed that we're going. A mild accusatory note, as if we were dragging John into it instead of vice-versa."

"A dependable type?"

"Who, Millicent? Yes, I would say so, very. A bit of a cold fish is Millicent, but sharp. Not a flutterer." Penny gnawed her lower lip. "John does have a vivid imagination. Underneath his proper Bostonian exterior lurks, I suspect, a raging romantic. I hope he hasn't gone off half-cocked on this."

"He's a good man when the chips are down," Toby observed mildly, "as we both have reason to know."

Penny looked at her watch. "Well, since we don't have to be social, I might as well do some work. I ought to get over to Harvard and chat with Joe about the anthropological symposium we're organizing for this summer in Chicago. Will you be OK? I'll be back for dinner."

"Happy as a lark. I shall seek my own room and stretch out. Mr. Lefau's style appears to be a little turgid; I think I'd appreciate it more in a supine position." Toby helped himself to another snort from his hip flask.

"Then, you'd better stretch out here; John might call." Penny looked with some disapproval at his drink. "Go easy on that stuff. We don't want you arriving in New Orleans with a hangover. All you've got to do to get ice and soda is to press a button, you know."

Toby appeared outraged. "This happens to be Napoleon special-stock five-star brandy—it does not need to be polluted! And I have been known to consume a whole bottle without visible effect."

"Umm, that's a matter of opinion," she growled and stomped out.

When Penny returned several hours later, it was to find Toby stretched out on the bed, peacefully snoring, the book open on his chest. She shook him awake. "Dinnertime! Any calls?"

He came to, pouting like an elderly baby. "Not a thing."

She dithered. "Maybe I'd better try and call him before we eat; otherwise, he might miss us." But when she called the hotel, it was only to be told that there was no reply from Mr. Everett's suite. "Must be out on the town," she grumbled. "Oh, well, 'sufficient unto the day is the evil thereof.' Let's eat."

John Everett descended the elegant marble steps of the St. Louis Hotel and proceeded through the large glass doors giving onto St. Louis Street. There he hesitated on the pavement, looking first to his left toward the semidarkness of conservative Chartres Street and then to his right where the brighter vistas of Royal and Bourbon streets beckoned. It was a chilly, damp night, the low-scudding clouds belly-heavy with unshed rain.

"A cab, sir?" The ornately costumed doorman, who in spite of his Ruritanian frills looked like an ex-boxer, eyed him speculatively.

"No, thank you." But John still hovered uncertainly, not sure, now that he was out here in the hurly-burly of the French Quarter, that he wanted to leave the hushed security of his suite, which but a few minutes before had seemed to him so claustrophobic.

"The night tour of New Orleans is just about to leave," the doorman invited. "They still have a few seats, I think. If you are a stranger to the city, sir, I highly recommend it." He beckoned surreptitiously to a young girl in a bright-red jacket, who came hurrying up.

"Well, no, I don't think——" John began.

"Our tour includes a drink at the Top o' the Mart and a visit to two top nightclubs, and the evening ends in the traditional New Orleans way with *café au lait* and *beignets* at the French Market," the girl said in a high, clear voice. "The Red Coach Tour price includes drinks, cover charges, and tips, and there is preferred seating everywhere." She gave

John a bright, winning smile; she was very young, a harbinger of spring on this raw winter's night.

He succumbed to the smile. "Oh, all right."

She relieved him of twenty-five dollars and with another bright smile indicated the huge, glossy bus that was parked at the curb. Bemusedly he got in and found a vacant seat behind the driver, next to an elderly man who was staring steadfastly out the window, a gloomy expression on his face. With John's arrival, the bus had gorged its fill, and its door hissed shut with a definitive snap as it started to pull gingerly away from the curb into the narrow, crowded streets of the Quarter.

What the hell am I doing this for? John thought dazedly. *What is the matter with me? I came here to think things out, not to act like some half-witted tourist.*

The girl had started up a chatty commentary on the night streets they were edging through, all gay with the purple, green, and gold colors of Carnival, but he shut out her determined voice and edged back into the private world that had been his for the past several months, a world of pain and restlessness and confusion, but one that was as persistent as an aching tooth. This flight to New Orleans ahead of time had been a spur-of-the-moment decision. He had seized it because he had been desperate to get away from Boston and from Millicent, eager to have some time to think things out before Penny and Toby arrived and before he had to face the Lefaus *en masse*. Yet now that he was here in all this alien atmosphere of frantic, self-conscious gaiety, he found it harder than ever to think. Damn it, he *had* to. . . .

For the thousandth time he found himself wishing he had never been tempted by Jules Lefau, never set eyes on the man. But Lefau's offer had been so beguiling, so opportune. Cosby and Son had been feeling the pinch like every other publishing house, and the Lefau order had meant the difference between letting two of the younger employees go and keeping them on until things, optimistically, got better again. John remembered the surge of pride and pleasure he had felt when he looked up Lefau in *Who's Who* and reflected what an accolade it was for the reputation of Cosby's to be sought out by such a prestigious man. Now that he thought about it in retrospect, it seemed bizarre, almost sinister. There were plenty of publishing firms in the South; why hadn't Lefau used one of them? Or in New York, where there were scores, many of them dedicated to vanity publishing? Why Boston, why Cosby's, why . . .?

When the letters started, John had mentioned them to Millicent more or less as a joke. Her reaction had startled him and emphasized the gulf that with such unseen stealth had been widening between them. She had been horrified, not so much at the letters but at the thought that he had trifled with the good name of Cosby's, of which one of her great-grandfathers had been a founder, by allowing such a thing as a vanity book to come out under its imprint. In vain John had tried to point out to her the harder realities of the modern publishing world, but his wife could not, or would not, understand. Even when he became increasingly concerned and alarmed as the letters took an uglier turn, she had continued to treat the whole matter, himself included, with an icy disdain. There was just no talking to her anymore, no joy in being with her anymore. . . .

The bus hissed to a stop, jolting him from his reverie. Sheeplike, he allowed himself to be jostled out into the ultramodern lobby of the International Trade Mart and then into an elevator for a giddy ride up to the revolving cocktail lounge at its skyscraping top. He found himself seated at a table with his morose bus companion and four elderly women, who eyed them with speculation. Two of them beamed an invitation at him and then volunteered the information that they were sisters from Canton, Ohio, and wasn't this all too exciting and fascinating for words—my, would you just look at that view!

A hovering waiter saved him from replying. "Scotch and soda," he ordered as the ladies twittered about their own choice of drinks and then started to bombard the waiter with questions about what they were seeing from their slowly revolving eyrie.

The lights of the city hung like a choker of multi-colored diamonds around the dusky throat of the Mississippi, upon which their tower seemed to be floating. Only in one section was the gay sparkle muted to the point of darkness, and John realized he was looking at the outlined long quadrangle of the French Quarter. *The city had a dark, sinister heart*, he thought and again was startled by his own fancies. As a counterpoint, his elderly neighbor turned and addressed him for the first time. "By the look of this lot, these here southerners don't seem much concerned with the energy crisis," he grumbled in a heavy New England accent. "Eyah, if they had to pay the fuel bills where I come from, they'd sing a different tune. Will you look at all that waste!"

The ladies, glad to see some semblance of life in their male companions, immediately mounted a spirited defense of the New Orleans city fathers. "It's Carnival, after all!" they chorused and took it from there. John quietly downed his scotch, ordered another, and lapsed back into reverie.

He knew now what Millicent was after: she wanted him to retire. She wanted them to uproot and go to California to be near their doctor son, who was practicing in the Bay Area. Well, he wasn't about to. Hell, he was only fifty-eight, and he felt a lot younger than that. He liked what he did; he liked Boston and all it stood for. He was not about to be pushed on the shelf; she had no right. . . . His sense of grievance grew. A soft hand touched his shoulder, and there was the bright smile of his springlike guide. "We are ready to move on to the Hotel Bayou cabaret," she announced.

The bus swallowed them again and was off, moving now through the broader streets of the new city. The trouble with Millicent was that she had a jealous nature, John thought bitterly. Look how negatively she had reacted to the news that Penny was coming on this trip. And he had never given her any cause to doubt him. Not that he hadn't been tempted . . . It was really extremely aggravating. He had tried to explain, tried to cajole Millicent into coming along, too. "Lefau would like us *all* to be his guests. It will make our presence there a lot more natural if we go as a group to the Carnival. It will give Penny and Sir Tobias some necessary cover, if they are to conduct an investigation."

"If you think I am going along as a camouflage to the snooping activities of that weird pair, you have another think coming," she had sniffed. "I am still getting very snide remarks from my garden club over your involvement with them in that extraordinary affair on Cape Cod. I really don't see why you have to get mixed up with them at all. After all, she is only one of your *lesser* authors."

It was hardly the moment to reveal that he had egged

Penny on into the Cape Cod mystery. At the time, he had enjoyed every moment of it, including his own part in the affair, but now that things were closer to home he was not so sure about it. He worried about the tiny anthropologist, of whom he had become very fond over the long years of their friendship. Danger and excitement to Penny were like red flags to a bull; she tended to rush at things head on. What if he were leading her once more into danger? Yet Lefau had been so insistent, so pressing. He was back to that again—the strange, enigmatic Jules Lefau.

The bus once more ground to a stop, and they were herded out. He looked around him in some bewilderment; they seemed to be on the very outskirts of the city, a tatty area of used-car lots and small, darkened factories, in which the square block of the Hotel Bayou stood in a depressing park of asphalt. It appeared, in spite of Carnival, semideserted. This time they ended up in a smallish dance hall where a middle-aged combo was playing dance music of the fifties and a heavily made-up singer of uncertain years was crooning voluptuously at a mike. The group settled down. Another Scotch and soda appeared. The leader of the combo made a little speech about Carnival and his own achievements and halfheartedly plugged a record of his band, which by its outdated jacket looked as if it had been remaindered for years. *Losers,* John thought, looking them over carefully, *losers to a man. They don't even believe in themselves anymore.* As if picking up his thought, the singer gave the group a tremulous, timid smile and began with soulful intensity to sing the theme song of Carnival, *"If ever I ceased to love . . ."*

John was usually so good at summing people up—it was one reason for his success in business—but Jules Lefau so far had eluded him entirely. True, John had not had much contact with southern gentlemen, particularly Creole aristocrats, but even so, he found it impossible to penetrate Lefau's reserve or to fathom the workings of his mind. When Lefau had finally admitted to receiving the threats, he had scoffed at John's suggestion that maybe it was some business rival, some embittered client of his bank who was behind them. "Really, Mr. Everett, New Orleans is not New York City; we do not conduct ourselves like Mafia hoods!" He had been equally negative about the suggestion that the threats could have originated within the Comus krewe. "I do not think you realize how close we all are in the krewe—linked by blood, common interests, common goals. Yes, there have been scandals, there have been tragedies in Comus over its long history, but if someone within the krewe were at all apprehensive about my disclosures, he would come to me and discuss it openly, not bombard us both with a series of cheap, theatrical anonymous letters." And yet, underneath, John could sense that Lefau was apprehensive, even afraid, his fear outweighed only by his abhorrence of any kind of publicity. Hence this present elaborate subterfuge and pantomime, which they had orchestrated to get Penny and Toby on the scene. What did Jules Lefau know? What did he suspect?

The crooning had stopped and some halfhearted dancing among the group had begun. A smartly dressed woman, her white hair stylishly cut, loomed over John. "Would you care to dance?" she asked with a coy smile.

It so startled him that his response was abrupt to the point of rudeness. "I don't dance."

Her face froze, and she snapped, "Oh, I'm so *sorry* to have disturbed you," then added in an overloud voice when she had returned to her companions, "You wonder why some people come on a tour like this, when they seem determined not to enjoy themselves."

Embarrassed and hoping to stave off any further confrontations, John plunged into the glossy booklet that had been presented as part of the tour: "A Guide to New Orleans by Day and Night." There was a section on Mardi Gras, which he read with some attention. Two sentences struck out at him: "In 1857 the Mystick krewe of Comus became New Orleans' first Carnival organization, whose ball and parade are still the grand finale of our Mardi Gras." And "There is a private, mysterious, and secret part of Carnival shared only by the krewe members and their fortunate guests. . . ." In spite of himself, John felt a small thrill of excitement. He was going to be part of this secret, mysterious circle, thanks to Lefau. It was a new experience, a new adventure. Hell, why should he worry? What could this anonymous letter-writing kook do to him, John Everett, Boston Brahmin, highly respectable and respected publisher and man of means? He had been letting his imagination run riot, and that was absurd. This had nothing to do with him; it was not part of his world at all! He would savor Carnival as an experience, present Lefau with his books, and not worry about it further. When Mardi Gras was over, he would return to Boston and put the whole thing out of his head. Now he would enjoy . . .

He looked up, firm in his new resolution, thinking to make his peace with the smart-looking woman at the next table and invite her to dance, but he found he was too late. The band had stopped playing and the bus group were already on their feet and shuffling toward the door. On the way back into town John listened patiently to a monologue from his New England companion on how Arab oil was buying up New Orleans bit by bit and that before you knew it, "we'll have an alliance between these here southerners and those Arabs to squeeze the North out of its last nickel." "They just don't like us down here," his confidante concluded as they drew up before a flashing sign of Bourbon Street that announced LE NIGHTCLUB in purple flashes. "No, they're just plain out to get us northern folks. So you just better watch yourself, sir."

John was more than a little thankful that in the ensuing rush for seats in the small club they were separated, and he found himself wedged into a corner with one of the sisters from Canton as his neighbor. No sooner was the group seated and drinks brought than the show crashed into action. It was a one-woman affair, but the woman was decorative, and her generous endowments displayed in the minimum of spangles and sequins sent a sudden pang of pure sensuality through John's plump loins. She sang, she told mildly pornographic jokes, she sat on bald men's laps and kissed their pates, she dragged fat, middle-aged men onto the stage and made them rhumba with her: she was a ball of fire—and John was quietly grateful that he was embedded in the back of the room, beyond her avid reach. The noise level was unbearably high, and, with the heat of the closely packed room and the cumulative effect of the Scotches he had downed, he began to get a pounding headache. When the show had screamed to its ear-shattering conclusion and they had jostled their way out onto Bourbon Street, he decided that enough was enough and that he would slip away.

The cool night air was like a benison to his throbbing temples, and so he elected to stroll down Bourbon Street, which was still wide awake and buzzing with life, before seeking the quieter fastnesses of his hotel. He was still feeling aroused and stimulated, and he looked almost hungrily at the nude pinups, at the blazing signs that proclaimed TOPLESS WAITRESSES, BOTTOMLESS WAITERS, and was embraced by the overwhelming tide of commercial sex that permeated the night air of Bourbon Street. He walked slowly, so that he was a natural target for the barkers that stood outside the seedier clubs touting for customers. One actually clutched at his arm. "Finest strip show in the city. Best goddamn counter strippers you'll ever see. Come on in and enjoy!" As he spoke the doors swung open and a drunk lurched through, revealing at the same time a stark-naked girl, her arms raised above her head in triumphant finale, standing on the bar.

John burst out laughing. "What's left to see?" he inquired and shook himself free. But as he walked farther, reading the obscenities printed on the T-shirts that flapped from the street stalls in the light wind, rebuffing the night ladies and their more insistent pimps, his desire was gradually replaced by a feeling of disgust as the puritan in him reasserted itself. At the same time, nature began to call rather insistently, and to satisfy it he turned onto the more decorous St. Peter Street to find a quieter bar or restaurant with a handy men's room. Pat O'Brien's, a name he had read about, caught his eye. He hurried in there and, after a quick conference with a waiter, found the relief he sought. When he reemerged, he was caught up once more by the genial atmosphere and the cheerful crowd and decided on a final nightcap. The same waiter ushered him to a minute table, urged him to try the Hurricane Special, to which John meekly agreed, and hurried off. John looked around at the cheerful, relaxed crowd. Enjoy, he instructed himself sternly, enjoy! Tomorrow Penny and Toby would be here, and the game—whatever it was—would be afoot. But tonight was his.

His drink, of intimidating size, arrived, and his waiter whispered, "We're very crowded tonight, sir. Would you mind sharing your table with a lady?"

John looked up to see a spectacularly striking woman, beautifully dressed in a cream-colored *haute mode* suit, with a multitude of thin gold chains around her slim neck, standing at the waiter's elbow. "Not at all," he gulped and stood up politely as the vision seated herself beside him. Her hair was long and a lustrous blue-black; her skin, the color and bloom of ripe peaches; her eyes, a deep, warm brown; and her wide, sensuous mouth was parted in a polite smile of acknowledgment, revealing perfect, pearllike teeth. She gave her own order to the waiter in a low, musical voice, and John braced himself expectantly for further developments. He was disappointed when none came.

She sat quietly, her head turned in profile to him, watching the entertainers on the small stage, and made no attempt at conversation. Only when her drink arrived was there a brief moment of confusion when her scarlet leather handbag was dislodged from the table and he bent down to retrieve it for her. Thinking this might be an opening, he handed it back with "They don't give us much room, do they?"

"No," she agreed with a polite smile of thanks, and that, unfortunately, was that.

John sipped his drink, which was rum-based and very strong to his taste, sneaking surreptitious glances at his table companion's perfect profile and savoring her perfume, which tantalized with its faint orange fragrance. He finally identified it with a little thrill of triumph. Frangipani, that was it! The exotic delicacy of frangipani. Suddenly the room began to swim before his eyes and the lights to dim. *Damn, I shouldn't have mixed my drinks*, was his last coherent thought as he staggered to his feet. He swayed and almost fell and was seized in a whirling, roaring vortex. He was conscious only of an arm going around his shoulders, steadying him, the scent of frangipani, and a low voice saying, "I'll help you"— then blackness and a whispering void.

When he came to, the top of his head felt as if it would implode, his mouth tasted like the inside of a garbage can, and there was a continuous roaring in his ears. *Where am I?* was his first panic-stricken thought, and he squinted his eyes open to find himself staring at the star-spangled ceiling of his ornate suite in the St. Louis Hotel. The light was unbearably painful, and he closed his eyes again, thankful for small mercies: at least he was where he belonged. The roaring continued, and it gradually percolated through to his numb mind that it was the roar of a vacuum cleaner being operated in the outer room of his suite. The panic returned. What time was it? What if Penny and Toby arrived to find him like this?

With an agonizing heave, he turned on his side to look at the traveling clock on his night table, and went cold with shock: the other twin bed was occupied. He saw the long swirl of lustrous blue-black hair, the perfection of the naked peach-colored back, and one slim arm above the covers. Instinctively he glanced down at himself, causing an acute stab of pain, to find he was in his shirt and undershorts. A groan bubbled to his lips. "Oh God, what have I done?" He had to get her out of here fast! Suddenly the room seemed permeated sickeningly with the scent of frangipani, and he felt like retching.

He struggled out of bed, gritting his teeth against the pain in his head, and laid an urgent hand on the girl's bare shoulder. "Wake up!" The head flopped toward him, revealing the perfect features distorted into a hideous caricature, the tongue protruding between blue lips. She was dead, strangled, the profusion of golden chains around her neck knotted into a cruel garrote from which tiny rivulets of dark blood patterned her throat. But that was not the worst horror: through one of her full, dark-nippled breasts had been driven a skewer, topped by a red-and-black-colored square worked in coarse wool that looked like an obscene badge.

As John bent over her, stupid with shock, the door opened. A large black woman, vacuum cleaner in hand, started to enter. "Oh, I'se sorry, suh. You didn't have no sign up, so . . ." Then she saw what was on the bed. For a second she stood paralyzed, her eyes slowly dilating with fear; then she started to back slowly away, her thick mouth opening wide. "*Murder!*" she screamed at the top of her voice. "Help, dear Lawd, help! It's bloody murder!"

CHAPTER 3

"Anything exciting in the book?" Penny inquired over dinner in the Logan Hilton's elaborate but thinly populated dining room. The dinner so far had not been very exciting, so she felt in need of further stimulation.

Toby shrugged. "I now know a lot more than I thought I would ever want to about Mardi Gras and the Comus krewe. Lefau throws around a great many names which mean nothing to me at the moment, but on the whole I'd say it was perfectly innocuous and more than a little dull. He relates the odd scandal, the odd tragedy, but nothing that seems to amount to anything."

"What sort of tragedy?"

"*Tragedy* is perhaps too strong a word. There's been a lot of infighting between families for the top spot over the years, the inevitable 'honorable' duel here and there, one princess who eloped in the middle of a Grand Ball with an '*Anglo*'—a heinous crime, apparently—one young blue blood who had the bad taste to blow his brains out during another Grand Ball, amid dark suspicions that he had been siphoning off the Carnival funds; but there's nothing at this juncture that you can really point to and say, 'That's what it's all about.' "

"How annoying," Penny commented and dived with gusto into her fresh strawberry shortcake. "Well, let's hope John will be brimming with bright ideas when we see him tomorrow."

In the morning they had a mild row over a perennial point of difference. Toby's philosophy about planes was that the later you boarded them the less bored you got and that they would always wait for you. Penny was a nervous traveler and

31

was convinced that any plane she was booked on would sneak off without her unless she was there at least half an hour before they told her to be. Over the years it had developed into a seesaw battle, with honors about even; this time she won.

"On the way back you can miss all the planes you like," she said magnanimously as she pushed the grumbling Toby into the hotel elevator, "but now I am very anxious to get there; so *allons-y!*"

Behind them in her deserted room the phone began a frantic shrilling, which went on and on and on. . . .

"Phew, isn't it *hot*!" Penny gasped as they wrestled their bags through the New Orleans airport. "I think I've brought all the wrong clothes." They were both still dressed for the cold damp of England and the snows of Boston, so that the muggy, mild March day of the Mississippi delta seemed like a steam bath.

"No porters in sight, not even a luggage cart," Toby grumbled beside her. "Fine sort of setup!"

They shouldered their way out of the exit doors of the airport to confront a whole bevy of redcaps leaning on their trolleys and listening with interest to a loud-voiced altercation that was going on between the traffic controller, a Yellow Cab driver, and the owner of a gray cab that was defiantly slewed in front of the Yellow Cab's hood. The last named was a huge black man, his hair done in a miltitude of tiny braids, heavily beaded at their ends. He was wearing a violently patterned shirt with violet pants and sported one gold earring hooped through his large ear. As Penny and Toby tottered out under their burdens, he broke off his bellowing, strode toward them with menace writ large on his bearded face, seized their four bags as if they were packed with thistledown, and flung them into the open trunk of the cab. Willy-nilly, they followed the bags and with some trepidation climbed into the back seat as he slammed the trunk shut and, with a final warning growl at the intimidated Yellow Cab driver, hurled his great bulk behind the wheel and shot away from the curb. The couple exchanged alarmed glances, before a huge grin flashed at them in the rearview mirror.

"Sorry about that, folks," the vision roared, "but those

damn yellow-belly cabs are shafting us independents the whole time. Got to fight every inch of the way, yeah. Ah been waitin' in line for mah turn, and then two of 'em tried to box me in. Well, I'll box them!'' He let out a triumphant bellow of laughter and shifted into top gear, so that the seedy environs of the airport melted into one confused blur as they sped toward the city. ''Where 'bouts can Ah take you?''

''The St. Louis Hotel,'' Toby said in a faint voice, his eyes firmly shut. ''And we are *not* in a hurry.''

''That's a mighty nice place, mighty nice. You goin' to be here for the Mardi Gras?''

''Er, yes,'' said Penny.

''Then, you sure come to the right place at the right time. Anything you want to see or do, you just contact me. Ah'll see you don't get into no clip joints. Mean Gene's mah name, driving's mah game.'' Again the big grin flashed.

''Mean Gene?'' Penny echoed, intrigued.

''Heard of Mean Joe Green, the football player, ain't ya? Him and me is look-alikes; so Ah'm Mean Gene. Not that Ah'm no football player. Lost a kneecap in 'Nam, so that was *out*. But Ah'm one up on him—Ah'm a *jazz*man.'' His deep voice took on a note of resonant pride. ''Yes, sir, when you see the Zulu parade comin', Ah'll be up there with mah group playin' for St. Peter hisself. That's mah group, the Knights of St. Pierre. We plays all over town—Preservation Hall, Bourbon Street. . . .''

Penny was beginning to enjoy herself. ''I love jazz! What do you play?''

''You name it, Ah plays it—double-bass, tenor sax, and Ah can toot a *mean* trumpet!'' He beamed at her in the mirror.

''So, if you are a jazzman, what are you doing driving a cab?'' she demanded.

''Ah likes people,'' came the surprising answer, ''and when you do nothin' but play jazz, man, that's a mighty lonely life—just you and the group and the music. So Ah drives by day and plays by night.''

''Good enough.'' She smiled at him. ''I know how you feel, because I like people, too.''

''Ah'm never wrong. Ah just *knew* you did. You're a nice lady. What's your name?''

"Dr. Penelope Spring."

"Doctor, eh? That's good—we can use all the doctors we can get," he roared. Penny decided not to explain. "Your old man there a doctor, too?"

Penny shot an amused glance at Toby, whose blue eyes had popped open in indignation. "No, he's a distinguished visitor to our shores. Sir Tobias Glendower."

"Oh, a sir. Ain't that like a lord or something?" His grin became roguish. "Well, we got some of them, too. We got Duke Ellington, Count Basie, and next week this place'll be crawling with kings and queens and princesses. He'll feel right at home. Why, Ah'm going to be a baron myself—Baron Samedi."

"The voodoo *loa* of death!" she ejaculated without thinking.

"You know about that, do you?" Now he was serious. " 'Course, Ah'm not into that stuff, Ah'm a Baptist. It's just for the Zulu carnival."

"You'll certainly make a very impressive Baron Samedi," she said dryly.

"How come you know about voodoo?" he asked. "Ah can tell you ain't from around these parts."

"Oh, I spent some time in Haiti and the islands." She didn't elaborate.

He shook his head, making the beads rattle. "That's a *bad* scene, man. Nice lady like you don't want to mess with things like that. Those old voodoo people down there were strictly bad news. No, Ah wants no part of that." He fell silent for a minute as they reached the narrowest streets of the French Quarter and the traffic demanded all his attention. He slid skillfully into a narrow parking space in front of the hotel and turned to her. "This is it. You want me to pick you up for a sight-seeing tour later on?"

"If we do, I'll be sure to get in touch." Penny beamed companionably at him. "But we aren't actually staying here, just going to meet a friend."

"Where you staying at, then? Places are mighty hard to come by in the city during Carnival."

"We're staying outside of town, at the Lefau place."

His lips pursed in a silent whistle. "You just said a mighty important name, lady. You must be mighty fancy folks—ol' Lefau's goin' to be King of Comus this year." He got out and unloaded the bags, fending off the doorman of the hotel with a growl, and shepherded Penny and Toby inside and up the marble steps to the reception desk. The young man behind the desk recoiled slightly as Gene loomed over him and remained paralyzed as the big man fished out a tiny card and pressed it upon Penny. "Ah works out of the Basin Street stand. You call there, they'll always know where Ah'm at." He accepted the fare and a substantial tip from Toby, who was still very much on his dignity, and with a final growled admonition to the desk clerk to "Look after this nice lady, y'hear," took his magnificent departure.

The desk clerk came out of his paralysis and said with icy disapproval, "You have reservations?"

"Er, no," Toby rumbled. "We are here to meet a friend in the hotel. Would you phone Mr. John Everett's suite and tell him we've arrived. He is expecting us."

The clerk's pale face went a shade paler. "Just a moment," he stuttered and disappeared into the manager's office. After a minute he emerged and said, "Please, would you step in and see the manager for a moment."

Penny and Toby exchanged puzzled glances as they followed him in. An impressive-looking gray-haired man was standing behind the desk as they entered. "May I ask who you are?" he inquired stiffly. Even more mystified, they gave their names. "And you had an appointment with Mr. John Everett for this morning?"

"Why, yes! We were to meet Mr. Everett here and then proceed with him to the Lefau plantation. Why these questions?" Penny was becoming indignant. "We wish to see Mr. Everett at once!"

"I am afraid that will be impossible," the manager said slowly. "You see, Mr. Everett is no longer here. He was arrested this morning and conveyed to police headquarters. I'm sorry, but I must ask you to leave."

"Arrested!" Penny gasped. "Whatever for?"

"Suspicion of murder," the manager said coldly. "It appears to be an open-and-shut case—he was caught red-handed."

CHAPTER 4

"Captain Beauregard will see you now." The young policeman ushered Penny and Toby from the waiting room into the bright, fluorescent-lit corridor. Despite the fact that the building was a modern one, there was still the air of slight seediness and incipient despair about it that stamps police stations the world over.

As they walked behind the officer, Toby said in an urgent undertone to Penny, who was bristling with indignation, "Will you please let me handle this? You know the irritating effect you usually have on policemen, and if we are to be of any use to John at all, we've simply got to keep on the good side of them. We've already failed in our first objective—to prevent something from happening. Keep that firmly in mind, and play along with me. I've got an idea."

They were shown into a small, square, harshly lit office where a large, broad-shouldered man was gazing moodily out the window at the now-teeming skies. His most remarkable feature was a pair of exceedingly bushy eyebrows, which, when drawn down over his dark, deep-set eyes as they presently were, made him into an intimidating figure. He was blue-chinned, and the dark pouches under his eyes signaled a man who for days had not had his natural quota of sleep. Penny's heart sank at the sight of him. He turned as they entered and impatiently waved them to chairs, seating himself behind the desk.

"So," he said in a soft drawl, looking at the note pad before him, "Dr. Spring and Sir Tobias Glendower, I have some questions to ask you concering Mr. John Everett, who is suspected of the murder of Arlette Gray of this city. The prisoner has stated that you and he were meeting here on business. Please tell me the nature of that business.''

Toby cleared his throat. ''Before saying anything, Captain Beauregard, may I ask a favor of you? Would you call, at my expense, Detective Barnabas Eldredge at the state police post at South Yarmouth, Massachusetts, and ask him about me and my colleague here? I could also refer you to Inspector Abrams of the Jerusalem police and Inspector Hamit Bey of the Bergama police, but I realize time is of the essence, and this one call should suffice. I am afraid we cannot say anything until you have done that.''

Beauregard was startled by this unusual approach. He looked keenly at Sir Tobias, who gazed back with guileless blue eyes, and then at the worried face of Penny. ''All right,'' he agreed. ''Wait here.'' And he went into the outer office.

''What are you up to?'' Penny hissed as the door closed.

''Just trust me,'' Toby murmured. ''I've got a hunch about this.''

''Are you really going to tell him why we're here? What about Lefau?''

''Our prime interest in all this is John Everett. If it becomes necessary, yes, I think we should tell Beauregard all we know. Which, after all, is not a hell of a lot,'' Toby growled. ''But if we can only get him to believe in *us,* I've a feeling it will be a great help.''

After a seemingly endless wait, Beauregard came back in, looking thoughtful and a little bewildered. He slumped into his desk chair and looked at them with a grim smile. ''Amateur sleuths—that's just about all I need right now!''

''Amateur sleuths, perhaps, but with a one-hundred-percent success rating up to now. Please bear that in mind.'' Sir Tobias was firm.

''But what the hell has that got to do with the present situation? Are you telling me that you were involved with John Everett on a *case*?''

''Yes,'' Toby said simply, ''I'm saying just that. Mr. Everett had been threatened with disgrace and death by someone in this city. We were here to look into these threats and to prevent them. We were too late. But before I explain all this, would you mind telling us the circumstances of this murder and the evidence against Mr. Everett? We know nothing save that he has been arrested on suspicion of murder, and, knowing him as well as we do, we find this a fantastic charge. If you will be frank with us, we will be frank with you, and it may save a great deal of time all the way around.''

Their eyes locked for a long moment; then Beauregard nodded. ''Right. Well, the facts are these: The murder victim was Arlette Gray, age twenty-seven, mulatto, born in Haiti, emigrated to New Orleans ten years ago. Occupation: officially a photographers' model, unofficially a call girl.'' Penny's spirits sank even lower. ''John Everett was discovered by a cleaning woman around nine A.M., in his bedroom in the St. Louis Hotel, bending over the body. The victim was nude and had been strangled with her own gold jewelry. She had been dead approximately six hours, putting the time of death about three o'clock this morning. We'll know more definitely after the autopsy, which is being performed right now. When he was taken into custody, Mr. Everett appeared dazed and confused and claimed he could neither remember anything nor explain anything.'' He paused.

Penny opened her mouth for the first time. ''What did he say happened after he arrived in New Orleans?''

Beauregard looked at his notes. ''He claims he ate dinner at the hotel, then went on a Red Coach sight-seeing tour of the city. He left the tour before its conclusion and ended up in Pat O'Brien's bar on St. Peter Street. He admits that the victim shared a table with him in the bar but claims he became very sick there and recalls nothing between the time he was at the table and when he woke up this morning to find the dead girl beside him. He also claims that he was awakened by the sounds of the cleaning woman and had only just discovered the body himself when she entered and gave the alarm.''

''And yet you have booked him only on suspicion of murder, not murder.'' Penny pounced. ''Why?''

Beauregard favored her with a grim look. ''Because there are several circumstances that have to be clarified before we charge him with murder one. He was so dazed when he was brought in that we gave him a blood test. As well as alcohol, it revealed traces of sodium amytal—in other words, a Mickey Finn, which *could* account for a mental blackout and symptoms such as he described. Secondly, the night clerk reports that Mr. Everett arrived back at the hotel 'dead drunk,' in his words, and was supported by the victim and a cabdriver. Thirdly, there is one bizarre aspect to the killing that does not quite fit in with the pattern of an ordinary sex murder. The dead girl's breast was mutilated by an iron skewer of unusual design, which had a sort of emblem attached to it that no one here can identify.''

"May I see it?" Penny asked quickly.

Beauregard considered, then said, "Why not?" His tone was weary. He took up a manila envelope and decanted its plastic-wrapped contents onto the desk. Penny stared and gasped. "You know what it is?" he asked quickly.

"I recognize the emblem." She was breathless with excitement. "It's a voodoo sign, a *vévé* of one of their chief gods. It's the symbol of Ghede, the *loa* of death and resurrection. The black and red colors are the colors of Ghede. And the girl was from Haiti!" She looked at him triumphantly. "This has the earmarks of a sacrifice. That's what she was—a sacrifice!"

Beauregard looked at Penny with deepening suspicion. "Are you sure about these facts?"

"Of course I'm sure!" she was indignant. "It's my job, after all; I'm an anthropologist. I spent a year some time ago down in Haiti and Santo Domingo, looking into the native religions." She omitted the fact that she had been kicked out of Haiti by the Duvalier government of the time, which had not appreciated her research. She peered closer at the skewer. "And that looks like a handmade skewer of pure iron. That also would fit. The cold iron would help keep the girl's spirit from approaching the living. Was the cabdriver who came in with them black? If so, he should be looked for immediately."

Beauregard let out an exasperated sigh. "Naturally, we are looking for him, but have you any idea of the number of black cabdrivers in this city and the difficulties of getting such information during Carnival? Anyway, we are wasting time. What was your business here?"

Toby hastily cut in. "The threats centered around a book that Mr. Everett is putting out from his Boston publishing house. The anonymous letter writer threatened both him and the author with dire happenings should the book appear, as it is scheduled to do at Mardi Gras. He and the author thought we might be able to trace the source of these threats."

"What was the book?"

"A history of the Comus krewe and of Mardi Gras."

Beauregard looked suitably blank. "And the author?"

Toby hesitated a second. "Jules Lefau."

The policeman let out a soft exclamation. "So that's why . . ."

"Mr. Lefau has already been in touch with you?" Toby said with quick hope.

Beauregard passed a weary hand over his face. "Mr. Lefau's lawyers have been swarming over us like a hive of bees," he said dryly. "As a result, though this is practically unheard of in a murder case, the prisoner is shortly going to be released on fifty-five thousand dollars' bail, put up by Lefau on his personal surety. If Lefau is mixed up in this . . ." He wiped at his eyes with his hands, like a tired child. "God, what a *mess*! I don't think I want to hear any more. This city is enough of a madhouse during Carnival: I've been averaging about three hours' sleep a night, and everyone else here, too. Now you tell me one of our leading citizens is connected in some way with one of the messiest murders we've had in years, one that the press are going to be onto like wolves."

Toby looked at him with sympathy. "Well, so far as we are concerned, there is not much more to hear. Apart from the fact that the letters have no identifying fingerprints, that's all we know at the moment. I think this murder implicating John Everett may be a setup. If Lefau is the real target, what better way for the letter writer to show he means business, to show he is capable of carrying out his threats? You may feel we are here to tamper with justice, but that is not the case. I suggest we may be of value to you, because we will be working on the inside: we will be guests of Mr. Lefau from now until Mardi Gras. To you we may seem an unlikely pair of detectives, but believe me, Captain, both Dr. Spring and I know what we are doing and how to get information. Anything we find cognate to this case we will pass on to you. You evidently have your hands more than full during this busy season; well, now you have two extra pairs of hands. We would like to help." He sounded impressively sincere.

"Fair enough," the big man muttered. "Until Carnival is over, we are going to have neither the time nor the manpower to devote to this case. But once it is over"—he looked up, his dark eyes hard—"we are going to get to the bottom of it. And if John Everett is our man, Lefau or no Lefau, we'll get him."

"We understand that," Toby rumbled placatingly. "But may we see Mr. Everett now?"

Beauregard gave a harassed glance at the wall clock. "OK. Lefau's lawyer should have completed the arrangements; we'll not be able to hold him any longer. I believe he is being taken to the Lefau plantation."

They all stood up. "One more thing," Toby persevered. "Would it be possible for you to let us have the results of the autopsy on the dead girl and any other background facts on her? It may help."

Beauregard gave a reluctant nod. "All right."

"Do you have a picture of her you could let us have, also?" Penny put in. "I may be able to locate that cabdriver through a cab-driving friend of mine." Toby looked faintly shocked, but again the large man nodded and opened a folder on his desk. He slid a glossy five-by-seven picture out of it and handed it to Penny. "Goodness, she was beautiful!" she exclaimed.

"Not when I saw her," he returned grimly. "But, yes, she was a doll—a real living doll."

Their first sight of John Everett was a shock. His small, portly figure seemed to have shrunk in on itself, and he had the crumpled, battered look of a man much buffeted by fate: his round face unshaven, his mild blue eyes bloodshot and frightened—there was nothing left of the cheerful, philosophical, poised little man Penny had known for the past thirty years. Over him towered the cadaverous figure of a Lefau lawyer, disapproval on his austere face. An equally tall thin black man with a fine-boned face, thin lips, and deep-set hooded eyes, dressed in a sober black suit, stood slightly behind him as Penny rushed up to John and gave him a reassuring hug.

The lawyer looked at her with equal disapproval and turned to Toby. "Mr. Lefau has sent his majordomo, Henri Legros" —he indicated the black man with a slight nod—"to escort you all back to the plantation. Please give him the instructions as to where to pick up your baggage. I have a few details to take care of here, but Mr. Everett is free to go."

"If you would follow me?" Henri's voice was high and harsh, and he spoke with a heavy French accent. He escorted them out of the police headquarters to a white Mercedes-Benz limousine parked illegally at the curb; a uniformed cop was looking at it with intense disapproval. Penny and John hastily scrambled into the back seat as Toby, with more dignity, allowed himself to be seated in the front by the aloof driver.

Once inside, Penny turned to her shaken friend. "Are you all right?" she said in an urgent whisper. "They didn't rough you up or anything, did they?"

John raised dazed eyes to her. "No, nothing like that."

"Well then, cheer up! Everything's going to be all right now. Just tell me everything that happened, would you? Once we get to Lefau's, we may not have the chance for a private talk."

"Hell, everything is *not* all right," he said dully. "I may be a murderer."

"*You*! Go on, of course not. You've been framed. How can you even think such a thing!"

"I wish I could be that sure." He pressed his hands wearily to his temples. "If only I could remember."

"What *do* you remember of last night? Think, John. It's very important."

Haltingly he told her of the events of the evening before. "I wouldn't say I'd been behaving normally the whole evening, but after the bar I scarcely remember a thing, and what I do remember is no comfort." He gave a little shiver. "The trouble is, I don't know whether I was dreaming it or not."

"Well, go on."

He looked shamefaced. "I recall an erotic sequence . . . and a woman laughing . . . and a feeling of terrible anger. Suppose I did try and she rejected me? Suppose I did it then in a blind fury?"

"John, you're not thinking straight," Penny whispered. "Look at your hands."

He looked wonderingly at his small, well-kept hands. "What about them?"

She turned them over to reveal unblemished palms. "The girl was strangled by the gold chains she wore around her neck. Anyone using that much force on her would have lacerated his own hands *unless* he was wearing gloves. Beauregard says the only gloves of yours they found were a pair of light pigskin, neatly packed in your suitcase—without a mark on them, incidentally. Can you seriously believe, if the scenario had been as you describe it, that in a fit of furious anger at being rejected you would have gone to your suitcase, unpacked the gloves, strangled her so neatly that not a spot of blood or mark was left on them, and then *re*packed them?''

He looked at her, then back at his hands, with dawning hope. ''Then, you don't think I . . . ?''

''Of course not! John, you were set up. Someone slipped you a Mickey Finn. Possibly it was the girl herself—she could have done it when you were retrieving her handbag from under the table. Then, before you blacked out completely, she and her accomplice hauled you back to the hotel.''

''But that would mean she connived in her own death!''

''Not really.'' Penny was thoughtful. ''Maybe all she thought was going to happen was to take some compromising pictures of you and her in bed—blackmail. Maybe that was all that was *supposed* to happen, but something went wrong and she was murdered. Our anonymous friend's object was still accomplished: you were on the hook either way.''

''But *who*? No one can get into the St. Louis Hotel that late at night without the night clerk's seeing him.''

Penny shrugged. ''That's as may be; it's too early to tell yet. But there's the cabdriver, and it's entirely possible that someone was in the hotel waiting for you to be brought back, someone who had strolled in earlier, while there were plenty of people around, and had hidden out. Look, it's unlikely you could have got the Mickey Finn as early as the nightclub, or it would have hit you sooner. It *had* to be when you were in the bar, and that seems to narrow the field to the girl and the waiter there. In view of everything else, most likely the girl.''

''But how could they possibly have *known* all this?'' John protested. ''I was just wandering; it was just happenstance that I went into Pat O'Brien's.''

''You could have been followed. It would have been easy enough for someone who was out to get you to find out you'd gone off on the night tour. Anyone can find out the approximate times you'd be at the various stops. They could have watched you from the time you came out of the nightclub and separated from the group, followed you along Bourbon Street, seen you settle, and that was it."

"It's all so incredible," he fussed, but he looked relieved, "all so *organized*."

"That was a voodoo sign on her," Penny said grimly, "and if there is voodoo involved, it is not a matter of *one* operator; voodoo *is* organized. We may be in much deeper waters than we know. But what the hell this has to do with the book or with Lefau I just cannot imagine at this juncture."

He began to look wretched again. "What on earth am I going to say to Millicent? How can I explain?"

"Very little until you get back home. I've already phoned her," Penny said firmly. "In fact, she was hell-bent on flying to your rescue, but I vetoed that. I was certain you would not want her involved in this mess. But I shouldn't worry too much. Millicent is blaming herself for not coming with you; so you can have a merry old sackcloth-and-ashes session *à deux* when you get back together again. In the meantime, I suggested she fly out to your son's place for a while, so that if any Boston reporters get wind of this, she won't have them to deal with. She thought it was an excellent idea."

John let out a relieved sigh. "Thank God for that! I don't think I could have coped with Millicent at the moment."

Toby had been keeping one eye on their deep conversation in the rearview mirror. Since it had been conducted in whispers, he hadn't been able to make out a word above the muted roar of the powerful engine, and Henri, driving steadily and sedately, was totally uncommuncative; so Toby devoted himself to watching the slowly unfolding scenery and trying to keep track of their direction. They had started heading north toward Lake Pontchartrain but then had turned sharply west on Route 61 past the airport; now they were angling north again, and he surmised they were following the meanderings of the river, although he had caught no glimpse of it. They were no longer on the main road and for some time had been following along a long white wall adorned with a menacing chevaux-de-frise. The car began to slow, and in the wall appeared two soaring wrought-iron gates of such exquisite workmanship that they looked like a symphony of iron lace. Henri produced a little black box from his pocket and pressed a button, the gates swung silently open, and the car picked up speed again along a tree-lined avenue. The car veered around a large ornamental fountain onto a wide sweep of gravel and drew up before the portico of a typical columned antebellum southern mansion, where twin staircases in the same exquisite wrought iron soared up in a horseshoe shape to the colonnaded patio before the huge front doors.

As the car came to a stop, one of the doors opened, and a man stepped out onto the terrace. He was slim and of but medium height though he held himself very erect. His longish silver-gray hair was elaborately cut and styled. Although his clothes were casual, they, too, were of such impeccable cut and neatness that he looked almost dandified. He stood, leaning his hands lightly on the railing of the patio, watching until they had all got out; then he started down one of the staircases toward them as they moved toward the house. His thin, fine-featured face broke into a welcoming smile, revealing small white teeth, the incisors singularly pointed and long. He halted on the bottom stair, looking down at them. "Welcome," he said in a pleasant, light tenor voice. "Welcome to *La Maison de la Dame Dansante*." He bowed to Penny. "I am your host, Jules Lefau."

CHAPTER 5

"The House of the Dancing Lady—such a charming name! I am sure there must be a story behind it." Penny was being extremely affable to her host. In part this was to make up for Toby, who had lapsed into a mood of dour taciturnity on arrival, as if his own congeniality had been totally expended on Captain Beauregard and he was not about to overstrain himself.

"In the Bayou country there is a story about everything." Jules Lefau was being just as charming, equally as if the furthest thing from his mind was the fact that one of his guests was under suspicion of murder and he himself a target of ominous threats. "There are several stories about the dancing lady. It is said that my first ancestor here, who came with Bienville, settled in this remote spot and that his wife, who was used to the life of the French court, went a little mad with the loneliness and would dance the stately dances of the time in a clearing he had made in the forest. Another story is that the name was given by the builders of this present house—that would be about 1840. They were twins, and the elder by about five minutes thought it so unfair that his younger twin be deprived of his inheritance that he built a remarkable house. It is, in effect, a twin house, a double house. After the fatiguing day you have had, I do not propose to drag you on the grand tour—in any case, there would scarcely be time before dinner—but tomorrow I would like to show it to you."

"That would be delightful," Penny said.

"Anyway, while the brothers enjoyed their joint owner-ship, their wives apparently did not. The wife of the older

46

was a proud, jealous woman, but deeply religious; that of the younger was beautiful, gay, and a little light-headed. In the house the will of the older brother's wife prevailed and no dancing was allowed, but the younger to spite her would dance on the lawn in the moonlight, swathed in all manner of outlandish, and presumably scanty, garments. Some say on a bright, moonlit night she dances still and that when she does, it is a sign of great misfortune.'' He gave a Gallic shrug and smiled at Penny. "I have never seen her myself.''

Jules Lefau intrigued her. Although for nearly three hundred years the Lefaus had been part of the American scene, there was still an indefinable air of foreignness about him. His gestures, his appearance, even his precise speech, which was that of a well-educated foreigner not speaking his native tongue—all added to the impression that he was in America but not of it. She found him fascinating and could hardly wait to meet the rest of the Lefaus, none of whom had as yet been in evidence.

Jules glanced at a delicate Louis Seize ormulu clock that was chiming beguilingly from the marble mantle of a *petit salon* in which they had been having before-dinner drinks and which was furnished throughout with the graceful pieces from that exquisite period of French artistry. "Would you care for another drink? I think there is just time before we must dress.'' He gave a little rueful grimace. "We do not normally keep such state, but during Carnival we return to the old ways and are rather formal. I hope you do not mind.''

"Not at all. It will be an interesting change for me. And thank you, but no more; that gin fizz was excellent but rather strong,'' Penny returned.

"Then, perhaps we should go.'' Jules got up and addressed Toby, who had been talking quietly with John Everett. "Sir Tobias, I am very eager to have your expert opinion on the claret we will be having at dinner tonight. It's a Yon-Figeac '75. I would most value your thoughts on it.''

Toby's blue eyes were almost steely as he looked at his host. "Certainly, I would be happy to oblige,'' he replied pompously. "Yon-Figeac happens to be one of my favorite vintages.'' But he said nothing further and appeared to sink into an even deeper gloom.

"What is the matter with you?'' Penny whispered in his ear

as Henri ushered them on their way to their rooms. "Loosen up a bit, will you? Lefau is knocking himself out to be nice and you're acting like a stuffed owl. He really *is* extremely thoughtful. Do you know I found a whole box of *marrons glacés* on my night table? My *favorite* candy!"

"Exactly," Toby growled obscurely and disappeared into his own room with a bang.

Penny wandered around her own room, munching *marrons glacés* and trying to decide which of the formal dresses she had brought she should wear. The more she looked at them, the shabbier and more out-of-date they appeared. "Oh, dear!" she muttered as her watch showed her it was five of eight. "Dinner at eight—I'd better get a move on." She scrambled with undignified haste into a kaftan of cream wool, lovingly embroidered for her with barbaric designs in multicolored wools by a Kazak woman she had befriended. Its oddity suited her own peculiar charms rather well, she thought, as she hastily reduced her hair to some sort of order and, with a despairing look at her face, decided there was really nothing further she could do about *that*. She skittered down the long corridor and the magnificent staircase to find her host, resplendent in black velvet dinner jacket and ruffled shirt, waiting for her expectantly in the hallway.

"Ah, there you are, Dr. Spring. Our little party is complete." He turned to a lighted doorway just inside the entrance and raised his voice slightly. "We are ready to go in," he said and offered her his arm.

They proceeded into a formal dining room, dimly lit by two great silver candelabra on the long mahogany table. Jules Lefau seated her on his right and then stood waiting courteously for his wife, entering on Sir Tobias's arm, to be seated at the far opposite end. When Penny got her first glimpse of Toby, she nearly let forth a yelp of despair and began to perspire quietly into her wool kaftan, which she realized belatedly was far too warm for the occasion.

Toby was clad in an old-fashioned waistcoated dinner suit of such antiquity that it was green with age. Across the waistcoat was slung a gold hunter watch and chain, and topping off the monstrosity, on his stiff shirt front, which bulged, nestled the Order of Merit, slung rather crookedly on its ribbon. *What the devil is he up to?* she thought wildly. She

knew full well he had a perfectly acceptable modern dinner
jacket and shirt in his bags; she also knew for a fact his Order
of Merit had not left its velvet box since the queen had
presented him with it and that he abhorred the very thought of
wearing it. She looked anxiously at his face, which told her
nothing save that he had progressed from looking like a
stuffed owl to looking like a boiled one. *Is he drunk?* flashed
through her mind before her attention was claimed by her
host, introductions commenced, and she gathered her wits
together to collate her first impressions of the Lefau family.

"I am sorry to rush you in like this," Jules Lefau was
saying charmingly, "but I fear we are on a very tight sched-
ule. My wife, Eleanor, has to meet with the Comus women's
committee tonight, and I, alas, with the program committee.
And Benedict here"—he indicated his elder son, who was on
Penny's right—"has to go down to the city to see how the
floats are progressing."

"Oh, I know how busy you all must be," Penny responded
politely. "My fault entirely for being so late."

The long and sumptuous dinner commenced, and Penny,
who loved food anyway and good food to distraction, found it
very hard to concentrate on her fellow diners. What mainly
struck her about the Lefaus was their disparity. Unlike his
father, Benedict was very large, beefy, fair of hair and skin,
blue of eye, and on the clumsy side. His wife, Grace, across
the table from Penny, had even fairer hair but with a brunette
skin and dark eyes, and what would have been a striking face
was marred by a thick-lipped mouth that drooped disconso-
lately at the corners. She had nothing to say for herself. Next
to her was the small, dark-haired younger son, Vincent, with
very dark, thoughtful eyes, and he also was silent. Penny
could catch only glimpses of his sister, next to Benedict's big
bulk, but she saw a beautiful, regular profile and a mass of
chestnut hair as Juliette talked with animation to her partner,
John Everett, seated on Eleanor Lefau's left, opposite Toby.
The hostess was only dimly visible, but she appeared to be
almost the same size as her husband, deep-bosomed, dark-
haired, and with high-colored, strong features: a handsome
woman rather than a beautiful one.

For a while it puzzled Penny as to who the slim young girl
with the short, bobbed fair hair could be on Toby's right. She

could not see her face, which was turned toward Toby and listening to him with rapt attention. By a process of elimination Penny concluded this must be Celeste, which startled her. Jules Lefau was fifty-five but did not look it; his sister, according to John's genealogy, must be sixty-five and *certainly* did not look it. Her interest aroused, Penny determined to get a closer look at the amazing Celeste at the first opportunity.

"Where's Deacon?" Jules Lefau asked Henri, who was replenishing their wineglasses.

"I haven't seen him all evening, *m'sieu*." The harsh voice was modulated into a sibilant whisper.

"Hmm, that's strange." Jules's brows knitted. He turned to Penny with a little smile of apology. "Every man has his weakness—mine is Deacon, my hunting dog. Terribly spoiled, I'm afraid. He is never known to miss a meal, for I have the bad habit of feeding him tidbits at table. But he is a remarkable dog—more like a friend than an animal—and I think he is as devoted to me as I to him."

Penny had been straining to hear what Toby was going on at such length about at the other end of the table. He was using his sonorous lecturer's rumble, and when she managed to tune in, she was startled to hear him describing in boring, interminable detail an excavation he had conducted at Troezen in Greece. It was a dig that he had found highly unsatisfactory and that normally never crossed his lips. Toby, when libated with good wine—and this was very good wine they were drinking—could be one of the world's wittiest and most interesting dinner companions; now he was being deliberately and ponderously boring. *Why?* she thought frantically. *What can he be up to?*

Henri materialized at her side and murmured something into his master's ear. Jules Lefau gave out a little exclamation of annoyance and dabbed at his lips. "Will you excuse us," he said to her. "A business phone call. Benedict, I'll need you. I am afraid I will have to leave you in my sister's hands for the rest of the evening," he went on as the blond giant lumbered to his feet. "Please feel free to do whatever you please, and forgive us for all this unmannerly disturbance."

His going began a general exodus. Eleanor Lefau swept out, and the two younger children followed her. "Shall we take coffee in the salon?'' Celeste said in a silvery voice, still concentrating on Sir Tobias. They migrated to the chandelier-lit splendors of a *grand salon* furnished in the heavy, ornate style of Louis Quatorze, and Penny for the first time got a clear look at Celeste. Her girlish figure was as slim as a wand, her fine, fair hair done in a short, curly bob that had been fashionable in the thirties and was once more back in style. At first glance her face, with its thin, fine nose, delicately molded lips, and large gray eyes, confirmed this impression of girlishness, but closer inspection revealed a fine network of lines that creased the fair, faded skin and wattled the slim throat. At one time Celeste Lefau had been a very fair flower indeed, but now that flower was faded, and the pale eyes under the finely etched fair brows were sorrowful and haunted. *Rich and pretty—I wonder why she never married*, Penny thought as Celeste gracefully dispensed coffee and polite, inconsequential chitchat to her three guests.

Grace Lefau had settled onto one of the stiff couches and was gazing sullenly at the older woman, without making the least effort to join in the conversation. Penny felt a twinge of irritation. God damn it! If she hadn't enough manners to help Celeste with her guests, why didn't she just leave? She was on the point of saying something snappish to the sulky blonde, then decided that would never do, so jumped up and started to examine the portraits in heavy gilt frames that lined the pale-cream walls. Celeste joined her and began to explain the many and various Lefaus.

Penny stopped before one portrait with a gasp of admiration. ''What a perfectly heavenly portrait of you!''

Celeste looked at her, a strange expression in her faded eyes. ''Look a little closer, Dr. Spring.''

Penny looked at the nameplate underneath. PERNELL LEFAU, it read, 1890-1935. She was the exact double of Celeste, even to the hairstyle. ''Why, the resemblance is uncanny!'' Penny exclaimed, peering at the picture.

''My mother. It was painted the year she was Queen of Comus, exactly fifty years ago,'' Celeste said in a dreamy voice. ''That is why Jules is having the exact costumes reproduced for this year's anniversary. And this is my father.'' She passed to the next picture, where a man dressed in heavy cloth of gold stared at them with dark, mocking eyes. "Also in his costume as King of Comus."

Penny didn't much care for the looks of him; there was a sardonic twist to the heavy, cruel mouth, and in looks, if not in coloring, he favored his grandson rather than the elegant Jules.

Henri again loomed behind them, beckoned Celeste aside, and whispered to her. Her delicate lips clamped into a determined line of a sudden, and for the first time Penny saw a faint resemblance to her brother.

"Does it have to be now?" Celeste asked sharply. More murmuring, and she turned to Penny with an exasperated sigh. "Oh dear, how very tiresome! I shall have to leave you for a while. A domestic matter."

Toby and John, tiring of their own company, had joined them. Celeste hurried over to the couch and the petulant Grace, and Toby had time to say into Penny's ear, "I am about to suggest a walk in the park. Accept!" before Celeste hurried back, an apologetic smile on her lips.

"Really, you must think us terribly rude, all of us leaving like this. My nephew's wife has a bad migraine and is about to retire. I don't know . . ." She hovered uncertainly.

"Please do not disturb yourself on our account," Toby said pompously. "We realize what a busy time this is for you all. I was about to suggest a walk outside to Dr. Spring and Mr. Everett before retiring. I see the rain has ended. Is there any reason we should not go?"

"Why, no, of course not," Celeste dithered with a quick look at Henri, who was gazing fixedly at Toby. "Henri will not lock up the house for another hour at least. The only thing is that I shouldn't venture too far in the dark; the grounds are rather extensive, and you might get lost. Also, if you go out by these doors, keep right rather than left; to the left it gets very swampy and unpleasant close to the river."

"I think, if you don't mind, I'll follow Mrs. Lefau's example and turn in," John Everett said with a wan smile. "It's been a hard day."

"Then, I shall bid you all good night. Shall we go?" Toby took a firm grip on Penny's elbow and steered her toward the French doors giving onto the stone terrace, leaving the small group gazing after them.

Once outside and the doors closed, Penny shook her elbow free and turned on him. "Do you mind telling me what the hell you are up to? Not only do you *look* like a complete buffoon, but you've been acting the fool the whole evening. Why?"

Toby had produced his pipe from some hidden pocket and filled and lit it before replying. He exhaled a large cloud of blue smoke with a satisfied sigh. "Phew! That was a strain!" He began to chuckle. "Really had you going, did I?" He started toward the sward of lawn beneath the terrace, lit by a fitful moon. "Well, I had a very good reason. Let's get farther away from the house, and I'll fill you in."

Still mystified, Penny trotted along beside him as he stalked out on the lawn toward the banked magnolias and oleanders around it. His next remark completely flabbergasted her. "How many people know you have a weakness for *marrons glacés*?"

"It's not a deep, dark secret," she spluttered, "but not a lot. Why?"

"Yon-Figeac is one of the smaller and not particularly well known vineyards of the Bordeaux region, and yet I have always liked its product better than any other claret. Only half a dozen people in the world know that."

"Toby," she squeaked in exasperation, "will you get to the point, if there is one? I don't even begin to see what you are getting at."

"What I'm getting at is that Jules Lefau has obviously done some *very* deep research on both of us, research that must have taken a good deal of time and money. Ask yourself why."

"All right, I'll buy it—why?"

Toby appeared to go off on a tangent. "What would you say our outstanding characteristics are?"

Again this took her breath away. "What a question! Er, well, we're both very good at our jobs, and we're a bit odd. What of it?"

He brushed this aside. "Odd, indeed!" he snorted. "Apart from that, then?"

"I've no idea."

"Would you say we were people of solid reputation and

integrity—and of a certain eminence—whose word is gener-
ally accepted?'' he prompted.

"Yes, I suppose so."

"So that if we witnessed something and testified to it, we
would be believed?''

"Yes."

"That's it, then. That's why I think we're here—to witness
something."

"But what?" Penny wailed.

Toby waved his pipe grandly. "Ah, as to that, I haven't
the faintest idea as yet."

"And what's it got to do with your dressing up in a
comic-opera suit and playing the pompous idiot?''

"Because, if Jules Lefau is as devious as I think he is,
that's precisely the impression I want him to get—a boring, eminent old ass, whose reputation is a lot greater than his abili-
ties, instead of vice-versa," Toby added with breathtaking
conceit. "*I* am going to hide my light under a very large
bushel while we are here, and I'd advise you to do the same,
at least until we know what he is up to."

They had passed through the close-banked magnolias and
were now among huge live oaks, whose trailing fingers of
Spanish moss sent little shivers up Penny's spine as they
gently reached out and touched her face in the light night
wind.

"He's a very interesting man," she murmured.

"Umm. I noticed you were finding him so, but don't get
swept away by it," Toby growled. "Did you know your neck
is purple?''

Penny scrubbed irritably at her neckline. "Oh, rats! It's
these hand-dyed wools; they always run, and you got me so
nervous in there I was perspiring like crazy. I hope it comes
off. Hey!'' She stopped suddenly. "We're bearing off to the
left. We'll end up in the swamp at this rate!''

"Not if we go cautiously. It's just that until we get to know
the household a bit better, I'm not prepared to believe any of
them. I *think* Celeste is probably all right, but I just want to
see for myself."

Penny suddenly clutched at his arm. "Toby, what's that?"
A scudding cloud crossed the moon, and they were plunged

into momentary darkness. "I thought I saw something large and dark on the ground ahead."

They froze until the moon reappeared, and then Toby let out an exclamation. "You're right!"

They hurried toward the large shape. It was a huge Irish wolfhound—and it was very dead.

Penny let out a gasp. "I hope it's not Deacon."

"Deacon?"

"Lefau's favorite dog. He missed it at dinner."

"There's something very queer here." Toby was bending over the stiffened carcass. "Damn! I wish I had my flashlight." With a grimace of distaste he started to drag the dog from the shade of the tree into a moonlit clearing, where he knelt down, struck some matches, and appeared to be feeling the body.

"What is it?" Penny breathed.

He got up with a little shudder. "Well, it's hard to say for certain without a better light, but I'd say the dog's throat was cut, and then someone cut its heart out."

"Oh, my God! An affair of beef hearts and black crepe paper."

"What on earth are you babbling about?" Toby was testy.

"I was thinking of the famous row between Marie Laveau and the *hungan* Jim Alexander. It's the voodoo theme again." She glanced uneasily around and quoted. " 'To effect the death of an enemy, take the heart of an animal close to the intended victim, cover it with black crepe paper, and stick it through and through with black-headed pins, saying the incantations. Place it near to your victim, and he will be dead within a week.' Oh, Toby, what is going on? I'm sure that's Lefau's dog."

"Hmm, yes, it seems to be getting pretty nasty. I think we'd better head back to the house." He started to hustle her away, casting backward glances as he went. "No sense in pressing our luck."

When they reached the safety of the lit terrace, they were both a little out of breath. "We won't say a word of this to anyone," he admonished, "but first thing tomorrow we'd best try and make a search of the house. If you're right—and you usually are on this sort of thing—there's a dog's heart around here somewhere, and when we find it, we'll know who is in danger. We'd better call it a night now.''

Her thoughts in a whirl, Penny got ready for bed. Turning out the light, she went to the window to open it—and stood transfixed. Her bedroom looked out over a vista cleared through the magnolias to another, smaller version of the main fountain, its soaring waters spraying silver rays into the moonlight. Dark against them was the figure of a woman—and she was dancing.

CHAPTER 6

"I think the less we say about any of this, the better." Toby was firm.

"Not even about the dancing lady?" Penny, although the morning was bright with sunlight, gave a little shiver. "That really was spooky. I just can't get over it."

"You couldn't make out who it was?"

"No, not even the color of the hair or skin. She seemed to be dressed in something filmy, because you could see it flapping against the water, spraying as she danced."

"And you say she just disappeared?"

"Yes. I watched her for about five minutes, and then I blinked my eyes to clear my vision—everything was getting blurry, I was staring so hard—and, hup, when I opened them again, she was gone, vanished."

"You know, you *were* pretty tired, and we'd just had a rather upsetting experience," Toby said dubiously. "Are you sure it wasn't some trick of the moonlight on the bushes?"

"Oh, really, Toby, you ought to know me better than that! When I say I saw something, I *saw* it. Besides, I nipped out first thing this morning to check on the bush situation. There's nothing near that fountain that would account for it. She was whirling like a dervish, and for branches to be that active, you'd have to have a howling gale. Last night there was only a gentle breeze. I do hope she wasn't a ghost; I wouldn't care for that at all."

"Ghosts!" Toby snorted, then made a little shushing gesture as their host appeared in the doorway of the small room in which they were breakfasting. He was dressed in a conservative three-piece, light-gray business suit, and his air of total immaculateness made them both feel dowdy.

"I have to go into the city in about half an hour, but I was wondering if you would care for a quick tour of the house," he said in his precise voice. "I can give you a general idea of the place, and then you may wander at your leisure. My wife is in town having a fitting for her Carnival dress, but she should be back to entertain you at luncheon. And there is always Celeste." He hesitated a second. "I shall be back about six, and I thought perhaps then we might have a talk about this other wretched business." Since he did not elaborate, they weren't quite sure whether he was referring to the murder or the threats.

"I'd love to see the house," Penny said eagerly. "And Sir Tobias is fascinated by southern plantation architecture."

Toby, who had resumed his stuffed-owl expression, nodded agreement.

"Well, then, let's get started." Jules led them out into the marble-floored hall, from which twin staircases soared in a horseshoe of marble and delicate ironwork balustrades up to the second story; the walls were French gray, the moldings picked out in gold leaf.

"How exquisite all the ironwork is!" Penny exclaimed. "Your front gates are really a masterpiece."

"Yes, they are rather fine, aren't they? All the ironwork was done by the same craftsman, a rather interesting character called Daumeny Glapion. He was one of the many love children of Louis Glapion and the famous—or perhaps I should say infamous—Marie Laveau."

"Ah, the voodoo queen," Penny said, avoiding looking at Toby.

"Oh, so you have heard of her? Yes, the very same. Not that she had anything to do with his work. Now, as to the layout: This was the elder brother's house I was telling you about last night. He put it up on the site of the original Lefau house, which he pulled down because he did not think it stylish enough to suit the rising family fortunes. It has been changed around a lot over the years—my father did a lot of renovating—but the basic idea is the same. At present it houses my wife and me and our two children in the left wing, as well as the guest rooms in the right wing. However—" He advanced on two huge gray-and-gold double doors that stood between the two staircases and threw them wide, revealing another hall beyond of equal size. He beckoned them through and smiled at the amazed look on their faces as they saw identical twin staircases soaring upward, the only difference being that on this side the walls were ivory and gold. "As I said, this was the younger brother's house—identical in every respect to the other half."

"And this housed the dancing lady?" Penny inquired.

Jules shrugged. "Perhaps. But now we have converted it into two completely separate dwellings. My sister, Celeste, occupies the wing on the left, and my elder son and his wife that to the right. Since Celeste, being unmarried, does not require quite so much space, the modern kitchens and domestic offices are now in this left wing, adjoining our dining room. Of course, in the old days they were all outside, along with the sla——er, servants' quarters."

"And now they live in the house?"

"The few permanent ones we have." He grimaced. "Like so many other things that have changed in the South, domestic help is becoming harder and harder to find. Besides Henri, who has his own quarters over the garage, we have only three that live in: Celeste's personal maid, who used to be my old nanny; her daughter, who looks after my son's ménage; and Elviny Brosse, our cook." He grinned at Penny. "You will really have to make her acquaintance; she is quite a character— as cantankerous as all get-out, but a superb cook. Other than that we have a floating population of servants who come in for the day and go home at night. Luckily, Henri takes care of all that, or my wife would swiftly be driven mad!"

At the mention of his name, Henri suddenly materialized in the double doorway, once more clad in his dark suit and wearing a chauffeur's cap. "We should be going, m'sieu," he said abruptly. "Mr. Everett is waiting in the car. He has to go to the police again."

Jules gave a cluck of impatience. "Already? Then, I am afraid this has been a very short tour. But please feel free to explore on your own," he said as Henri retreated.

"I am most interested in the construction of these houses— particularly the roofs," Toby rumbled stodgily. "Would it be all right if I inspected your rafters?"

Jules looked a little taken aback. "Why, er, of course. I imagine there is some access through the attics. I must confess I have never been up there myself. The servants should know; perhaps when Henri gets back? Oh, one thing—if you are exploring the grounds at all, would you keep an eye out for my dog? He's a large Irish wolfhound but very amiable. I can't think where he has got to." For a second he looked vulnerable and a little lost. "I've told my son Vincent to look for him, but this is such a big place." He bowed to Penny with a little smile. "Until this evening, then." And he was gone, leaving behind the fragrance of an extremely expensive aftershave lotion.

Penny inhaled. "Goodness, that smells wonderful! You ought to get some." Toby, who had only recently got to the newfangled idea of shaving cream, looked disapproving. "So now what," Penny went on when she was sure they were alone, "a general wander or straight to the attics?"

"They strike me as being the most likely place, if your suspicions are correct. Anyway, we might as well be methodical and work from the top down."

"The servants are going to think it mighty queer if they catch us searching their rooms," Penny fussed.

"Then, one of us had better search while the other keeps 'cave,' " said Sir Tobias, for a second looking impishly like the Winchester schoolboy he had been in the long ago.

They went back into Jules's house, toiled up the marble staircase, and, bearing to the left, after several false starts located behind one of the ornate doors a humbler, wooden staircase that led up to the third-floor attic rooms. Some of the rooms were completely empty, others scattered with miscellaneous discarded household bric-a-brac that yielded nothing but clouds of dust.

Only one room showed signs of human occupancy, and an item in it elicited a little yelp from Penny. It was a photograph in a small silver frame, showing a dusky, heavy-faced woman in an old-fashioned *tignon* headdress. "Do you know who that is?" she asked Toby excitedly but didn't wait for an answer. "It's Malvina Latour."

"So?"

"Malvina Latour was also a famous voodoo queen in New Orleans—sometime in the 1890s, I think. She took over when

Marie Laveau—the second one, the daughter of the first—did her disappearing act. I wonder whose room this is." Penny hunted around for clues like an excited terrier and triumphantly came up with some letters. "It's Elviny Brosse's, the cook's. I am certainly going to want a word with *her* later on!"

Toby had been keeping an eye out at the door and was getting restless. "I think we are going about this the wrong way. You wait here; I want to check on something," he said suddenly. When he returned after a short interval, he looked satisfied. "We need to find some opening into the eaves. I collected my flashlight and yours. You mentioned that this death sign had to be placed near the intended victim. Well, if that is the case, the most likely place would be *over* the main bedroom."

"Or *in* it," Penny interjected. "We haven't looked there yet."

"First things first. We're here now."

They located what they sought in the final empty room on the third floor—a small wooden doorway that led into hollow darkness where their flashlights revealed nothing but joists and rafters. "This *should* stretch right over it." Toby launched himself along a large beam.

"For heaven's sake, be careful, Toby! If you slip, you'll go clean through the plaster ceiling. You don't want to break your neck or bust your other leg!" Penny exclaimed, flashing her light around.

He gave a sudden exclamation and knelt down precariously. "Come and take a look at his."

She inched along the beam and joined him. Their flashlights illuminated a small package that nestled between two joists. It was swathed in black crepe paper and was stuck so full of black-headed pins that it looked like a sinister pomander.

"Bingo," Penny said in a faint voice. "So Jules *is* the intended victim, just as John was, and the link is voodoo. Rather knocks your theory about him into a cocked hat, doesn't it?"

Toby's brow was furrowed as he got up and shooed her back along the beam in front of him. "Not necessarily." He was thoughtful. "We need a lot more information before we can say that."

They did a mutual brushing-down when they got back to the attic room, sending clouds of dust swirling into the still air, and stood staring at each other. "I think we should tell him when he gets back," Penny said. "I mean, he's bound to know something is up when the dog is found mutilated like that; so why keep him in the dark?"

"*If* the dog is found," Toby replied. "I think we should go back and see if it's still there. When we found it, it was still in full *rigor mortis*; so it hadn't been dead long. Animals go into *rigor* a lot quicker than humans, and it passes off faster, too."

"Can you find the spot again? It was dark, and things look so different in the light."

"I think so. A photographic memory does have its uses," he returned and led the way downstairs and out of the house. He paused a moment on the terrace and then set off at a determined lope, Penny trotting beside him. When they got to the live oaks, he slowed his pace and started to veer to the left. After a while he stopped and said quietly, "Just as I feared, it's gone."

"How can you be sure this is the place? There must be dozens of clearings like this."

"There's a big rock over there that I noticed last night. Also"—he bent down and picked up something white with a red tip—"I lit some matches trying to get a clearer look at the dog after I dragged him out. Here's one that I dropped."

"How do you know it's yours?"

"Because it's an English Swan Vesta match"—he produced a box from his pocket and rattled it at her—"and I very much doubt that anyone else around here would have such a thing."

"Oh," she said blankly. "So where does that leave us?"

"It leaves us with the fact that whoever killed the dog and hid the heart believes in what he is doing and doesn't want Lefau to be aware of it."

"I'm not sure that's good voodoo practice," Penny said. "Half of African magic is based on the premise that if your victim knows he is under attack, you'll succeed quicker."

"Umm. Well, I don't see much sense in hunting around for the body; it could take forever and wouldn't get us much further. I feel a strong need for more information. I'd like to get out of here, on the quiet, and go into the city. There's a lot of checking I'd like to do on the book and the Lefau background in general.''

"Me, too," Penny agreed. "I'd like to check into the current voodoo scene, and a good place to start would be the Voodoo Museum on Bourbon Street. The question is, how *do* we get out of here?"

"Maybe Henri has returned; we can get him to drive us in or at least borrow one of the cars," Toby said as they retraced their steps. "The garage is over there." It stood at some remove from the house, but when they reached it, the four spaces in it were empty. "Damn!" he exploded. "Well, I certainly don't want to hang around until somebody shows up. We'll just have to call a cab."

"It'll cost a small fortune all the way from here!" Penny protested, ever practical.

Toby shrugged indifferently. "I'm sure Lefau will reimburse us—not that it's all that important if he doesn't.''

"Yes, but do you have enough money? I've got only fifteen dollars on me."

He stopped dead. "Oh!" He got out his wallet and glared gloomily at its contents. "Damnation, I used the few dollars I had to pay the airport cab. I've got a hundred pounds in sterling and traveler's checks. I meant to change them yesterday, but in all the hoo-ha over John, I never got the chance."

"Then, we'll have to hitch; there's bound to be something come along the river road. We can pay our way with my fifteen, and you can change yours when we get to the city," she said brightly.

The prospect did not cheer Sir Tobias, but he followed her as she picked up her purse and headed down the long drive to the main gates. Here a further obstacle presented itself: the gates were firmly shut, and there was no clue as to how to open them.

"I suppose you have to have one of those black boxes," Toby said glumly as he rattled the delicate ironwork and peered through the bars.

Penny frowned. "That doesn't make sense. There must be another, smaller gate the family uses. They wouldn't bother to cart around one of those gadgets the whole time."

"I didn't notice any other openings in that wall when we drove in yesterday."

"Well then, let's look in the other direction." She started off at a brisk trot along the inside line of the high wall and in a few minutes was rewarded by the sight of a small, heavy door set into the wall. It was bolted and had a heavy Yale lock but could be opened from the inside. "I don't think we'd better leave it open, on general security principles; so once we're out, we won't be able to get back. But who cares!" she commented.

They emerged onto the country road with a certain feeling of relief, and before long Penny's energetic thumb was rewarded when a truck laden with fresh vegetables, driven by a sandy-haired youth, drew up. "Ten dollars to take us into the city?" Penny inquired, wise in the ways of world barter.

The youth looked at her calculatingly. "Reckon if you made it fifteen, I could do that," he drawled. "Even if it's out of my way."

"Done," she said promptly, and they were off and running.

The young man dropped them outside a bank on Canal Street, where Toby immediately replenished their coffers and split the proceeds fifty-fifty with Penny.

They bent over a street map that he had thoughtfully picked up at the airport. "I think the best bet is for me to find you," Penny said. "You're going to be at the library all day?" He nodded. "I don't know where I'm going to be, so I'll plan to meet you outside the main entrance at, say, five o'clock. We should be able to get back some way by six o'clock to meet with Lefau."

"I think I'll rent a car," Toby said. "It'll be simpler in the long run."

Penny didn't put up her usual protest about unnecessary expense. "The public libarary is on Loyola Avenue. You just go along South Rampart here and turn right, and Loyola is the next one over."

"I am quite capable of reading a street map," he boomed icily.

"Yes, but I want to take the map with *me*," she returned.

"Oh, all right," he grumbled. "Well, see you later, and good hunting." They went their separate ways.

Toby paused briefly before the clean, modern lines of the

library, admiring its unusual design, then plunged into its all-glass interior, where he was directed to the top floor for historical records and newspapers. When he emerged from the elevator, his heart sank at the sight of the huge banks of microfilm machines. Never completely at ease in the modern age—his infinite preference was fifth century B.C. Greece—he considered a particular abomination all the gadgets forced by the twentieth century on the serious scholar. He was anything but a handyman, and machines, it seemed to him, had a way of sensing this and acting up on his very approach. Inquiry at the large central desk confirmed his worst fears: all the material he was interested in was on microfilm. He sighed inwardly as he filled in the obligatory card stating his name, address, and object of research: The hard-faced blonde who had been waiting impatiently for it thawed visibly as she read his title and the address of the Lefau plantation. With some ceremony she ushered Toby to the catalogs and then seated him at a machine.

"You are familiar with the operation of these machines, Sir, er, Tobias?" she asked coyly.

"Umm, no, not this particular model," he lied.

"Then, I'll thread this one for you and get you started, and then you can see how to do the others," she chirped. With dazzling speed she threaded, turned knobs, adjusted, focused, and stepped back. "There, now, you're all set! If you need any further help, be sure and call me."

"Thank you very much. I'll, er, do that," Toby said with a weak smile and, collecting his wits, started to work.

The pile of notes beside his little black notebook grew steadily, although he was not sure he was getting anywhere. To complicate matters, the knob fixing the picture had a tendency to slip, and he began to feel like a tennis spectator as his head moved from side to side trying to read the moving image as it flicked by. He had become so absorbed in what he was doing that he was only dimly conscious of a small hand that from time to time would reach out and adjust it for him. The pile of reels grew, and so did his excitement. Finally a pile of them slipped off the desk with a clatter, and as he bent to retrieve them, he saw by his watch that it was after two o'clock and became aware that he had a fierce thirst and a very stiff neck. He simply had to have a drink. He ambled over to the main desk, where the hard-faced blonde had been replaced by a mild-eyed young man, and was directed across the street to a Howard Johnson's.

In total abstraction Toby wandered out of the library, across the broad street, oblivious to blaring horns and incipient disaster, and entered the near-empty restaurant. He came to only when beer and a sandwich, which he supposed he must have ordered, appeared before him. He downed the beer quickly, ordered another, and peered at his notebook, his lips pursed in a silent whistle of wonderment. He could hardly wait to tell Penny about his findings, but for the life of him he could not see how it all fitted in with this voodoo business. . . .

"Sir Tobias." His name spoken by a soft voice startled him, and he looked up to see that a young, dark-haired girl had seated herself in the same booth and was watching him with an anxious pair of vivid blue eyes. She had very pink cheeks. "Sir Tobias, I'm sorry to interrupt your lunch, but I wonder if I could help you in any way." She sounded breathless.

Toby was aghast. At best he was never very good with the female of the species; now all sorts of terror-stricken thoughts flitted through his mind. "Umm, help me? In what way?" he managed to get out.

"Well, I noticed you were having some trouble with your microfilm machine—they are a nuisance if you're not used to them. I work there, you see. My name is Mimi Gardiner." She went even pinker of cheek. "Perhaps I should explain. The other librarian told me who you were, and, well, you've made so much difference to my life that I'd like to do anything I can to help you."

"I! Made a difference! How?"

"The 'Jesus' document in Palestine—your finding it made a lot of difference to me. I'd lost my faith, you see, and now I've got it back. After the publicity about it, I read everything I could find about you, Sir Tobias—sort of like a fan?" Her voice sank to a whisper. "If you are here working on a case, I'd like to help: research, finding records, anything. I can stay in the library after hours, you know."

He gathered his wits and looked at her searchingly, noting for the first time that she was a remarkably pretty girl. "No, no case," he said hurriedly. "Just some research—genealogical, mostly. But if you would really care to help——"

"Oh, I *would*!" She appeared delighted.

"Then"—he consulted his notebook with alacrity—"I would like all the information you can find out about the following." She whipped out a notepad from her purse and waited, pencil poised. "Gaston Duchamps and his mother, Arlette Duchamps. Also the parents of Eleanor Duchamps, who was born in 1940. The parents of Pernell Lefau, wife of Jules Lefau, born 1890, died 1935. Anything you can find on the family of Grace Harmon, born in Baton Rouge in 1951, married Benedict Lefau in 1978."

"Anything in particular you want to know about all of them?" Mimi asked as her pencil flew over the pad.

"No, just everything and anything you can find. It will save me a great deal of time, and I shall be infinitely obliged to you."

"How shall I get the information to you? Where are you staying?"

Caution reasserted itself. "I'd better get in touch with you," Toby said. "I can reach you at the library?"

She tore a leaf from the pad and scribbled two numbers on it. "This is my library extension, and this is my home phone. Call either one."

"Extremely good of you. May I buy you a drink?"

"No, I must get back." She went pink again. "This was my coffee break."

"Then, I'll return with you." He rose and signaled for his check. "And perhaps when we get back up there, you can show me how to operate that infernal machine properly."

"Gladly. It'll be a pleasure." Mimi dimpled. "As it is, I've been doing it all morning."

CHAPTER 7

After leaving Toby, Penny zoomed straight for her objective—the Voodoo Museum on Bourbon Street—ignoring the cacophony and the swirling morning crowds of the Quarter, which normally would have stimulated and delighted her. She was a little nonplussed to find the museum housed in a tiny shop, which had all the earmarks of a tourist trap. She entered its small, cluttered interior to face shelves of fake voodoo bric-a-brac; jars of "Follow Me" water and "Fame and Success" elixir jostled boxes of assorted *gris-gris* charms and rather dog-eared pamphlets on Marie Laveau and voodoo in New Orleans. A pale woman in a plain black dress and with a worried expression stood behind the piled-up counter. There was no sign of the museum, but a poster on the counter caught Penny's eye. UNDERGROUND VOODOO TOUR, it proclaimed. *See the Voodoo Museum, a voodoo church, famous Congo Square, Marie Laveau's house and tomb, have refreshments at the Voodoo Lounge, plus other interesting sights.* For ten dollars it seemed the very thing. "I'd like to take the tour," Penny said firmly.

It did nothing to cheer the woman up. "Oh, yes?" she said in a faint, husky voice. "The only thing is that the guide hasn't shown up yet this morning. I don't know where he is. Would you care to wait? Perhaps you could see the museum while you do so."

"Where is it?" Penny looked around her.

The woman indicated a rather tired-looking curtain. "Through there." Her spirits seemed to revive a little. "It's really very interesting. I'll put the lights on for you."

"Will the guide be very long?" Penny asked.

"Oh, no. He should be here any minute," she was assured, "and you can go on the tour right away."

Penny parted with the ten dollars and was let through the curtain into the museum, which was so dimly lit that she had to strain to read the labels. It opened with a tableau of the younger Marie Laveau busy at work, apparently whomping up potions in a caldron. The manikin was minus a hand. "That went last Carnival," the woman told her sadly, "and we haven't been able to replace it." Beyond the tableau was an assortment of voodoo drums and figurines of voodoo gods that had been found in Louisiana; there were cases of *gris-gris* charms and smaller voodoo objects. One item at which Penny stared long and hard was a shriveled beef heart swathed in black crepe paper and stuck full of pins. DEATH GRIS-GRIS, the label read simply. The pattern of the pins was exactly the same as the one that nestled in the rafters of the Lefau house. One thing that intrigued her was the fact that none of the really sacred items of voodoo, none of the operating paraphernalia of the voodoo *mambos* and *hungans,* such as the sacred *ogans* and *assons,* were on display. She wondered if that meant what she thought it did.

A figure clad in a long green robe suddenly appeared through a hidden door, causing her to start. For a moment in the dim light she thought it was Henri, but a closer inspection showed the man was lighter of skin, though he had the same tall, thin figure, the same fine features, and the same hooded, deep-set eyes. He glared at her for a second and then swept by her with a swirl of robes, carrying with him a distinct aura of menace. Intrigued, Penny waited for him to return, while continuing with her inspection.

When he didn't come back, she wandered back through the curtain. "The guide here yet?"

The woman looked apologetic. "Not yet, but soon, very soon."

"Who was the tall man in the green robe?"

"Oh, that's our *hungan,* Hungan Thomas." The woman began to look worried again. "He's from Martinique, and very good. Would you care to have a reading from him? People come from all over for one, but he does have some free time today."

"Maybe later. Is there much voodoo activity in the city?" Penny tried to sound casual.

"Now? None at all." The woman was suddenly, sharply positive. "It was all in the past; other parts of America have it, but not here. Most of our trade is mail order or tourist." She hesitated. "Look, why don't you go back to your hotel and wait, and I'll direct the guide when he comes to pick you up there? No extra charge. I'm sorry about holding you up like this."

Oh, no. You don't get rid of me that easily, Penny thought. "No problem," she said aloud. "I'll wait. I'll buy a couple of those booklets and read them over in the corner, out of your way." She did just that, but as she leafed through the pamphlets, she kept a sharp eye on what was going on in the shop.

The *hungan* reappeared and went back through the curtain, shortly followed by two young girls who giggled their way in for a "reading." The stray tourist would come in and wander around, and, more interestingly, the occasional black woman who would whisper to the woman behind the counter and receive something from under it. Finally, a stocky young man with dark, curly hair and horn-rimmed spectacles wandered in and began a vehement low-voiced conversation with the woman, who came out from behind the counter and approached Penny. She appeared flustered. "The guide is here and could take you now, but he has to take a group on a plantation tour in an hour; so, in view of that, you'll be somewhat rushed. Would you like your money back and come some other time?"

"No, that's all right." Penny got up. "Just so long as he can give me the information I want and show me the main places of interest."

"Oh, all right," the woman said reluctantly and, raising her voice, "Mr. Dixon! Paul! Here is the lady who wants the voodoo tour."

The young man came over and smiled at her muzzily. "We'll start with the museum," he said in a slurred voice.

He's either drunk or stoned, Penny thought and, looking closer at his eyes, decided it was the latter. "I've seen that, so let's skip it," she said quickly. "Let's get on the road."

Outside, and beyond the hearing of the woman, she said, "Now, look. I happen to know quite a bit about all this, so you can skip the usual tourist spiel. What I mainly want from you is to show me the way to the points of interest, and most of all I want you to tell me what is going on here now in New Orleans. You're a student, aren't you? Tulane?''

He gazed at her through his fog. ''That's right.''

''Not anthropology, by any chance?''

''No, a history major, but I'm minoring in anthro. Why?''

''My name is Penelope Spring. I just thought you might have heard of me.''

''The *Sex in the South Pacific* Spring? Why, yes, I've read some of your books.'' He essayed a faint grin. ''Well, wha'd'ya know—a VIP!'' He staggered slightly.

''Are you all right?'' Penny said crossly. ''What have you been into, anyway?''

Paul made an effort to pull himself together. ''Just popped one too many pills with my beer last night,'' he confessed. ''I'll be OK.''

''That's dumb.'' She was sharp.

''I know, but it helps take the pressure off sometimes,'' he agreed amiably. ''What was it you wanted to know again?''

''What's going on in voodoo *now* here in New Orleans?''

He shrugged. ''I'm not the person to ask. Nothing, so far as I know. Though, now you come to mention it, ol' Hungan Thomas has been a bit uptight recently, as if somebody'd been stepping on his toes. There was some talk of a voodoo bash up at the lake a while ago, but the locals sometimes do that hoping to get the TV people interested. There isn't even a voodoo church here like there is in some places—St. Louis has one, I believe.''

''You've heard of nothing unusual in any of these voodoo sites you visit?'' She was grasping at straws.

They had been walking north on Toulouse and had reached the busy eight-lane highway of Rampart. Paul stopped, indicating the old church islanded in the middle of its traffic lanes. ''That's our first stop—our Lady of Guadalupe, the so-called voodoo church because in the grotto to Our Lady outside they used to make voodoo offerings to Erzulie, one of their main goddesses. Come to think of it, the priest did mention to me that they've had a lot more voodoo graffiti than normal lately. But there's really nothing to see; they scrub them off and remove the *gris-gris* as soon as they're found.''

''So let's skip that, too. Where next?''

''The tomb of Marie Laveau—the older one—in St. Louis Number One, the cemetery just beyond the church.'' Paul guided Penny across. ''That's *always* got graffiti.'' He led her through the gates of the quiet, walled cemetery and along a little path to the left, running by the wall; then with a sudden zig to the right they were standing in front of a tall white vault whose lettering proclaimed it as the last resting place of Marie Laveau, ''the Widow of Paris,'' and also of Louis-Christophe Daumeny de Glapion, her longtime lover, and sundry other Glapions. The whitewashed face of the tomb was covered with little red crosses, and there were small bunches of flowers, some real, some plastic, scattered on the ground before the tomb. Penny's guide bent down and picked up a crumbled bit of brick and handed it to her. ''Go ahead! Everyone else does. Stamp three times with your right foot, turn around, make a wish, and mark your cross.''

I wish I could get a worthwhile bit of information, Penny thought gloomily, doing as she was bidden. ''Now where?''

''The site of Marie Laveau's house on St. Ann Street, by way of Congo Square.''

Congo Square—the very heart of covert voodoo activity in old New Orleans—turned out to be a weed-covered wasteland of bare earth, encompassed by high iron railings, in which a few dispirited-looking trees drooped.

''So you don't know of any *mambos* or *hungans* operating in the city?'' Penny persisted.

''Well''—Paul was hesitant—''I just don't have the right color skin to know much about this, but I *have* heard that a lot of blacks consult a very old woman called Mama Tio, who operates out of a little church—I can't recall its name—in the black section near here.''

''Would you show me where that is?'' Penny asked quickly.

''Oh, OK, it's not much out of our way.'' The young man led her into a maze of poor little streets beyond Congo Square to a neat, white-painted church. It was firmly locked, and there was no indication of when its meetings were held.

''Damn!'' Penny said in frustration.

"It's probably open on Sundays," Paul volunteered. "You could come back then."

"I can't wait that long, unfortunately."

They retraced their steps, crossed Rampart again, and walked a little way down St. Ann. Paul halted before two small, white frame houses. "This was the site of Marie Laveau's home. It was torn down about 1910—long after she had died, of course—and these two houses were put on the site."

Penny gazed blankly at their shuttered faces; she seemed to be getting nowhere at all.

"The tour ends with a drink at the Voodoo Lounge," Paul said, brightening, "and, frankly, I could use one."

"So could I," she agreed with alacrity.

"We can cut down Burgundy and go through the hotel. The lounge is back on Rampart," he said, suiting his actions to his words.

Seated at the bar of the dimly lit lounge, he indicated an ornately carved decoration of wood behind it. "That's supposed to be the headboard of Marie Laveau's bed."

Penny peered at it. "Is it?"

He shrugged. "I don't know. Probably not. Look, I'm sorry this has been such a bust."

"Not your fault," she said absently. "I don't suppose the voodoo shop keeps records of its transactions, does it? Where it sends supplies, and so forth?" He shook his head.

She drained her drink with a sigh. "Well, I'd better be getting off. If you do happen to hear anything, would you give me a call? It really is quite important."

The drink seemed to have revived him. "Sure. Where are you staying?"

"Out at the Lefau plantation. Damn! I don't have the number, and it's probably unlisted."

"Now, that's a familiar name." He smiled. "You'll know Henri, then; I could send a message through him."

Her interest quickened. "*You* know him?"

"Yes. He's quite a character. Often drops in at the shop; he and Hungan Thomas are buddies. Did you know he was on Papa Doc Duvalier's kill list in Haiti? Had quite a time getting out, so I'm told."

"So he's Haitian?" Now she was really interested.

"Yes. Got out about ten or eleven years ago when there

was some sort of shake-up down there. One of the Lefaus helped him.''

"Do you know which one?" He shook his head. "Actually, I think I'll contact you, if I may," she went on. "Are you usually there?"

"Only on Mondays and Thursdays. This is a part-time job. The rest of the time I'm supposed to be studying."

"Well, don't pop too many pills," she charged. They parted amiably, and she hurried off to her next destination—a cab stand on Basin Street.

There was no sign of the huge figure of Mean Gene, and only after Penny had made it quite clear to all the other cabdrivers that she had no intention of going anywhere did one of them reluctantly part with the information that Gene was off with the Knights of St. Pierre, practicing up for the Zulu parade. "They does it in an old garage in the two-hundred block of North Rampart. You can't miss it; it's the only one there."

Really, she thought as she hurried back along Basin Street, *at this rate I'll be worn out before I've got anything done.*

The Knights of St. Pierre were easy enough to find, the sounds of their delicately interwoven brassy themes reaching out to her over the roar of the traffic along Rampart. She hesitated a moment before the peeling green paint of the garage doors, listening with pleasure to their interplay. "They're good," she muttered, "very good indeed." And she plunged inside.

The bare interior of the garage was brightly lit with naked bulbs, and as she came through the door the music faltered, staggered, and finally died. Mean Gene, a trumpet looking like a child's toy in his huge hands, let out a bellow of recognition. "Why, it's the doctor lady! Come on in and meet the group!"

Penny duly met Joe the piano, Al the double bass, Hiram the trombone, and the unfortunately named Cyril the clarinet. "Are you all cabdrivers?" she asked hopefully.

"No, just Hiram, Al, and me. Why? You need a cab?"

"No, but I badly need your help. You remember you took us to the St. Louis Hotel to meet a friend? Well, that friend is in serious trouble. He's accused of murdering the girl who was killed there, and I desperately need to locate the cabdriver who brought them back to the hotel that night—two nights ago it was, at around two in the morning.''

They looked at her blankly. ''What murder?''

''Why, the murder of Arlette Gray. She was a call girl. You must have seen it in the papers.''

They shook their heads. Joe the piano produced a much-crumpled paper from his coat, and they pored over it. There was nothing.

''It must have been in yesterday's,'' Penny said.

From another pocket he produced a paper of the day before. They pored over that; still nothing.

She thought quickly. Was this the long arm of Lefau, or was Beauregard keeping it quiet for some other reason? Well, she had let the cat out of the bag now, so she might as well plunge on. ''The girl *was* murdered, and there seems to be some voodoo involved.''

''She colored?'' Gene asked in a stern voice.

''A mulatto from Haiti.''

The group looked at one another in grim silence. ''Dat explains it, lady,'' said Hiram the trombone. ''Dey don't pay much mind when one of us gets it.''

'' 'Specially during Carnival,'' Al the double bass chimed in. ''No, dey doesn't want to frighten off de tourists.'' They gazed at her with closed faces.

Oh, dear, she thought, *that's torn it,* but she said with spirit, ''Well, *I* don't intend to let it go. My friend is in trouble, and the girl's murderer has to be found. I intend to find him. The girl and this cabdriver brought my friend, who had been given a Mickey Finn, back to the hotel. I'm not saying the cabdriver was involved; all I want to do is to find him and talk to him. I thought you might be able to help me, and I'll gladly pay for the information.'' She got out the photo of Arlette Gray that Beauregard had given her and showed it to them. ''Do any of you know her?''

''Why dat's de Angel!'' Al exclaimed. ''Ah knows her. Used to drive her back to her place on St. Ann all de time. Right nice place she had there, had it fixed up all fancy, and she always used to smell so good. Never did know her right name though, but all of us called her de Angel 'cause she was mighty pretty.''

''Whereabouts on St. Ann?'' Penny asked quickly.

He furrowed his brow in thought. "Think it was 1016, left-hand side going up between Burgundy and Rampart."

That's incredible, Penny thought, for he had named one of the little frame houses that stood on the site of Marie Laveau's house. "There's another thing," she went on. "Do any of you know how I can get in touch with Mama Tio?"

There was dead silence for a moment; then Cyril the clarinet said nervously, "Ah knows her." The rest looked at him with disapproval.

"What do you want to see her for?" Mean Gene growled.

At that moment Penny's punctual stomach gurgled and, looking at her watch, she saw it was past lunchtime. "Look, I'm sorry I interrupted your practice," she said a little desperately, "but if you would all be my guests, I'll be able to explain it better over lunch."

With the exception of Mean Gene, this seemed to cheer them up. "How you feel about soul food, lady?" Al asked.

Secure in the knowledge that she would be fed another sumptuous Lefau dinner, Penny agreed cheerfully that it was just the thing. They locked up the garage, repaired to a tiny restaurant half a block down Rampart, and over a plate of hamhocks and greens—which she happily found very tasty—Penny explained all she dared about what had happened so far.

Again with the exception of Mean Gene, they were fascinated, but he continued to gaze at her morosely. Finally he broke his silence. "Ah just don't see why you wants to get mixed up in all this for. What can a doctor lady like you do about it?"

A sudden inspiration came to her. "Do you remember Washington Thompson, the football player?"

Gene nodded. "L.A. Rams. Went on the dope and got hisself killed."

"And *I* found his killer," Penny asserted. "Sir Tobias and I are good at it. We've solved several cases, and we both enjoy doing what we're good at—just like you and jazz. I not only want to solve this murder but to prevent other murders from happening, and I think they may if I don't move fast. There's voodoo mixed up in this somehow, and that's why I want to see Mama Tio."

"She don't usually see white folks," Cyril put in dubiously.

"I just want to ask her a few questions," Penny persisted. "I'd gladly pay for it."

"She don't take money—not when she's using her gift," Cyril said, "but she's mighty partial to snuff."

"Please, then, would you—could you—fix it up for me?"

They all looked at Mean Gene, who nodded slowly. "OK, we're in."

Hiram disappeared to get the snuff, Cyril to make the arrangements, and in a short time, with the entire complement of Knights as escort, Penny found herself in front of a decayed-looking frame house not half a block from the little white church.

Inside it was incredibly hot. A very old black woman, her face seamed into a thousand creases, sat hunched over a coal stove. The room was heavy with the smell of incense and a medley of herbs, which hung from the open rafters in bunches. Cyril was spokesman and, after a low-voiced conversation, he handed the old woman a pound package of snuff. The clawlike hands of the *mambo* clutched possessively as a surprisingly bright pair of beady eyes peered through the greenish gloom at Penny. "What you want to know?" she said in a husky whisper.

"There is black voodoo going on in this city," Penny said with more certainty than she felt. "I must find its roots, for it is evil. I need names, Mama Tio."

"Come closer," the old woman croaked. She stared into Penny's mild hazel eyes as if trying to plumb her very soul. "The voodoo is black, but the skin is white," Mama Tio whispered. "Remember Clemence Alexander as you seek. And take care, for the Sect Rouge is here. I can say no more." She paused. "But if you want more, my *loa* tells me you will find it closer to you. Ask Elviny Brosse. . . ."

CHAPTER 8

Penny hurried along Loyola Avenue. It was a little after five, and she could see Toby standing outside the library looking disapprovingly at a small red car parked at the curb. As he spotted her, he began to lope toward her and she to run toward him, so that it looked for all the world like the fade-out shot of an old romantic movie, where the lovers rush into each other's arms and the music soars. In this case they both put on the brakes as they came face-to-face and said in unison, "Wait until you hear what I've found out!"

"Oh, good," Penny went on. "We'll have plenty to talk about on the way back to the plantation. Have you figured out how we're going to do that, by the way?"

"Hired a car." Toby waved a demonstrative arm. "That red thing was all I could get. Seems cars are in short supply during Carnival."

"Well, it beats thumbing," she retorted, scrambling inside. "Do you want to drive, or shall I?"

"You drive, I'll navigate," he instructed. "And we're in no hurry; so, for heaven's sake, watch what you are about."

"OK, then, you go first with your info," Penny said, trying to figure out where everything was at once as they shot away from the curb and Toby set the course.

"To get the et ceteras out of the way first," he began, "I called Beauregard this afternoon for the results of the autopsy, and, for what it's worth, it's another tiny swing in John's favor. The woman had *not* had sexual intercourse that night; so the sex-murder angle is no longer as tenable. Furthermore, Beauregard has turned up a sizable bank account in her name with regular monthly payments, which looks as if she was either being kept or getting blackmail payments. They are checking on the real source of those payments now, since they were made from some sort of holding company. Also, John, at his own insistence, took a lie-detector test and came up clean. So that's another point in his favor.''

"Do you realize there has not been a word about the murder in the papers?"

"No, but it doesn't surprise me," he returned, lighting up his pipe. "The very name of Lefau in this city seems to get everyone treading on eggs.''

"So what did you get from the records?"

Toby went through his patting-all-pockets routine and came out with sheaves of notes. "So much stuff I haven't had time to digest most of it yet. But here are just a few interesting nuggets to chew on. Item one: That line Lefau fed you about the House of the Dancing lady seems to be so much malar-key. It is never referred to in the records as anything but Lefau's, and only in some social notes of the past forty years has it been referred to by its more romantic title. I've got an assistant working further on that—she's very good."

Penny's eyebrows rose a fraction, but she said nothing.

"Item two," Toby went on, "Grace Harmon, Benedict's wife, was from a Baton Rouge family, and yet they got married in Las Vegas, and there was absolutely *no* fanfare in either the Baton Rouge or New Orleans papers of the kind you'd expect when an heir of Benedict's proportions marries. It's as if they hopped off and got married on the quiet without parental blessing. And she, by the way, is several years older than he is. Item three—and this is where I could really kick myself for not spotting it sooner—is about one of the trage-dies in the book. Remember, I told you about a young man who blew his brains out at a Grand Ball? Well, his name was Gaston Duchamps; he was Eleanor Lefau's uncle, her father's younger brother. And what is more, one of the main rivalries through the years for the control of Comus has been between the Duchamps family and the Lefaus. Jules's second marriage was a real Romeo and Juliet affair: he married into the enemy camp." Toby frowned at his notes. "I haven't been able to sort all the links out yet, but when Jules said the Comus krewe were related by blood, he wasn't kidding. They are an incredibly interbred lot, and there is some connection between

Pernell Lefau—that is, Jules's mother—and Arlette Duchamps, the mother of Gaston and Pierre, Eleanor's father. I *think* they were first cousins, but I haven't worked out how yet.''

"Arlette again," Penny commented.

Toby shrugged. "Well, I don't put much stock in that; it's a fairly common French girl's name. But what it all does seem to point to is that we may have been dead right in thinking Jules was afraid the threats were coming from close to home. There no doubt about it, if anyone had reason to get uptight about that book, it would be the Duchamps family. Again, there's a lot more to find out, but it seems that up to the time of Jules's father, the fortunes and prestige of the Duchamps and the Lefaus were equal. But the older Jules was a real wheeler-dealer, and under him the Lefaus suddenly shot ahead. That would be enough for resentment right there, even without the other scandal. The only thing I do *not* see is how this voodoo angle comes into it.''

"I think I can add a bit to that," Penny said. "And a lot more, I hope, after I've talked to Elviny Brosse." Rapidly she filled Toby in on her voodoo trip and her talk with Mama Tio. "Clemence Alexander," she explained, "was the wife of the famous *hungan* Jim Alexander. She was also a *mambo*, one of the few pure white *mambos* that ever operated here—most of them were mulatto and the rest black. What Mama Tio was trying to tell me in her offbeat way was that there *is* voodoo going on here, and its leader is a white *mambo*.''

"What's all this about the Sect Rouge?" Toby asked.

Penny grimaced. "That's the really nasty part. Very little is known about it, but it is a sort of secret society existing within the framework of voodoo—a killer cult, not too dissimilar from the Thugs of India, dedicated to murder and all the negative aspects of voodoo magic. Some of Duvalier's hit men, the *Tontons macoutes,* were supposed to be in it. If Jules Lefau is up against that, things could get very ugly indeed—particularly if, on the face of your evidence and mine, the most likely person to be that white *mambo* is Eleanor Duchamps. We are going to have to find out a lot more about her and the sinister Henri. He's Haitian, which could tie him in with the dead girl; he's also cozy with a male *hungan*—another sinister character, I'd say—who operates out of the Voodoo Museum. And yet he was apparently a refugee from

Haiti, which does not really *fit*." She fell into a worried silence.

"It's beginning to look as if Jules Lefau is in some real danger, but the thing that puzzles me is why John should have been framed. I mean, that doesn't make sense at all." Toby frowned.

"Maybe it was just part of the softening-up process to get Jules really scared before the ax falls on him."

"Possible, but not probable when you consider the risks involved in any murder." Toby cogitated. "Unless the whole thing is a giant smoke screen and this voodoo business just window dressing, with no real purpose at all."

They had reached the gates of the plantation and found that it was a lot easier to get in than it had been to get out, there being an intercom box built into one of the pillars. It crackled to life the minute Toby touched the button, amazingly answered by Celeste, whose silvery tones contained a faint acidity. "Oh, *there* you are! We were very worried about you, having no idea you had left the plantation."

"Er, spur-of-the-moment thing, spur of the moment, change of scene, breath of fresh air, y'know," Toby boomed, reverting to his stuffed-owl role. "We're outside the main gates. Would you let us in?"

The gates opened smoothly, and Penny drove through. "Aren't you going to abandon your 'Asinine Algy' role?" she said as he got back in and the gates shut with an ominous clang behind them. "Apart from the strain of keeping it up, what's the use anymore?"

He shook his head. "I think I'll keep it up for a while, until we get closer to these people. After our powwow with Jules, I'm going to corral Celeste—who seems, in spite of everything, to be quite partial to me—and do a bit of quiet pumping. Are you going after the servants?"

"I think I'll try the other distaff Lefaus first. Though they dash in and out so much it isn't going to be easy. It's amazing how much time and energy they expend on all this, especially when you think it lasts for only a few hours of one day. Do you know what they have in mind for this year's Comus procession?"

"No, I was too busy being boring, I'm afraid."

"Jules Lefau is going to re-create the whole thing as it was when his father and mother were King and Queen of Comus fifty years ago: the floats, the dresses—they are even going so far as to wear wigs and lifemasks to stimulate Jules Senior and Pernell.'' Penny gave a little shudder. "I think it's all a bit macabre myself, all this aping of the dead.''

They drew up before the house to see Celeste's slim form standing rigidly on the patio and realized they had been followed up the drive by a Rolls containing Jules and Henri and John.

"Do we tell him about the dog?'' Penny whispered as the second carload disembarked.

"We'll see what he has to say first, but, yes, I believe we should. Let's not say anything about what I've been up to, though,'' Toby muttered back. As he glanced up at the patio to find Celeste had disappeared, a relieved-looking John Everett came up to them with their host, who appeared preoccupied.

"I passed the lie-detector test,'' John said thankfully to Penny. "It may not let me off the hook so far as the police are concerned, but at least it puts my own mind at rest. God, you can't imagine how worried I've been! I'm just off to call Millicent. I'm hoping that will calm her down.'' He sounded none too sure of himself.

"I'm glad''—Penny smiled at him encouragingly—''but I told you so all along!'' Then, to her host, "And we wondered if we could have a talk with you now, Mr. Lefau. There is something you should know.''

Jules cast a harassed glance at his watch. "Yes, of course, Dr. Spring. Unfortunately, again I shall be unable to spend much time with you. Tonight my wife and I have to preside over the last ball of the season prior to the Grand Ball, and most of the household will be coming with us. Alas, I could not include you, since it is only for krewe members, but the Grand Ball will be different. I am afraid you will be a small party for dinner tonight—just Celeste and Vincent. Will you follow me?'' He led them to the library, which was situated to the left of the main entrance, and saw them seated in the red leather chairs with which the library was furnished. He remained standing, as if poised for flight, and looked inquiringly at them.

Toby had begun the snaillike process of lighting up his pipe, so Penny took this as a sign that she should be the spokeswoman. "I'm afraid we have some rather unpleasant news for you," she began hesitantly. "Your dog, Deacon—is dead, and in circumstances that lead me to believe voodoo was again involved, just as it was in Arlette Gray's murder, and that in consequence you, yourself, may be in some danger. Sir Tobias and I have been in New Orleans today making inquiries along that line, but I believe the focus of the danger is here on this estate, although I hesitated to make any inquiries here without consulting you first."

A nerve had leaped under Jules's left eyes as she told of the dog, but beyond a tightening of his lips he showed no other emotion. "What circumstances?" he asked huskily.

Penny glanced over at Toby, who had resumed his stuffed-owl expression and stance and was encircled by a rakish halo of blue tobacco smoke. By his totally blank expression, she gathered he wanted no part in the explanation, so she struggled gamely on. "We found the dog during our walk last night in the grounds. Its throat had been cut and the heart removed. When we returned to the spot today, the body had been taken away, but we did find the heart. When we explored your house this morning, we found it covered with black crepe paper and stuck full of pins—the voodoo death sign."

"Where was it?" He had gone very white.

"In the rafters located above the master bedroom. I think there is danger to you and would urge, if it is at all possible, that you leave here until we can find out more."

He looked sick and stricken and, for the moment, every one of his fifty-five years. "You did not inform the police of this, I hope."

It was a strange reaction, which jolted Penny. "No, we thought we should talk with you first. But, Mr. Lefau, we will *have* to talk to members of your household. I think, in light of these events, polite subterfuge is no longer possible."

Again his reaction was not what she expected. "We were planning to move to our Royal Street house in two days' time for the final preparations, in any case. I'm afraid I cannot permit my family to be upset. We are under considerable strain as it is, with Mardi Gras so near. I will take whatever steps are necessary to see that nothing further happens. Please do not concern yourselves anymore. You are my guests; let us leave it at that."

Now she was annoyed. "Really, Mr. Lefau, I don't think you fully understand the situation. We are here to help you and to clear our friend of this ridiculous murder charge. You are in *danger*. You can't turn us off like a tap, nor can you turn your back on this situation! We know you are a man of great power and influence—as is witnessed by the fact that no word of the murder has as yet appeared in the press—but whoever is at the back of this is also not without power, of a different sort, and has already demonstrated that by striking very close to home. Mardi Gras is only a week away, and the killer could strike at you and yours anytime between now and then. Short of announcing that you are not going ahead with the book publication and publicity, I can think of nothing that will turn the killer from his avowed purpose, *unless* you let us go ahead with our investigations."

Jules's mouth clamped in a determined line. "The book comes out. I will not be intimidated."

"Then, you have to let us investigate. I *must* talk with Elviny Brosse."

Penny could have sworn a flicker of relief appeared for a second in his eyes, before he said coldly, "Very well. If you wish to question the servants, go ahead, but I beg you to be circumspect. All the house servants have been with us a very long time and arc highly valued. I find it incredible that they should be involved."

"Mr. Lefau," she said firmly, "are you seriously telling me you believe an outsider could have got into your grounds, killed your dog, and then placed its heart in a very inaccessible part of your house without *somebody* inside knowing? If you do think that, well, you must know more about all this than we do, and it would be only fair to tell us."

He was saved from answering by the opening of the library door as Eleanor Lefau swept in. "Jules!" she said imperiously. "You really *must* come. I am almost at my wits' end. Grace is being very difficult again, and Benedict is no help at all with her."

Jules's smooth diplomatic front reappeared on the instant. "Yes, my dear, I'll be right with you. But since you are here, I'd like you to meet our guest, Dr. Penelope Spring, whom, due to all this hurly-burly we're in, you have not properly greeted."

Eleanor nodded grandly at Penny. "Yes. How do you do, Dr. Spring. I very much regret the cavalier treatment you have been receiving since your arrival and beg you to forgive us. Things will be a lot better when we move to the Royal Street house, and I shall have more time to devote to you." Her tone turned waspish as she looked at her husband. "I can't think why you insisted on staying out here so long. I'll be thankful, as always, to get away from this madhouse! Come along, now. You must settle this with Grace." She swept out again.

Jules hesitated for a second, an unfathomable look in his dark eyes, then smiled apologetically at Penny and Toby. "You really will have to excuse me. As I said, we are all under a lot of tension just now," and he followed his wife out, leaving them gazing at one another.

"So what did you make of that?" said Penny.

"No love lost, by the sounds of it, between our suspect number one and her stepfamily," Toby observed. "Very much the grand lady, isn't she? And our host's feet seem to be getting on the cold side." He looked at the phone. "I think I'll give Beauregard another call."

"You're going to blow the whistle already! But we don't have anything concrete," Penny said in alarm.

"No, no, of course not." He was impatient. "Besides, I've already told him most of what I've got. With John's safety at stake, I'm not going to make the same mistake we've made in our other murder cases by keeping the police in the dark. I just want to know if he has come up with any other information on Arlette Gray."

Toby got through, and his main part in the ensuing conversation was a series of 'Yes, I sees,' reducing Penny to a state of irritated agitation. "So?" she demanded when he hung up.

"Umm. *Very* interesting," he said maddeningly. "They've found out that the holding company is backed by one of the many Lefau enterprises. Apart from the fact that the checks to Arlette Gray came from that enterprise, that's as far as they can get. But *one* of the Lefaus must have authorized those payments. The trouble of it is, it could be *any* of them, with the exception of Vincent, the youngest."

"You mean the women, as well?'

"Yes, even Juliette, since her eighteenth birthday was last

year. They are all involved in the Lefau trust. Beauregard is still digging, but he doesn't hold out too much hope of getting much further.''

Penny looked at her watch. ''I don't think I'd better tackle Elviny Brosse now; she'll be in the middle of getting dinner. I'll wait until after. What are you going to do—go for your moonlight walk with Celeste?''

''I think I'll do that after dinner, too,'' Toby said uneasily. ''I'm not looking forward to it. I think I'm going to collate my notes to see if I've missed anything and figure out what Mimi should work on tomorrow.''

''Mimi?''

''Yes, this girl in the library. Very helpful she's been, very helpful indeed. Saved me all sorts of time.''

''How did you manage that?''

''Oh, she volunteered.'' Toby described their meeting. ''Pretty young thing and very enthusiastic,'' he concluded.

''How odd!'' Penny sniffed. ''Then, I think I'll have a chat with John and alert him to keep out of your way with Celeste this evening.'' She got up. ''You're cutting quite a swathe with the females, it seems. But just remember one thing, Toby: John thought Arlette Gray was a very pretty young thing, too, and see how that ended!'' And with that Parthian shot she was gone.

Dinner was a very informal affair compared to the night before. Since there were only five of them, they did not dress up, and they ate at a round table in the small room in which they had breakfasted. They were waited upon by one very old black woman and a younger one who looked exactly like her, whom Penny deduced correctly to be Jules's old nanny and her daughter. Henri, presumably, was escorting his employers to the ball.

Only one thing of interest arose during dinner, which in substance was equally as long and sumptuous as the night before. The subject of the book was introduced by Toby, and Celeste, for once, abandoned her amiable chitchat. ''We all have been very upset with Jules over this,'' she stated firmly. ''Eleanor and I tried to dissuade him; even Benedict could not see the sense of it. We felt he had no business disclosing the history of Comus to public gaze. But he can be so stubborn when he chooses.''

"I imagine it will have a very limited readership," Penny observed mildly.

"But *nobody* has any right to know these things," Celeste returned with a flash of her gray eyes. "It's nobody's business but ours."

After dinner John excused himself to make some business calls, and Penny did a quiet disappearing act, leaving Toby, somewhat uneasily, a clear field. "Would you care for a walk?" he invited. "It is another very fine night."

With dismaying alacrity, Celeste agreed and, as they descended from the terrace to the lawn, took his arm, thereby causing him a further twinge of alarm. "I often walk like this at night," she confided. "I never tire of the beauty of my home."

"You live here all the time?" he asked.

"Oh, yes, and most of the year—save for the hot summer months and at Christmas—I have it all to myself. Eleanor much prefers living in the Royal Street house, and Benedict and Grace, who have an apartment there in the old *garçonnière,* prefer it, too. This year has been exceptional: Jules, for some strange reason, insisted they stay on after Christmas."

So he had taken those threats more seriously than he appeared to, Toby thought. "Don't you find it lonely?" he asked. He deliberately had been walking in the direction of the night before, to see what her reaction would be, but there was none.

"Lonely?" She gave a little tinkly laugh. "Why, no! I have the company of all the Lefaus who have ever lived here."

Oh-oh, a little barmy, just as I feared, Toby gloomed. "Dr. Spring showed me a portrait of your mother," he went on aloud. "A remarkable likeness to you, if I may say so."

"You think so?" Celeste was coy. "My mother was such a saint, and taken from us, alas, too soon, too soon. Jules was only ten when she died, and my father was taken from us shortly after; so in a sense I have had to be father and mother to him." She sighed lightly.

"A very heavy responsibility." He thought this was the right thing to say.

"Oh, yes, and Jules has always been so headstrong! I feel I have failed him in so many ways by not being firmer. His marriages . . ." Her voice trailed away, and she shook her head sadly.

Toby felt she was looking for some encouragement, but he couldn't think of what to say; so they strolled on in silence for a minute.

"His first wife was a *northerner*," Celeste finally continued unprompted. "Now, I would not say this to everyone, but you as an English aristocrat will understand." Toby's grandfather had been a Welsh country doctor, but he let it pass as his companion expounded, "Northerners, I find, are so lacking in sensibility and sensitivity. They appear to think that money is the answer to everything. I am afraid that attitude is *very* apparent in Benedict: no sense of family at all. Now, Eleanor understands these things—after our own family, her family is the best stock in New Orleans—but, alas, she has not inherited their better characteristics. A very cold and very domineering person, I regret to say. Sometimes I feel she does not understand Jules at all." She sighed again.

Toby was in a quandary. He would have liked to pursue the subject of the Duchamps but did not wish to betray his, by now, extensive knowledge. "Er, like the English aristocracy, the Creole families are very interlinked, are they not?" he said lamely.

Her answer was sharp and to the point. "My mother was first cousin to Eleanor's father's mother, which makes Eleanor and Jules merely second cousins. The danger lies only when third cousins marry."

Toby was a little startled by this inaccurate piece of biological lore but, feeling she had grown a little tense, hurried to change the subject. "You do not participate in all the Carnival festivities?"

"Oh, but *yes*! I shall be at the Grand Ball, as always and as is my right." Again she laughed her tinkly little laugh but on a shriller note. "Carnival has so many sweet-sad memories for me. Why, fifty years ago, when my father and mother were king and queen, I was crown princess. I was just sixteen. And had my father lived but a few months longer, I would have been queen!" Again she tensed up.

"And a very gracious queen you would have made," Toby said gallantly.

Celeste stopped and looked up at him. "It is said by the

Creoles that once one has been Queen of Carnival, life is complete and there is nothing left to live for. Do you think that could be true?''

"Er, I've no idea," he said in uneasy confusion at the weird question, and as he took a hurried step forward, his foot squelched ankle-deep in mud.

"One more step and you'll be hip-deep in the marsh, Sir Tobias," she said calmly. "I think we had better turn around; we are almost at the river."

They reversed direction and headed back for the house in silence. To break it, Toby asked, "What kind of plantation was this originally?''

"Indigo mostly, and a little cotton, but it has not been worked as such in years; no profit in it," Celeste said with surprising briskness.

"Are there any other habitations on the estate besides the main house?''

"Not anymore. The old slave quarters were torn down many years ago—you can still see the foundations if you are interested. There are a few shacks in the woods, for gardeners and the like. We prefer to be by ourselves." She sounded remote.

"Just you and the dancing lady, eh?" He attempted to be jocular. "Have you seen her?''

She laughed. "Oh, really, Sir Tobias, I'm surprised at you! You've been listening to Jules's fairy stories. He has such a romantic mind at times. Why, the next thing you know, he'll have you believing in voodoo, like poor, ignorant Elviny Brosse!''

CHAPTER 9

Penny waited until the coast was clear, then headed for the kitchens. They came as quite a shock after the rest of the house, which had been furnished throughout in variations of all the great periods of French furniture styles, for here the twentieth century reigned supreme, with gleaming tiles, bright lights, and every electrical gadget known to man. At a Formica-topped table sat two figures, one the younger maid who had waited on them at dinner, the other a woman with a strong, stern face, immaculate in a white coverall, with a white *tignon* covering her gray hair. As Penny entered, the younger woman got up politely, but the older remained seated, the only indication of surprise shown by her coffee cup, which she held suspended between table and mouth. Inwardly cursing the presence of the girl, Penny said brightly, "I am so sorry to disturb you like this, but I simply had to come and congratulate you on your magnificent cuisine. You must be Elviny Brosse; Mr. Lefau said I simply *had* to meet you. My name is Penelope Spring, and I'll be staying here until Mardi Gras."

"Thank you, Miz Spring, it's always nice to be appreciated." The voice was deep and had a southern drawl but was not uneducated. The dark eyes looked at her steadily.

"I have never tasted such a delicious pie," Penny rattled on. "Is that what's called shoofly pie, by any chance?"

"It is."

The younger woman had stowed her cup and saucer in the dishwasher and turned to the cook. "Ah'll say good night now, Elviny. Good night to you, ma'am." And she exited through a swing door to the right.

"Good night!" Penny heaved an inward sigh of relief.

Deciding on shock tactics, she walked over to the table, sat down in the vacated chair, and, leaning forward, said in an urgent whisper, "I come from Mama Tio. She said I must talk with you."

Elviny Brosse put her cup down with a small clatter and stared at her. "Mama Tio doesn't see white folks. What are you after?"

"Mama Tio did see *me*, and she told me about you and Malvina Latour."

"That's no secret." There was an edge of scorn in the deep voice. "Malvina was my great-grandmother, and I'm not ashamed to own to it."

"Or to own that you still keep to the old ways?"

"Mama Tio never told you nothing like that."

"Look, I'm not here to make trouble. I'm here for information, information that Mama Tio said only you could give me. I am here to help Mr. Lefau. There is a dead girl—murdered with a *vévé* of Ghede on her breast. There is Mr. Lefau's favorite dog with its throat cut and its heart cut out. I know where the heart is and what is on it, so don't pretend to me you don't know anything—I know better. Have you a grudge against Mr. Lefau? Something you can tell me about and I can do something about?"

This appeared to surprise the cook. "Land sakes, no! Mr. Jules is a good man!"

"Whom *someone* is threatening, someone right here. Help me to help him."

"I don't know anything about no dead girl, nor the dog, though he was a pesky creature. And you're all wrong, Miz Spring, no harm will come to Mr. Jules in *this* house."

Penny decided to switch tactics. "I have seen the dancing lady, the white *mambo*. I think you know who she is. I must talk to her; I want you to arrange it."

It was as if a steel shutter had clanged shut behind the black woman's eyes. "I don't know what you are talking about," she said sullenly. "And you'll have to excuse me; I've still got work to do." She got up.

Penny held her ground and hurled her last bolt. "The Sect Rouge is involved, and where that appears there is danger to everyone. If you are a true voodoo, you must understand that and help me."

The dark face blanched to gray, and Elviny made a sign fending off the evil eye. "Oh, no, not that! I know nothing of that," came the husky whisper, "but there is one here who might. . . ." The words died on her lips as she stood staring over Penny's shoulder.

Penny looked quickly behind her. Framed in the doorway stood Henri, gazing at them with his cold, hooded eyes. She felt a little trickle of ice up her spine as he moved on silent feet toward them. When he spoke, it was an anticlimax. "You got some supper you can heat up for me, Elviny? *M'sieu* sent me back for some papers. He's staying in town tonight after the ball, and I got to get the papers back to him before bringing the rest of 'em on home."

"Sure thing. Won't take but a minute." The black woman shuffled toward the refrigerator. "I'll be sure and let you have that recipe before you go, Miz Spring. Good night," she said in a dismissive tone. There was nothing for it but to retreat.

Penny made her way through the silent house and tapped lightly on Toby's door. It opened a tiny crack, and a suspicious blue eye peered out. "Oh, it's you," Toby grunted and opened the door wide. "I was afraid Celeste might have started to get some ideas about me."

"Getting like that, is it?" Penny slipped into the smoke-filled room. "Just wanted to see what you'd come up with."

"Want a brandy?" She shook her head, and he helped himself to a liberal snort with a contented sigh. "I did not get a lot for my considerable efforts. In sum: (a) she, Eleanor, and Benedict are all dead set against the book; (b) she doesn't think much of Eleanor or Benedict but approves of Juliette; (c) she is a bit loopy on the subject of the Lefaus; and (d) she thinks very little of Jules's story about the dancing lady and voodoo. In light of my own research, I find that interesting. Did you get anywhere?"

Penny sighed in her turn. "Not very far. My shock tactics didn't work, but I'm not sure any others would have, either. Elviny obviously knows something, but she isn't talking—*yet*. When I mentioned the Sect Rouge, she started to open up a little; but then Henri made an untimely appearance, and that was that. She was frightened, but whether it was of him or of his knowing she was talking about it I can't say. She was quite firm that Jules was in no danger. I am also certain she knows who the white *mambo* is, but at this stage wild horses aren't going to drag it out of her. I've got to find a lever. Maybe tomorrow I'll take another crack at Mama Tio, or even get a reading from Hungan Thomas, and see if I can get anything there. This is one of the many times in my life I've wished my skin was a different color; I'd get on faster. Oh, one more thing: I've got an uneasy feeling about that damned heart. I feel we should remove it.''

"Well, I don't." Toby was firm. "For one thing, I'm not going to go crawling around those rafters at dead of night, and for another, I think we should leave it in place and show it to Lefau *in situ*; then maybe he'll start taking us seriously.''

"Maybe you're right." But Penny was uneasy. "What were you thinking of for tomorrow?"

"I thought after breakfast we might go for another prowl through the grounds to get more of an idea of the lie of the land. Celeste mentioned some shacks; if voodoo is going on here, wouldn't they have drums and things? So presumably they would have to stash them somewhere outside.''

"Yes. Good thinking. Then, I'll hop into town. You coming, too?"

"No. I'll check in with Beauregard and Mimi by phone and then have another crack at the book to see if there's anything I missed and also read a history of the Lefaus. Celeste mentioned there's one in the library here.''

"So I'll say good night. I wish I felt better about all this," she fretted.

"You should have had some brandy," he admonished. "Remarkably good for settling the mind.''

"Or fuddling it," she riposted and stumped off to bed.

John Everett, who since the lie-detector test had recovered a lot of his normal ebullience, joined their expedition the next morning and listened raptly as Penny and Toby filled him in on their findings. This time they explored the grounds to the right of the mansion, where they located the foundations of the old slave quarters and one shack that yielded a miscellany of gardener's tools and one very grumpy old gardener. They wandered deeper into the live-oak woods.

Suddenly Penny stopped, sniffing the air like a hound. "Do you smell something?"

The two men obediently sniffed in unison. "Umm, a bonfire somewhere," Toby opined.

"Let's split up and find it," Penny suggested eagerly.

After a few minutes John's voice echoed excitedly from straight ahead. "Over here! I think we may be onto something!"

Penny and Toby joined him to see the charred circle of a large bonfire still smoldering. Around its perimeter lay scattered black and white cock feathers. The two men looked expectantly at Penny, who nodded. "Looks like a voodoo fire, all right." She picked up a white cock feather and twirled it thoughtfully. "Black *and* white cocks sacrificed, so it wasn't just a death ritual. And it obviously was held last night. This is far enough from the house so that if they did use drums, they wouldn't have been heard. Maybe my visit to Elviny stirred up some action."

Toby had been poking into the heart of the fire with a stick. He bent down, picked something out of it, burned his fingers, swore, and dropped it. He indicated what lay on the ground. "We have also discovered, I think, what became of the dog. If I am not mistaken, that bone is part of a dog's skeleton." He picked it up gingerly and put it in an old envelope. "Better collect some of those cock feathers, too, just in case *this* does a disappearing act on us. I feel I should tell Beauregard of this." Nobody disagreed.

"If I'm going to get anything accomplished in town today, I ought to be off," Penny said restlessly. "You want to come with me, John? I could use some company, and on the way in you can fill me in a bit on Eleanor and Juliette. I haven't had a chance to talk to either of them yet, and Toby's been so busy doing his boring act that he hasn't got any ideas about them."

"Yes, I'd be glad to. Beauregard wants me to stick around the city, but I don't have to stay put here," John agreed. They left Toby diligently picking bits of the dog out of the bonfire.

"You're a good judge of people, John," Penny said as they made their way to the small car sitting somewhat forlornly in the huge driveway. "What kind of person would you say Eleanor Lefau is?"

John pondered. "She was very standoffish at first, obviously didn't relish having a presumed murderer as a house guest. But Jules must have had a quiet word with her, because she turned amiable all of a sudden. I know your suspicions in this affair are running in her direction, but I must confess I can't see her in the role of a *dea ex machina*, particularly with this voodoo business. Of course, there *may* be hidden depths there, but on the surface she seems exactly what you'd expect—a rich, wellborn southern lady, very conscious of her position and determined to live up to it. Not a warm woman. Obviously does not care for her stepson and his wife, is very fond of the younger boy, but seems to pick on Juliette constantly, and unfairly, in my opinion."

"How about Celeste?"

"Kid gloves with her; handle with care at all times. She's far from being a stupid woman, and I have the feeling she does most of the household management and that she finds that useful: it leaves her free for her social activities, which seem to be the largest thing in her life. She doesn't appear to notice the other servants but is very matey with Henri, who is equally useful to her. She said something to me about how lucky they were to have found a man of superior education and training like Henri."

"That's interesting. What do you think of Juliette?"

John's face softened. "A very attractive girl, high-spirited; the rest of them seem a bit lackluster by comparison. I'd say that like so many of her generation, she's a bit rebellious and has some half-baked ideas, but nothing that time won't cure." He sighed nostalgically.

Penny was well aware that the older John grew, the larger and softer his heart had become to young and pretty faces; so she did not put too much store on this evaluation. "What sort of half-baked ideas?" she persisted.

"Oh, I don't know specifically, but her mother made some cracks about her 'hippie' artistic friends. She's been involved in some demonstrations, too. Apparently got kicked out of the exclusive convent school she was at. Crime unspecified, but I doubt it was anything more heinous than smoking pot. She gets under her mother's skin by refusing to take all this 'court' business of the Comus krewe too seriously."

"Is she in college?"

"No. She was asking me lots of questions about art schools in New York. Evidently she wants to get away from here, but her mother has vetoed that. I've got an idea Juliette may have a steady beau up north somewhere of whom Mama does not approve. I expect Mama is right, too—girls of that age never know who is good for them."

"Why, John, you're becoming quite the southerner!" Penny gibed. "We'll have to get you out of here fast before they make a Creole out of you!"

Bereft of their company and tiring of his dog-collecting after a while, Toby wandered deeper into the woods. It was quiet and warm, and he strolled puffing contentedly on his pipe, unwilling as yet to face the research he knew must be done back at the mansion. A certain fastidiousness had come upon him; the case, he reflected, had nasty undertones, and he did not much relish the unearthing of secrets that were part and parcel of any old family and over which history had drawn its merciful veil. Still, he had committed himself, and so it had to be done. With a sigh he was about to retrace his steps when a small shack almost hidden by bushes caught his eye. Closer inspection revealed a stout wooden door, securely padlocked. There was one very small, dirt-encrusted window through which he tried to peer. It was a vain effort, for even with his flashlight it was impossible to penetrate the murk. Something else to take up with Lefau. Toby wrote it down meticulously in his notebook and returned to the house.

There was no sign of anyone about as he made his way to the library; most of the household were evidently sleeping late after their all-night ball. He phoned Beauregard and told him of the bonfire and was told in return that the regular payments to Arlette Gray had started only eight months before. "Just before the threatening letters started," Toby observed. "Did your lab get anything out of them, by the way?"

"Nothing much more than the Boston police lab got," Beauregard said resignedly. "All mailed from different boxes in New Orleans, all on the same cheap paper, and the lettering on them cut from the *Times-Picayune*. Jules Lefau kept only two of his. Claims he threw the rest away, but they tell the same story."

"What's the position on John Everett now, then?" Toby

asked. "Obviously, *he* could not have sent them, and so that establishes a third party with animosity toward him."

"He's still our prime suspect until we can come up with a better one. You've got no definite links as yet between the book, this voodoo business, and the murder."

"We're working on it," Toby said grimly and hung up.

He called the library hoping for better cheer. Mimi Gardiner was apologetic. "I haven't had much time, but I do have a little information. Pernell Lefau and Arlette Duchamps were both de Lesseps; their fathers were brothers. They were quite a swinging twosome in their day—suffragettes and among the first wave of 'flappers' in New Orleans. It was quite shocking to the locals at the time. Even after they both were married, they kept on with their high jinks as 'mad moderns' all through the twenties. I've got all the details written down if they are of any interest to you."

"Oh, yes, yes indeed." Toby reflected that this version of Pernell Lefau was definitely at odds with Celeste's picture of her mother as a saint. "Anything else?"

"Just one thing. I'm not sure it's important, though. It's from a social column just before the Mardi Gras of fifty years ago, the one you're interested in. It says, 'One of the high points of the Comus Ball this year is rumored to be the announcement of a uniting of two of its most eminent families. I had this on the authority of the happy bride-to-be. Remember, when it is announced, you read it here first.' Now, I checked, and there was *no* such announcement. Of course, it could have been submerged in all the scandal that resulted from the suicide of Gaston Duchamps. Is that any good?"

"You are doing splendidly," Toby responded, deep in thought. "Keep it up! Anything further?"

"Just one little item. One of Grace Harmon's great-grandmothers moved to Baton Rouge from New Orleans just after the War between the States. Her name was Lefebre. I checked the name here, and the man who was her father was listed as an FMC."

"What does that mean?" Toby asked blankly.

"Free man of color. It's a term they used to use for mullattos, quadroons, and octoroons. It means she probably passed as white but had some Negro blood, a not too uncommon situation at that time."

"Well, thank you again. I'll be in touch with you shortly," Toby concluded.

Chewing on all these choice nuggets, he wandered around the library looking at its layout and found with a twinge of pleasure that it was provided with a leatherbound catalog. His estimation of Jules Lefau soared as he examined it lovingly. While he was locating the history of the Lefau family, published in New Orleans in 1925, another item just below it caught his eye. *Journal of Desiree Lefau. 1850–1883*. A quick check of his notes informed him she had been an unmarried daughter of the putative 'dancing lady.' "That might be interesting," he murmured, but when he went to locate it on the shelves, it was to find a small gap next to the Lefau history. His eyebrows lifted slightly at this, but he contented himself with the history and, settling into a red leather chair, began to read. After a while he decided he needed Jules's book and went up to his room to collect it. The house was still very quiet, but there was some evidence of activity, witnessed by the distant hum of a vacuum cleaner, and as he descended the staircase again, he heard a door open and shut in the left wing. He returned to his studies.

He had put the book down, open, in his lap to refill his pipe when something dropped on it with a sudden plop. He looked up, startled, to see a small dark stain on the ceiling above, and he held out his hand over the book. Another drop plopped into it, and he peered at it. It was reddish. He went a little green at the sight, his thoughts whirling frantically to place what lay above the library. "My God! It's blood!" he croaked and hurtled out of the chair.

He ran into the hallway in time to see Benedict Lefau's large figure coming through the double doors from his section of the twin house. "Quick!" Toby trumpeted. "Come with me!" He started to race up the stairs. "Your father—something may have happened." The blond giant thudded up after him. "The main bedroom—which door?" Toby demanded.

Benedict hurried ahead of him and, opening a door, peered in. Then he looked back, puzzled. "What is all this?"

Toby pushed past him into the room and looked around. The room, dominated by the great Seignouret bed, lay tranquil and empty in the pale sunshine, only the rumpled covers of the unmade bed marring its impeccable neatness. Toby plunged on to where a door stood ajar. He hurled it open to find himself in a dressing room. Again, it was empty.

"Really, Sir Tobias," Benedict said over his shoulder, "What on earth are you up to? This is my stepmother's dressing room!"

"Your father's, then," Toby said desperately and dashed out and through another closed door into a smaller version of the other dressing room. Again, nothing.

"My father isn't even here——" Benedict began on a rising note.

Toby brushed past him again. "That blood is coming from *somewhere* here," he said, looking frantically around.

"*What* blood?"

"It's oozing through the library ceiling," Toby yelled. "Think, man! Where else?"

Benedict paled and stood frozen. "The closet?"

Toby rushed back into the first dressing room and pulled open the louvered doors of a huge walk-in closet filled on three sides with racks of clothes. Behind him, Benedict pressed a wall switch, and a pale-pink neon light sprang to life. Toby recoiled. "Oh, dear God!" he whispered

Lying crumpled on the floor of the closet in a welter of blood lay a figure, its throat slashed from ear to ear and gleaming wetly. It was Eleanor Lefau.

CHAPTER 10

Penny's further onslaught on the voodoo question came to naught when she checked in at the Basin Street cabstand to see if her merry band of Knights had come up with any leads on the missing cabdriver. There was no sign of Mean Gene, but at the sight of Penny, Hiram the trombone went into an agitated dance. "We found him for you, lady. It was poor ol' Ken Stubbs, but he ain't about to go to de police, Ah can tell you that! He jes' don't jive with them."

"Well, this is Mr. Everett, Hiram," Penny said firmly, "the friend I was telling you about, and *we* must talk to him. It's extremely important."

"He runs out of a stand near the old market, but I ain't sure he'll even talk to you." Hiram was uneasy.

"Where's Mean Gene?" Penny asked, figuring the leader of the Knights may have more clout in every respect than his faithful band.

"He's out on the town, but he'll be back soon," Hiram assured her with evident relief. "Mebbe you'd better talk to him some more." Getting into his own cab, he drove off.

Penny and John went into a quiet conference, so that when Mean Gene did put in his magnificent appearance some ten minutes later, they had their campaign all laid out. Penny went straight to the point. "Mean Gene, how much do you make a day, driving?"

"This time of year a good day runs about seventy-five dollars; why?"

"This is Mr. Everett, the friend who has been framed. We'd like to hire you for the rest of the day for a hundred dollars. Fair enough?"

100

"What's the catch?"

"The catch is, we'd like you to take us to Ken Stubbs and persuade him to talk to us. We've got to know more about that night."

Mean Gene grinned slyly at her. "You surely are a persistent lady, but Ah can see you make a good friend. OK. You want me to lean on poor ol' Ken a little. You're on."

They piled into his cab and shot off to the French Market, where their objective was found chatting to a group of other drivers by a coffee stall.

"You stay here," Mean Gene ordered and proceeded to cut Ken Stubbs out of the crowd and bring him back to the cab. 'Poor old Ken' was not old, nor did he look particularly poor, but he did look worried, and at the sight of John Everett he recoiled slightly. "Now, you tell these folks exactly what happened that night you picked up the Angel," Mean Gene charged.

Ken's maroon eyes flicked nervously over them and away again, and he cleared his throat. "Well, de Angel came out of Pat O'Brien's and flagged me down. Said there was a john in there who'd got sick on her and would Ah take 'em to the St. Louis. Ah said sure, de Angel always bein' a good tipper. Ah goes inside, and there's dis man"—he nodded at John— "sort of propped against the wall, all glassy-eyed. Ah thought to mahself, 'He's got a skinful. De Angel sure won't get much joy outta him.' Well, we carries him into the cab, and Ah goes over to the hotel. 'Help me in with him and there'll be a five-spot in it for you,' she says to me. So we drags him between us on up to dis room, and when we got to de door, she hands me de money and says, 'Ah can manage now,' and that was it."

"What about the key?" Penny said quickly. "Did you get that from the night clerk?"

"I had it with me," John put in. "I only intended to go for a stroll, so I never handed it in."

"She had de key in her hand," Ken said, "but she never got to use it."

"Why not?"

" 'Cause somebody opened the door," he said simply.

Penny and John looked at each other in excitement. "Who?" they chorused.

"Ah don't know. Ah didn't see nobody. The door jest opened and she pushed him on through, and Ah left. So, as Ah said, Ah don't know nothin'."

"But this is very important," Penny said in high excitement. "Ken, you simply *must* tell this to the police. The fact that there was someone else already in that room is vital, even if you didn't see who it was. All you need to do is make a statement."

Mean Gene looked at her warningly. "Let me talk to him," he growled and pushed Ken out of the cab. After five minutes of heated argument during which the smaller man visibly wilted, Mean Gene stuck his head back into the cab. "OK," he said briefly, "we'll go to the police, but Ah said you'd pay for his time, OK?" They nodded.

Beauregard was not immediately available, and Penny became increasingly concerned as Ken, hypernervous at the threatening atmosphere, kept throwing desperate glances at the door. Only the hulking presence of Mean Gene kept him from bolting. When the summons finally came, Penny almost leaped through the door of Beauregard's office, propelling the unwilling Ken ahead of her. The story was retold, and Ken, gaining courage as he went along, blurted out at the end, "And dat's de God's truth of what happened, but Ah ain't about to go to no court to say it."

"Unless the case comes to trial, you won't have to," Beauregard said briefly. "The stenographer will now type up your statement and you can sign it, and that might well be the end of the matter. You can go with her, and after that you may leave."

With a sigh of relief Ken scurried out after the slim figure of the policewoman. Beauregard looked at Penny. "That was quick work, Dr. Spring. I'm impressed. We'll have to check on him, of course."

"Your thanks should go to Mean—er—Mr. Gene here," she said quickly. "He was the one who located Mr. Stubbs for me."

Beauregard looked curiously at the giant and then at John Everett. "Well, Mr. Everett, I wouldn't say you are completely in the clear yet, but it certainly looks less black, particularly in light of this other voodoo activity that appears to be going on at the Lefau estate, about which Sir Tobias has informed me.''

Penny looked at the big black. "Would you mind waiting for us outside? There is something else I should discuss with the captain here.''

"Sure thing. My time is your time." Gene swaggered out.

"I don't know how much Sir Tobias has told you," she went on after the door closed, ''but my research so far points to the fact that a *white* voodoo *mambo* seems to be involved. Now, we don't have enough concrete facts to back any of this up yet, but there *may* be a tie-in between the book and this voodoo business, in that we have uncovered a long-continuing rivalry between the Lefaus and the Duchamps, the family to which Eleanor Lefau belongs, and she may be the *mambo* in question.'' Quickly Penny outlined her thoughts on this. "I feel there is definite danger to Mr. Lefau, although we haven't convinced him of that yet. Is there anything you can do to protect him?''

Beauregard shook his head. "Nothing, until something happens or an attempt on him is made. We certainly can't move on the flimsy evidence of a slaughtered dog and an old black woman's hearsay! And I must point out that voodoo activity is not against the law; the voodoo church has been recognized as a religion in America since 1948—I looked that up.''

"But if you wait for something to happen, it may be too late! Surely——'' she began to protest.

The phone rang, and with a muttered excuse the captain picked it up. As he listened, his mouth set in a grim line. "How long ago was this?'' he barked, then wheeled on Penny. "How long have you been with Mr. Everett this morning?''

They looked at him in surprise. "Why, Sir Tobias and we breakfasted together, we all went for a walk in the plantation grounds, and then Mr. Everett came with me into the city,'' Penny said. "We've been together since about eight o'clock this morning.''

"At any time, did Mr. Everett absent himself?''

"Why, no, we've been together constantly.''

"The medical examiner there?'' Beauregard asked into the

phone. "Put him on . . . How long? . . . I see. All right, put on Benedict Lefau."

The voice at the other end was so loud and strident that even on the opposite side of the desk it could be heard. ". . . your fault for letting a psychotic killer roam free to kill again. I want him behind bars and hanged high!"

"Mr. Lefau, calm down!" Beauregard roared. "You're way out of line. Mr. Everett is quite out of it. He has been with Dr. Spring all morning, and for the past hour he has been either waiting to see me at police headquarters or sitting here in this office. We'll be right out." He slammed down the phone and stood up, leaning his hands on the desk. "That was the police of Pontchartrain Parish. There's been a murder at the Lefau plantation. *Now* we can move."

"Oh, no!" Penny gasped. "Not Jules!"

"No, no," Beauregard said, reaching for his hat, "and so much for your theories, Dr. Spring. The victim was Eleanor Lefau. Let's go."

"You'll have to drive us back to the car," Penny stuttered at Mean Gene as they rushed out. "We've got to get back to the Lefau place right away—another murder."

"Ah'll drive you," Gene insisted. "You hired me for the day, remember?"

Penny was so shaken that she didn't argue, but as they sped out of the city, she calmed down enough to tell Mean Gene the meager details.

"This sure is going to stir up some mighty big waves," he observed. "They can't keep this one quiet, that's for sure. Strikes me you could use all the help you can get. Want me to mosey round back when we get there and see what Ah can pick up in the kitchen quarter? Ah believe Ah knows one of the daily maids there."

"Yes—anything, everything, you can pick up," she agreed. "This has so flummoxed me that I don't know where we are now or what we're looking for."

Despite the fact that they broke every speed law en route, the police car with Beauregard had reached the plantation before them, and when Penny and John entered the main hall, it was a sea of uniforms. Toby was standing stiffly by; one look at his face told Penny that not only was he deeply upset, but he was in a towering rage. His eyes were like blue steel as she rushed up to him.

"So," he exploded, "I have fulfilled my purpose—I have borne witness to a murder."

"You don't think Jules . . .?"

"Yes, I do. That's precisely what I think," he ranted, "and, by God, if that is the case, he's not going to get away with it!"

"But he wasn't even here! How could he have done it?"

"That remains to be seen." Toby drew them toward the library, and when Penny and John were inside, he closed the door against the hubbub outside. Grimly he indicated the spot on the ceiling, now dried black. "She was murdered—butchered would be a better word—in the walk-in closet in her bedroom. Her throat was so deeply slashed that both the carotid artery and the jugular vein were severed; she bled so freely and so fast that the blood seeped through the cracks in the old wooden flooring of the closet and through the plaster of the ceiling. The body was still warm when Benedict and I found her. I may even have *heard* the murderer. . . ." He went on to describe in more detail the grim events of the morning.

Penny tried to collect her thoughts. "But who was in the house, and where were they during the time of the murder?"

"The police haven't got to that yet. Benedict threw the local parish police for a loop by insisting that John here was the crazy killer. He carried on like a madman, insisting they beat the grounds and shoot him down like a dog. I tried to tell them John could not have been involved, but he raved on so you'd have thought it was his wife who lay dead and not an unloved stepmother. Once they got the doctor's report and started to listen to me and what I had to say, well, then they called Beauregard, and you know the rest. From what little I've been able to make out, everyone was here save young Vincent, who was in school, and Jules Lefau, who has *yet* to be located. There has been no answer at the Royal Street house, where he was supposed to be spending the night."

"I still can't believe he's responsible," Penny said. "Maybe we just jumped to the wrong conclusion over the voodoo. Because Jules had been threatened, we naturally assumed that the death *gris-gris* was aimed at him, but it could equally well have been directed at Eleanor, since they shared the same room. Perhaps that's what Elviny was trying to tell me when she insisted he was in no danger. Perhaps Eleanor Lefau *was* the white *mambo* and this was a ritual killing, too. And perhaps the Sect Rouge, which is color-oriented and anti-white, was involved.''

"Perhaps!" Toby snorted. "And *perhaps* Jules Lefau wanted to get rid of his wife and set up this elaborate flimflam to suck us in as expert witnesses trumpeting in the ear of the police about voodoo and whatnot. You know damn well that if a wife is murdered, usually the first person they suspect is the husband—and normally with very good cause, too. I'm back to my original position: there had to be a reason why he was so all-fired anxious to get us on the scene.''

"Well, I think you are being totally biased about this," Penny flared back. "Are you asking me to believe he slaughtered a dog to which he was obviously very attached *and* had a perfectly innocent girl murdered just to put us on the wrong track? Now, that *is* wild!''

"How do you know Arlette Gray was perfectly innocent," Toby expostulated, "since she was so obviously involved in setting John up?'' They glared at one another.

John, who had kept out of the exchange, stepped into the breech. "I'd say," he told them peaceably, "that both of you are getting very worked up for very little reason. Until we know a lot more about this unfortunate murder and where everyone was, I would say that speculations are completely uncalled for. Why don't we wait and see what develops?''

They both turned their glares on him, but he was saved by the door opening and Captain Beauregard's head appearing around it.

"Ah, there you are!" the captain said with a frown. "Sir Tobias, I'd like you out here.''

They all trooped out into the hallway, where the uniforms had thinned out but where the Lefau family was now evident in full disarray. Celeste Lefau was deathly pale, with a fixed look to her eyes that Penny did not like at all. Juliette Lefau was sobbing hysterically in the arms of her grim-faced step-brother, and Grace Lefau was standing by her husband, looking at them both with an enigmatic expression in which, Penny thought, lurked a suggestion of satisfaction.

"Would you show us what you found in the attic?" Beauregard said and led the way upstairs, Toby and Penny in his wake. Toby collected a flashlight, and they made their way to the opening in the eaves.

"Go carefully," Toby charged Beauregard as they edged out along the beam. "It is just here." He shone the light into the rafters, but there was nothing. "Well, that's where it *was*," he said heavily and looked out at Penny.

"So now we have only your joint testimony but no evidence of the voodoo business," Beauregard complained. "Why the devil didn't you bring it in?"

"We wanted to leave it in place for your experts to give it a going-over. But we do have evidence of the dog." Toby reached into his pocket and pulled out the envelopes from the bonfire. "There are enough bones in here to identify the dog, and these are the remains of the cocks used for the rite, whatever it was. We can lead you to the site if it's important, but I am beginning to wonder if it is."

"They found the murder weapon," Beauregard informed them as he led the way downstairs again. "It was thrown into a corner of the closet—an old-fashioned razor, no prints on it. According to Celeste Lefau, it is one of a matched pair belonging to her father, Jules. It came from an old-fashioned dressing case in Mr. Lefau's dressing room; no prints on that, either. This is a very well kept house." His voice was doom-laden.

They had reached the bottom stair when the front door opened and a hush fell on the hall. Jules Lefau stood on the threshold, two uniformed policemen behind him. He was very pale but showed no visible emotion. At the sight of him, Juliette gave a shriek and hurtled, still sobbing, into his arms. He hugged her to him and whispered into her ear; then he looked at the gathering over her lovely aureole of hair.

"If there is a doctor still here, I would like him to give my daughter a sedative," he said in a tight voice. "If there isn't, please send for one." He looked at Benedict, an undefinable expression in his dark eyes, but Penny got the feeling that a definite message had passed between father and son.

"The police surgeon is upstairs making out his preliminary report." Beauregard jerked his head at one of the uniformed men but kept his eyes on Lefau. "Get him." Then, to Lefau, "We have been trying to contact you all morning, Mr. Lefau. Where were you?"

"In my Royal Street house, working." The voice was even and cool.

"Can you prove that?"

Jules Lefau's eyebrows rose a fraction. "It is not up to me to prove that; it is up to you to disprove it."

Beauregard's bushy brows drew down into a formidable frown. "Your wife has been most brutally *murdered*," he growled.

"So these officers informed me, and as soon as my daughter is taken care of, I would like to see her."

"You're too late for that," Beauregard snapped. "The body has been removed, pending an autopsy."

"I forbid an autopsy," Jules said imperiously.

"You are in no position to forbid it. I must ask you again, Mr. Lefau, to account for your movements since last night."

Juliette had been given a shot and had been led away upstairs by Celeste's old servant. Jules, now unencumbered, took several paces toward Beauregard, who seemed to tower over his elegant figure. "I would prefer a more civil tone, Captain, but I have no objections to telling you. I returned from the ball alone by cab at about four o'clock this morning. I let myself into my Royal Street house, dismissed the caretaker, who stays in the house when the family is not in residence, snatched a few hours' sleep, rose at eight o'clock, made myself some coffee, and worked in my study there until these officers came pounding on the door."

"You were called constantly by the parish police here after the murder was discovered; there was no answer at the Royal Street number."

"There was no answer for the simple reason that I had turned off the bell on the phone; I did not wish to be disturbed." Their eyes clashed and held.

"And you are prepared to make a statement to that effect?"

"I am, although I am a little surprised, in view of the

gravity of the situation, that I was not approached sooner by the police at the house.''

"The parish police were misled initially by the unfounded charges made by Mr. Benedict Lefau against Mr. Everett. That caused the delay.''

"Where was Mr. Everett at the time of the murder?'' Lefau did not look at John.

"In New Orleans with your guest, Dr. Spring.'' There was an edge of satisfaction in Beauregard's voice. "They were waiting at police headquarters to see me.''

"I see.'' Jules suddenly wheeled and went over to where Celeste was still standing rigidly on the outskirts of the group. He took her hand. "Celeste, my dear, this must be most shocking and distasteful to you. Why don't you withdraw to your rooms and let me summon Dr. Bell?''

The gray eyes seemed to look through him. "No,'' she said in a low voice. "What's done cannot be undone. I prefer to stay. If the family is in trouble, it is my right.''

"Of course, of course. As you wish.'' He patted her limp hand gently.

Eyes switched away from them as there came the sound of raised voices from beyond the closed front door, which burst open to reveal a tall man, his arm in the grasp of a policeman. "Let me go!'' he roared. "I intend to enter.''

He strode in and paused dramatically, allowing everyone to take in the fact that he was spectacularly handsome from the top of his elegantly silvered hair to the tips of his immaculately shined shoes. Then, ignoring them all, he strode over to Jules and towered over him. "So!'' he bellowed. "You have done it at last! You have murdered her. Is there to be no end to this?''

Celeste emerged from her trancelike state and flung herself between the two men. "François, no!'' she cried. "What are you saying? You are wrong! You are mad!''

"How can you say that? How can you defend them anymore after what they did to you?'' he roared. "This time we will not keep quiet; this time the Lefaus must pay!''

Celeste made a little blind gesture and turned away, covering her eyes.

Beauregard emerged from his state of shock and shouted, "Enough! Who the devil are you?''

The handsome head turned to him, the green eyes glittering with hate. "I am François de Lesseps Duchamps, Mrs. Lefau's brother and head of the Duchamps family. I know nothing of the circumstances of this murder, but I can tell you your murderer. He hated her as he hates all us Duchamps. Jules Lefau is your man!"

CHAPTER 11

"These Creoles are always so damned *theatrical*." Beauregard looked with exhausted eyes at Toby and Penny. "I know I've got a Creole name, but half of me is Irish and there's a hunk of German in me, too. I sometimes can't believe these Creole families! Those two will probably end up with sabers or pistols at the Dueling Oaks at dawn. They're beyond me!" He was about to take his leave of the Lefau household after hours of questioning and examining, of statements and more questioning, and was currently smarting from an amazing *volte-face* undergone by François Duchamps over the question of the autopsy. On this François had immediately allied himself with Jules, and between them they had had the mayor and half the city council on the phone. For once it had availed them nothing, but they had withdrawn in high dudgeon to continue their quarreling behind doors closed fast against the police:

"There's not a hope in hell of keeping *this* murder quiet," Beauregard continued morosely. "God! Coming on top of everything else, I don't know how I'm going to make it through these next six days! Do you realize there is not a single provable alibi among the lot of them? Juliette and Grace Lefau both claim to have been in bed at the time of the murder—which has been established as eleven A.M., by the way. Celeste Lefau claims she was walking in the grounds. Benedict says he was working in his library; no one saw him. The servants were all working in different rooms, with the exception of Elviny Brosse, who was seen by several of them as they went in and out the kitchen. Even so, the murder could have been done so fast there's nothing to say she

111

couldn't have nipped out for the ten minutes or so that it required. Henri Legros claims he was in the garage polishing the Rolls; no one saw him, either. And Jules, as you know, claims he was in New Orleans; again, no witnesses.''

"How about bloodstained clothing?'' Toby asked.

"Not a sign of any anywhere in the house,'' Beauregard said heavily. "Sometimes I wish Louisiana was still under French law so that they'd have to prove their innocence and not I their guilt; then I could arrest the whole kit and caboodle and sweat it out of them. It'll take *weeks* to check and cross-check all of this.''

Penny looked at him with sympathy. "You know, Captain, I certainly don't want to add to your burdens, but I was wondering if it wouldn't be easier to keep plugging away at the *simpler* murder—that of Arlette Gray. The two have to be connected in some way, and if we can find the connection, the way may be clearer. There are two things I would like to suggest, if I may. First, there must be an alien registry in city hall somewhere. I'd like to get the names of Haitians still in New Orleans that came in the same year as Arlette Gray and/or Henri Legros and talk to them. Then I'd very much like to have a look at Arlette Gray's house, if that can be arranged. I feel much might be gained by following the voodoo angle. Sir Tobias doesn't agree with me on this, but he is following up his own leads on the Duchamps-Lefau rivalry, which may again give you some kind of pointer. The worst of it is, after all this upset today, I feel we can scarcely stay on here ourselves as guests; so we'll lose the advantage of inside contact—though where we're to go I've no idea.''

John Everett had quietly rejoined the group. "I've already thought of that and done something about it. On an off chance I called up the Hotel Bayou, and they've got room for us. It's no great shakes, but at least it will give us a base of operations until we see what Lefau has in mind.'' He looked apologetically at them. "I have to stay on until I'm officially cleared, but if this is all getting too disagreeable for you I'd quite understand if you want to take off.''

"Certainly not,'' Toby said severely. "We've no intention of going off and leaving you in this mess. But if you are released in Jules's surety, don't you have to stay *here*?''

They all looked at Beauregard, who threw up his hands in

despair. "Normally, yes; under these circumstances, no. In fact, it might be a damn sight safer for Mr. Everett *not* to be here. One thing that did strike me today was that they were all disappointed here that Mr. Everett *wasn't* handily around to pin the blame on. It was a bit of luck he decided to go into the city with you, Dr. Spring; otherwise, I think he'd have been railroaded. I'll see what I can do about your other suggestions. Call me tomorrow." He took a gloomy departure.

"Well, I don't know about you two, but I'm starved," Penny said. "I doubt whether we're going to get fed here tonight; so let's throw some things in a bag and eat dinner en route to the Hotel Bayou." They suited their actions to the words and, having left a note behind as to their intentions—since none of the household were visible—piled into the little red car, chauffeured by Mean Gene, and headed for the city.

Dinner at Antoine's fully restored Penny's good humor and recharged her batteries. Dropping Mean Gene off at his cabstand, she arranged a rendezvous with him for the following morning. Then, once more behind the wheel of the red car, she said briskly to Toby, "So what's your plan of action for tomorrow? I'm going to take Gene with me to talk to the Haitians—he has a great knack for opening people up. Are you going back to your girlfriend in the library and tell her what you are really up to? You'd better keep John with you; then you'll both be safe."

Toby looked pained. "Yes, not much use keeping quiet about it now. I imagine the murder will be splashed all over tomorrow's papers. And if John's willing, yes, the more the merrier on the research. I'd like to follow up on the Grace Lefau angle."

John, who was looking replete and relaxed, nodded a sleepy assent and yawned.

"What's that?" Penny asked.

"I haven't had time to fill you in yet, but I've a question for you first. You say Clemence Alexander was a white *mambo* and that that was extremely unusual. Wasn't it even more unusual that she was married to a black man? I thought it was against the law down here at that time."

"Yes, it was, but there were ways of getting around it," Penny said. "But, in any case, Jim Alexander wasn't black. He was part Indian and part white with perhaps a little black blood as well, and although Clemence appeared white, she may well have had a smidgin of black blood in there, too. Why?"

"Because I've turned up the fact that Grace Lefau has a smidgin of black blood in *her*," Toby returned. "And in light of your remarks about *mambos* often being of mixed blood, I should think that if there is anything in this *mambo* business, she would be a more likely candidate than Eleanor Duchamps."

"Goodness! I wonder if the Lefaus are aware of that," Penny murmured. "I shouldn't think that would go down well at all, at all! Not that Grace Lefau would win any prizes, anyway, personality-wise. Still, on this other business, I may have given you a bum steer. Perhaps I'd better explain a bit more. You see, the picture I have given you is how things *used* to be in New Orleans. First of all, when the Laveaus, mother and daughter, ruled the roost here, a lot of white women used to attend the ceremonies and dances. Partly this was a protest against their own very circumscribed and secondary role in society—they really weren't in too different a position from the slaves they lorded it over—and partly it was because it gave them an exciting outlet from their otherwise dull lives. *But* very, very few of them were involved in the actual practice of voodoo. Similarly, the mixed-blood women were heavily into this kind of thing because it was one of *their* few means to power. Starting with the mixed-blood Sirènes, who came as refugees from Haiti after the eighteenth-century revolution there, it was about their only road to any kind of position in society. Otherwise, they were doomed to be either mistresses of Creoles or wives of other coloreds in a very humble station in life. Naturally, the 'with-it' ones like the Laveaus seized what chances they had and were fiercely competitive with one another for the top spots. That was the way it *was*.

"To move on to present-day circumstances, since the voo-doo church was recognized as a church in 1948, it has been almost entirely a *black* movement. Interestingly enough, it has been embraced mainly by middle-class blacks, apparently as a means to separate themselves both from the whites and from their own blue-collar class, who tend to be strongly Christian. In other words, there has been *no* modern white involvement. So what we have here is a maverick, or a throwback of some kind, and I'm not sure my strictures about mixed-blood *mambos* apply to this present situation. This is one of the reasons I'm so anxious to get some more on the sinister Henri. He's a far more likely candidate for the active practice of voodoo on all counts: he's from the right place, he's educated, and, if there is a white woman involved, he may well be her Svengali. It is very difficult for a white person to come by genuine voodoo knowledge.''

Her impromptu lecture had sent John off into a sound slumber, but it roused Toby to combat.

"Ummph," he grunted. "What you've just said could also support my own view that the voodoo is all flimflam to cover up the real motives behind all this."

"It *could* be," Penny agreed, "but I don't think so. There are too many little things that add up to someone into voodoo who actually believes in what they are doing."

"Such as?"

"Just two 'for instances,' though I could give you a lot more. Why, if they were going to frame John for Arlette Gray's murder, did they bother with that Ghede *vévé*? If that had not been found on the girl, no one would have thought twice about throwing the book at him or even bothered to look elsewhere. Again, why, if the intention was to keep our attention fixed on the voodoo angle, was the dog's heart removed from the attic after it had served its purpose? It just doesn't add up to me. No, I'm convinced that whoever is doing this believes in it themselves."

"But why now and why in connection with that damn book?" Toby worried on.

"There you've got me. I haven't a notion."

"I wonder"—he gave a reflective puff on his pipe—"if there is any significance in this. From what you've just said, I gather the white Creole women who went in for this kind of thing were rebels to their own society—am I right?" Penny nodded. "Well, both Pernell Lefau and her cousin Arlette, Eleanor's grandmother, were also rebels in their time: suffragettes, flappers of the most outrageous sort, and so on. How old would you say Elviny Brosse is?"

"It's hard to tell, but I'd say about sixty-five."

"Umm, so that would hardly fit," Toby grumbled. "It would make her about the same age as Celeste—too young to have had any influence on Celeste's mother."

"*She* had a mother," Penny pointed out, "who was one generation closer to the great Malvina Latour. It would be interesting to find out if she, too, had worked for the Lefaus."

"I wish I could have located that journal," he muttered.

"What journal?"

He told her about the missing book of Desiree Lefau's. "She was the daughter of the dancing lady," he went on. "Following on this idea of white women as rebels—the dancing lady was also one of that sort, by all accounts—the journal might give us some idea, especially since it covers the period when voodoo was the 'in' thing in New Orleans."

"In other words," Penny said, "you are looking for a sort of hereditary link between the white Lefau women and voodoo? And that would tie in with the book?"

"It's a possibility. Remote, I grant you, but a possibility. However, I think if I keep digging, I'll come up with a much better and more realistic motive."

"*Bonne chance!*" she retorted. "But *I'm* after Henri."

The next morning, having dropped off Toby and John at the library, she rendezvoused with Mean Gene and picked up the list of Haitians from the harassed Beauregard. They passed a highly frustrating morning. Despite the fact that the list contained only a handful of names, the owners were hard to locate and, when located, yielded nothing; none of them had heard of either Henri Legros or Arlette Gray.

It was midafternoon before Penny and Gene tracked down the final name on the list—a woman who was assistant to a dentist in a remote suburb of the city. She disclaimed any knowledge of Henri Legros but, on being shown Arlette's picture, showed some recognition. "We shared a cabin on the boat that brought us to Florida," she exclaimed. "I haven't seen her since, but I remember her because she was quite young, sixteen or so, and some man who saw her off asked me if I'd look after her on the trip."

"Did she tell you anything about herself or her family?" Penny asked eagerly. "Anything at all you can remember would help, believe me."

The woman concentrated. "It was all so long ago," she said, "but there was something—something I remember that put me off. I was just so thankful to be getting out. It was just after Papa Doc's death, and things were in confusion; so a lot of us managed to get away at that time. What was it, now . . .?'' She wrinkled her smooth brown forehead with her effort to recall. ''Oh, yes. She told me her father had been an army officer. The army were all in cahoots with Papa Doc and his bully boys, and my family had suffered much from the *Tontons Macoutes*. I really had no time for her after learning that.''

''Did she say anything else about her father?''

''Only that he was dead and she had no money. I couldn't help her. I was going to a refugee family who had slipped out secretly and had a lot of relatives left in Haiti. I was afraid to let her know about them; she could have been a Duvalier spy.''

''Was she met by anyone here?''

The dental assistant shook her head. ''No, there was no one. I don't know what she did or where she went. I've told you all I know.''

It seemed to be another dead end. Penny thanked her and left. On the way back into the heart of the city, she looked at her notes and fretted. ''I wish we had a picture of Henri. For all we know, he may have changed his name, like that woman we just left did, for safety purposes. The sight of him might stir up some memories.''

''Want me to get one for you?'' Mean Gene said amiably.

''Don't tell me you're a photographer as well as everything else!'' Penny exclaimed.

''Not me, but Ah got a friend who's a street photographer. Ah could give him the word.''

''That would be great. Several color shots would just fill the bill.'' She was delighted.

''What you want color pictures for?'' he chuckled. ''He'd come out jest the same in black and white.''

She laughed with him; they were so easy in each other's company now that neither was careful anymore. ''Have it your way, then!''

At the police station they parted company, Gene to seek out his photographer friend, Penny to report to Beauregard her meager gleanings and to pick up on another detail she had noticed, as well as to get the keys to Arlette Gray's house. Beauregard was unavailable, but she got the ear of a friendly policewoman and explained. ''I notice Henri Legros's time of entry to the U.S. is listed as some six months after Arlette Gray's. Are there any names among the aliens listed who entered the country at the same time?''

A long wait ensued, but when the information came through, it didn't help. Henri Legros had come in as a singleton by air from the Dominican Republic, and the first address he had listed when he registered as an alien was the Lefau plantation. Had someone there sent for him, or was it just happenstance? Something else she would have to check with Jules Lefau.

A further delay came when it transpired that no one but Beauregard either would or could give her permission to go to the house on St. Ann Street. By the time the captain did show up, Mean Gene had rejoined Penny with the news that his mission had been successfully accomplished and the photographer was now hanging around the Lefau building downtown, where Henri was bound to show up sooner or later. "Ah told him to look out for the Rolls or the white Mercedes. Ah took their numbers when Ah was out at the plantation.''

"Mean Gene, you have the makings of a great detective," Penny said. "I'd never have thought of that. You didn't get anything on him from that servant you know, did you?''

"Not much. She ain't been there too long, and he keeps pretty much to hisself. The only one he has much truck with is Elviny. The gal I know is mighty afraid of *her*—has a tongue on her like a whip.''

"Did she say anything to you about the Lefaus?'' Penny asked, feeling a twinge of guilt.

"Told me Juliette and her mother used to fight all the time but that she was a proper poppa's girl. Thinks a whole heap of Miz Celeste, who she says is a *real* lady. Gossip in the servants' hall is that Mr. Benedict has been playing around some and things are pretty sour between him and his missus. But that's about the size of it.''

"Umm," said Penny, busy with her own thoughts. "You know, there is one thing that doesn't fit about the story on Henri we've got so far. He's supposed to have been on Duvalier's hit list and had a hard time in Haiti, and yet he didn't arrive in America until a year after Papa Doc had died, when things there, by all accounts, had calmed down a lot and the power of the *Tontons Macoutes* had been broken. That just doesn't jibe. Damn, I wish I could go to Haiti! I could find out what I want to know in no time from my contacts there.''

"You surely are an eager beaver." Mean Gene grinned. "No keeping you still, is there? Well, if you get to go, Ah'm game. Always ready to see somewheres new."

"There doesn't seem much of a chance of that." She got up to intercept Beauregard, who was rushing into his office.

"I can't spare a man to go with you," he snapped as he handed her the keys, "so, for God's sake, lock up after you leave. Don't disarrange anything, and bring the keys right back. The place has been thoroughly searched; so I'm afraid you'll just be wasting your time."

It was already dark by the time Penny and Gene left the police station and drove through the French Quarter to the quiet darkness of St. Ann. "It's amazing how localized the crowds are," Penny observed as they got out on the deserted pavement in front of the white frame house. "Everybody is milling around Bourbon, Royal, and Burgundy."

"That's where the music is; so that's where the action is," the devout jazzman assured her.

They let themselves into the deserted house and after some groping located the light switches. The house sprang to muted life. The inside was sparsely furnished in ultramodern style, but every article was of good quality and in excellent taste; it was also extremely neat, with none of the feminine clutter Penny had somehow anticipated. She made for the bedroom, the most likely repository for clues that might have escaped the eye of a male policeman. It was equally neat and dominated by a queen-sized waterbed with an elegant satin cover. Penny riffled through a pile of fashion magazines on the bedside table and then turned her attention to the vanity, which ran along one whole wall of the room with a huge mirror above it. She went through it carefully, drawer by drawer, but it yielded nothing save an amazing array of cosmetics, a jewelry case with some choice pieces, and piles of expensive, filmy underclothes. Exasperated, she turned next to the small drawers in the two bedside tables. One gave up a crucifix and a rosary, and then in the other she found with a quickening excitement a leather photo folder with two color pictures. One was of a dusky-faced man in the uniform and insignia of an army major, the other of a lighter-skinned woman whose features were an older version of the dead girl's. Penny slipped the photos out of their frames in the hope of finding something on their backs. On the man's photo was written in a scrawly feminine hand, *"Jean Gris—né 1925, fusillé 1970."*

"So he was shot. I wonder who by?" Penny muttered. "And she just translated her name into English, Gray for Gris. Well, that doesn't give me much." There was nothing written on the woman's picture.

As a last resort Penny turned to the closet, which was jam-packed with expensive clothes, all in the same good taste. Fumbling along the shelf at the top of it, her hand encountered a small wrapped package, and, standing on tiptoe, she managed to grasp it. It was gaily wrapped in gift wrapping with a gold bow on top and gave out a liquid tinkle as she brought it down. "Well, what the heck—whoever it was for isn't likely to collect it now," she murmured and opened it up. There was a little white card inside, written in the same sprawly hand. "To you, my love, a little remembrance of me," it said in French. It was a heavy cut-glass bottle of an expensive men's cologne. Gingerly, Penny worked the stopper out and sniffed the heavy aroma.

Mean Gene, who had been examining the kitchen, came in. "Find anything?" he asked.

Penny was looking at the bottle in her hand, her face a study of mixed emotions. "More, I think, than I wanted to," she said grimly. She had recognized the distinctive scent—it was the same one she had remarked on Jules Lefau.

CHAPTER 12

"Er, Miss Gardiner, I wonder if I could have a private word with you. I'm afraid I have not been completely open with you and would like to give you an explanation." Toby was intimidated by the accusing vivid blue eyes that stared at him over the screaming murder headlines of a New Orleans daily.

"I have a coffee break in fifteen minutes," she said stiffly. "I could talk with you then."

"We'll meet you in the Howard Johnson coffee shop," he said with relief, and he and John Everett, looking remarkably like an upper-crust version of Mutt and Jeff, made their way across the road to the restaurant. There they were duly joined by the neat figure of Mini Gardiner, still very much on her dignity.

Toby introduced John and got down to cases. "Mr. Everett and Mr. Lefau had both been threatened," he stated. "Since it was a private, personal matter, Dr. Spring and I came to look into it for them in the hopes of heading off trouble. As you can see by this morning's papers, we have failed in our attempt, but at least now we can come into the open with our investigation. You have been a tremendous help to me, and I hope when you understand the circumstances you will continue to afford me your extremely valuable knowledge and assistance."

Mimi Gardiner thawed visibly and listened with fascination as he outlined the bare details of the case. When he finished, she leaned forward and whispered confidentially, "Of course I will help you in any way I can, Sir Tobias, but would you answer one question for me? It says nothing in the paper about the murder weapon. It wasn't by any chance an Arab dagger?''

This was so unexpected that the two men gaped at her in astonishment. ''Why, no,'' Toby said when he had got his breath back, ''but why, if I may ask, should you think such an extraordinary thing?''

Her color came up and the fair brow furrowed, making her look prettier than ever and eliciting a slight sigh from John. ''It has been worrying me ever since I learned Mrs. Lefau had been murdered. I don't want to tell this myself—I might get some of the details wrong—but could you possibly talk to my roommate? She works at the Historical Commission over on Royal.'' Her color deepened. ''You see, I was so excited about working for you that I told her about it, and, well, she told me something I think you should hear.''

Toby curbed his impatience. ''Certainly. When?''

Mimi glanced at the watch on her slim wrist. ''I have to get back now, but in about an hour's time I can make some excuse to go over to the commission. If you could keep an eye on me and follow me out, I'll take you over.''

Once back in the library, Toby was too much on the jump to concentrate on what he was doing, and he was further aggravated by the fact that John had settled down to use the microfilm machines as expertly as if he had been doing nothing else all his life. With relief Toby saw Mimi slip out from behind the desk; hastily collecting the absorbed John, he went out after her, braving the suspicious stares of the hard-faced blonde behind the desk.

''Shouldn't we get a cab?'' asked John Everett, who was not keen on walking.

''It's only a short distance!'' Mimi said with the enthusiasm of hearty youth, and she set them a brisk pace as they crossed the wide expanse of Canal Street and plunged into the crowds of the French Quarter.

John was puffing by the time they reached the elegant facade of the Gallier House, which housed the Historical Commission. They paid their way in and stood looking at the ground-floor exhibit while Mimi went off to find her friend. In due course she returned with a slim blonde, as pretty in a fair, fragile way as Mimi was in hers, who elicited another faint sigh from John, the impressionable.

"This is my roommate, Jean Rivers," Mimi said. "Perhaps it would be better for us if she seemed to be guiding you around as we talk."

"Why don't we take you both out to lunch?" John promptly suggested. "It's just about time, and we'd regard it as a privilege."

It was Toby's turn to sigh, but his was of exasperation, as the girls briefly consulted and decided this was a great idea. They repaired down the street to the splendors of Brennan's, and it was not until the ritual of cocktails and ordering had been gone through that the impatient Toby could get anyone's mind back to business.

"So, Miss Rivers," he said, glaring icily at John, who was having a great time, "Miss Gardiner tells me you have some information about Mrs. Lefau that may have some bearing on her murder—something about *Arabs*?"

The girl was taken aback. "I wouldn't say that. I mean, it may not have any bearing at all. Well . . . " she paused a little helplessly. "I think first I'll have to explain a bit about the Historical Commission before any of this makes sense.

"One of its purposes is to try and safeguard what's left of the old French Quarter. It has been a real uphill battle, with little in the way of resources and up against all manner of vested interests. It has only been in the last twenty years that we've been able to make the people of New Orleans aware of the fact that if they don't safeguard the Quarter, one of New Orleans's main attractions to the rest of the world will be lost forever. Our task has been complicated by the fact that after the War between the States the Quarter had become very run down, and some things just couldn't be saved in spite of all our efforts. The whole of old Rampart, for instance, has gone, and the old St. Louis Hotel could not be saved; but in recent years we have fought off other threats, such as the big highway they were planning to run along the waterfront, which would have just ruined Jackson Square."

Toby squirmed impatiently in his seat, and her tone sharpened. "All this may seem beside the point, but it isn't. In the past few years we have had to face a new threat—Arab oil. The Arabs, with their oil wealth, as you probably know, have been buying up land all over the United States." John Everett nodded gloomy agreement. "They have been active here and have been helped by the fact that many New Orleans families have oil and mercantile interests, so are willing to deal with them.

"Now, for some time a combine headed by Arabs has been after land at the edge of the Quarter. To be specific, a large block of land running from the waterfront through North Front, North Peters, and Decatur up to Chartres, and between Canal Street and St. Louis. Their aim is to build a modern skyscraper complex similar to the one around the International Trade Mart—a project that would just about finish the French Quarter. They have already acquired most of the land, but there is *one* parcel, a fairly large one that runs between Decatur and Chartres, that is—or I should say *was*—owned by a Lefau who had always been steadfast in her championship of the commission and the upkeep of the Quarter. It was Duchamps land and was part of Eleanor's dowry when she married Jules Lefau." Jean paused expectantly, but Toby said nothing. "Eleanor Lefau had always been one of our strongest supporters and champions," she repeated. "So long as she *lived,* they would never have got that land. But not all the Lefaus are so minded; in fact, quite the opposite." Again she paused and looked at Toby.

"Are you implying that now that she is dead, the land will belong to Jules Lefau and that he is in cahoots with the Arabs?" Toby asked.

Jean looked faintly shocked. "Oh, no, not Jules—*Benedict!* You may wonder how I know all this, but in a humble way I have been involved in all the action on this, and it has become very cloak-and-daggerish. We've been collecting evidence that the Arabs have been using intimidation to get hold of some of the land they've acquired so far. Most of it has been financial pressure of one kind or another, but we did have one case—a small shopkeeper on Decatur who was visited by a band of thugs in order to hurry up the sale. Benedict Lefau is in charge of the Lefau real estate holdings; his father concerns himself with their industrial and banking interests. But we did get hold of a couple memos from Benedict to one of these Arabs indicating that he was pretty deeply involved."

"It seems so incredible that anyone who is heir to so much

would be interested in such financial skulduggery," Toby reflected.

"For some people there is no such thing as *too* much money," Jean Rivers returned grimly.

Celeste's words echoed in Toby's mind: *"No sense of family. . . . The money syndrome is very evident in Benedict. . . ."* "Well, it certainly is a very interesting bit of information, for which I thank you, Miss Rivers," he said. "But I'm not sure how significant it is. As a motive for murder, it would seem to be an extreme long shot, based on the supposition that Eleanor Lefau died intestate, whereupon her holdings would devolve upon *Jules* Lefau and therefore pass ultimately to Benedict, but we have no idea if this supposition is even correct. For all we know, Eleanor Lefau may have willed her properties to someone who thought exactly as she did."

"Practically anyone would be easier to deal with than Eleanor Lefau," the fair girl said flatly. "As I said, she was fanatical on the subject, as her brother is, too."

"So François Duchamps is involved in your battles, too?"

"Very much so. It was a sore point with him that he did not hold any of the threatened property, which would have meant he could have entered directly into the fight."

"Does he know about Benedict's involvement with the Arabs?"

"Yes."

"Umm, I see." Toby was deep in thought. He had been intrigued by François's enigmatic remarks, which had brought such a violent reaction from Celeste. "Well, it gives us yet another line to pursue. Miss Gardiner!" he barked, causing the dark girl, who had been working her way contentedly through a serving of crepes Neptune, to jump. "I would be infinitely obliged if you would try and discover for me any links between the Duchamps and *Celeste* Lefau, and particularly any 'dirty dealings' any other Lefau might have inflicted on her."

"Present or past?"

"Probably past—something in the nature of a prohibited romance or marriage. I find it definitely strange that a sympathetic lady of considerable physical attraction and with her riches should have remained unmarried."

"Right on," Mimi said with a conspiratorial grin at John Everett, who positively preened.

The rest of the luncheon passed with Toby eliciting further details of the Duchamps involvement in the battle with the Arabs but without anything of further significance emerging. "How does Jules Lefau stand on the battle to save the Quarter, Miss Rivers?" he asked.

"He's never been directly involved, although he has always been generous with money, probably due to Mrs. Lefau's prompting. She did try to get the daughter involved for a while—Juliette even did some voluntary work at the Historical Commission—but it didn't work out. She wasn't very interested and was too involved with some boy who was always hanging around. I believe her mother found out about it, and after that there was no more Juliette."

"How did she strike you?"

"Oh, spoiled and a bit on the flaky side. A terrible temper. I remember one time her mother vetoed a party she wanted to go to, and Juliette carried on like a fishwife. But then, I don't have too much time for poor little rich girls." Jean Rivers compressed her pretty mouth into a thin line of disapproval.

"Was Mrs. Benedict Lefau ever involved in any of this?"

She shook her head. "I've never laid eyes on her. I don't think she and her mother-in-law got on too well, because whenever we had a drive on for volunteers, Mrs. Lefau never so much as mentioned Grace as a possibility."

"Have you managed to get anything else on her?" Toby asked Mimi.

"Only where she and Benedict went for their honeymoon—on a Caribbean cruise."

"To Haiti, by any chance?"

"I don't know, but I could probably find out. There is very little mention of Grace anywhere. I don't think she's very active—a nonjoiner, it seems."

John insisted on paying for the lunch, so Toby left him, to his delight, to escort Mimi back to the library, while he loped off to police headquarters for an update with Beauregard.

Toby found him in no happy frame of mind. "The city fathers are having conniption fits," the captain growled. "Despite François Duchamps's trumpetings, they insist on kid gloves all the way on Lefau. It's going to be damn difficult to break his story. The caretaker at Royal Street confirms the fact that Lefau dismissed him sometime before five A.M., and he went back to his own quarters, which are below the *garçonnière*. He didn't hear or see anything after that. But Lefau *does* keep a car there—a sports runabout. It would have been no problem for him to run out to the plantation, murder his wife, and get back again with no one being any the wiser. He got very stuffy with us when we asked him what the 'important' papers he had been working so hard on were, said it was none of our damn business. One thing for sure, he's certainly uptight, but, then again, that's understandable with all this happening so close to Carnival.''

"That's been canceled, I suppose," Toby observed.

Beauregard looked at him in astonishment. "You can't cancel *Comus!* Not at this stage. It would be like scrubbing half of Mardi Gras!''

"Yes, but surely he isn't going to participate—not with his wife murdered like that," Toby said in outrage.

"So far as I know, he is. I tell you, it is much too late for changes, particularly with all the costumes made and fitted.''

"But what about the queen?" Toby spluttered.

"Ah, that's a good question. I've no idea. I imagine that's one of the Lefaus will have to fight out among themselves. Maybe Juliette or Grace, I should think. You'll probably find out sooner than I.''

"We didn't go back to the plantation. Didn't Dr. Spring tell you?''

"No, haven't seen her. She dropped the keys back and left a message that she didn't come up with anything. She seems determined to prove the butler did it.'' Beauregard gave a grim chuckle. "We're doing some more checking on him, but I don't think there is much in it myself, just another red herring.''

"Well, I may have another for you.'' Toby told him about Benedict. It did nothing to cheer Beauregard.

"Yet another motive,'' he sighed, "and another long-shot lead to follow up. At this rate, the only one in the house without some motive to kill seems to be Celeste.'' They parted in mutual gloom.

Toby felt disinclined to return to the library or, in fact, to do anything more that day; so he returned to the hotel for a brief commune with his brandy flask and, he hoped, a lengthier one with Penny. There was no sign of her, but there were three separate and urgent messages for him to call François Duchamps. He fortified himself with a couple of drinks before returning the call.

"I've been trying to contact you all day." François Duchamps's voice was haughty and aggrieved. "I very much want to have a confidential talk with you, Sir Tobias. If I send a car for you, would you come to my office?"

"Oh, all right," Toby agreed cautiously. "May I ask what about?"

"I'd rather not say over the phone." Duchamps was abrupt. "My driver will pick you up in about twenty minutes."

The Duchamps building was yet another modern skyscraper in the business section, almost equal in magnitude to the Lefau building, and François Duchamps's office was a palatial lounge, complete with couches, tables, bar, and fireplace.

With Toby firmly in his grasp at last, François seemed singularly reluctant to come to the point. He plied Toby with drinks, offered him cigars, expatiated on the building and the booming economy of New Orleans, and would probably have gone on in this vein indefinitely if Toby had not firmly pointed out that if he wanted a confidential chat, he had better get on with it, because he, Toby, had other fish to fry. This seemed to disconcert his handsome host, who frowned, dithered, and finally said, "Well, Sir Tobias, I confess I have been making inquiries about you and your colleague, and you seem to have quite a remarkable record of success. I cannot believe your presence as guests at the Lefau plantation was just a fortuitous one. May I ask if Jules called you in and why he did so?"

Toby could see no harm in telling him that much. "The idea was Mr. John Everett's, the Boston publisher who is putting out Mr. Lefau's book and who is a personal friend of Dr. Spring's. There had been threats to the book and to himself, and we came in the hopes of averting further trouble. In this, so far, we have failed rather miserably."

"I see." Duchamps appeared to be pondering deeply. "In which case, since you are no longer guests of Jules's, I wonder if you would consider a proposition from me? I would be very grateful if you would undertake the investigation of my sister's death, and I would be prepared to offer you carte blanche as far as expenses or fees are concerned.''

Toby was in a quandary. He had no idea what their position was vis-à-vis the Lefau household anymore, nor did he have the faintest idea what Penny was up to; so he temporized. ''We are doing that anyway, Mr. Duchamps, since your sister's death seems to be tied in with everything else that has happened. And I am afraid I could not possibly give you an answer until I have consulted with Dr. Spring and Mr. Everett, in whose welfare we are most deeply concerned. However''— he paused heavily and, he hoped, dramatically— ''you could help in this process by giving us information that would be most difficult to obtain elsewhere and which might help clarify the motive behind all this seemingly insane series of events.''

''What sort of information?'' François said dubiously.

''I gather from reading Jules Lefau's book that there has been a long-standing rivalry between your two families, and indeed, of recent years, a certain amount of enmity. I was present when you made a definite accusation against Jules Lefau. What was the basis of that accusation? And you made a further enigmatic statement to Celeste Lefau. What was that about?''

François's handsome brows drew down into a formidable frown. ''That is a very long story, Sir Tobias, which I am quite agreable to reveal to you; but, to put it in a nutshell, Jules's father caused the tragic death of my uncle Gaston Duchamps. He and no other.''

''Er, it was my understanding that Gaston took his own life,'' Toby put in hesitantly.

''That is what is *said*''—François glowered—''but I am beginning to doubt even that. Even so, if he did take his own life, he was driven to it by Jules Senior.''

''But why?'' Toby persisted.

''Because Père Jules was a cruel, vindictive man; because he forbade the marriage between Gaston and Celeste—who were madly in love with one another—and for no reason, no reason at all!''

CHAPTER 13

Mean Gene looked in concern at Penny's worried little monkeylike face. "What you need is to get away from this for a bit," he stated firmly. "Tell you what. Me and the Knights are playing a gig in a club in the old Perdido section of town tonight. Why don't you come along and just listen to some good jazz and meet some of the real old-timers from the jazz world? We plays there to cheer 'em up at Carnival time. It's a bit like the old folks' home, but some of those cats are *real* characters."

Penny came out of her guilty reverie. She knew she had probably done an unforgivable thing in not telling Beauregard about her find at Arlette Gray's, but she could not bring herself to point the finger at Jules Lefau. She had tried to find comfort in the thought that there had to be dozens of rich men in the city who also used that brand of cologne and who could equally well have been Arlette's lovers; but with everything else considered, she realized it was not too likely. Was she letting the fact that she liked Jules Lefau as a man blind her? Toby had had his doubts from the outset, and Penny had the deepest respect for the way his mind worked. What if he had been right and she wrong all along? The way things were working out, all she had to put up against the suspicions that were tipping in Jules's direction was her own gut feeling that he was not involved. If only she could talk to him first. . . .

"Oh, I don't think so, Mean Gene," she said apologetically. "I'm not much in the mood."

"Just want Ah was sayin'. It'll cheer you up! Besides, you might get some information," he tempted. "Those old cats played at every party, every Carnival. They might know all these people you been tellin' me about.''

She brightened. ''Now, that's a thought! But it was all so long ago. Would any of them be old enough for that?''

''You betcha. Some of them are in their eighties, a few in their nineties, and they got their marbles still.''

''It won't get you into any kind of trouble, will it?''

''No way! Me and the Knights'll look after you, don't you worry. You on?''

''I'm on.''

They collected the instruments and the Knights and set off for Jerusalem Hall, which turned out to be a decrepit nineteenth-century building nestled in among a host of new building projects. ''The old-timers are sure goin' to miss this,'' Gene told her. ''It's scheduled for demolition this year, but it certainly had its great moments. Jelly Roll Morton used to play here reg'lar.''

The interior was as moth-eaten as the exterior, but the old black faces on the crowd seated on the plain wooden chairs around scarred wooden tables were cheerful, and the charged atmosphere redolent with the fumes of cheap cigars and beer.

The Knights set up their instruments on a battered platform in the middle of the hall, and Mean Gene indicated a table adjacent to it and off to the side. ''You set yourself right there, and Ah'll see what Ah can rustle up for you.'' This he did by waving his arms, raising his voice, and bellowing, for the hall did not run to such newfangled luxuries as a microphone. ''Folks,'' he roared, ''Ah'd like you to meet a friend of mine all the way from northern parts, a mighty fine lady who's interested in our Mardi Gras. Now, she's here on mighty important business and would like to hear from any old-timers that played in the Carnival of fifty years back.'' He grinned hugely. ''That'll cut out all you youngsters of sixty, but before you all get those chins waggin', the Knights'll play our first set. Tonight is our tribute to Thelonious Monk, that real cool cat of the fifties.'' The Knights plunged into a spirited version of ''Bright Mississippi.''

Penny looked around her with interest. Some members of the audience were watching her with equal interest, but the majority had their attention firmly fixed on the dais, blissful expressions on their faces. A huge schooner of beer was plopped before her, and a young black with a white apron tied around his middle whispered, "From Mean Gene." "Bright Mississippi" ended, and the tempo stepped up for "Five-Spot Blues," slowed again for the complicated "Monk's Dream," and wound up with an existential version of "Body and Soul." The audience loved it, and the hall rocked as Mean Gene left the platform and joined Penny at the table. He wiped sweat from his forehead with a meaty forearm and took a huge swallow of beer. "Five-minute break. Should see some action now."

"I'm enjoying the music so much that I don't care if no one shows up," Penny assured him, and she meant it.

"If you like your jazz good and hot, this city is *the* place to be," he said with the assurance of one who knows his own worth.

An elderly figure shuffled toward the table and looked expectantly at Mean Gene with an alert but rheumy eye.

"Why, it's Sweet Daddy Coglan," Mean Gene exclaimed. "You're in luck! Come and sit down, Sweet Daddy, and meet Dr. Spring."

The old man lowered himself carefully into a chair and nodded his curly white head at her. "What for you want to know, lady?" he said in a husky voice. "Ah played in all the Carnivals from 1915 on. Started mah playin' over in Storyville in 1910; so Ah goes back a long ways."

"Then, you're just the man for me," Penny said. "But first, how about something to drink?"

"Beer'd do fine," he croaked.

She looked inquiringly at Mean Gene. "They serve boilermakers here?" He nodded and left the two alone together. "Then, how about a boilermaker for you, Sweet Daddy?" Penny suggested.

The rheumy eyes brightened. "Why, that'd be a real treat," the old man wheezed. And when the shot glass of whiskey arrived with the schooner of beer, he took a reverent sip of it.

Penny looked at the neat but shabby suit and the carefully darned knitted waistcoat and felt a little catch in her throat. *Damn!* she thought. *This is no time to get on my soapbox; this is business.* She cleared her throat of its constriction and said, "What I'm looking for, Sweet Daddy, is someone who played at the Comus Ball of fifty years ago and also someone who can tell me anything about two Creole girls who were flappers back then—their names were Arlette Duchamps and Pernell Lefau.''

His face fell. ''Ah didn't play at Comus that year; Ah played at the Zulu Ball—but what were those names again, lady?''

Penny repeated them and the old face turned inward and peered backward into time. Finally he brightened. ''Sure, Ah knows who you mean—the de Lesseps girls!''

''That's right,'' Penny said eagerly. ''You remember them?''

''Do Ah remember them!'' Sweet Daddy gave out a wheezy chuckle. ''Who could ever forget them! They set this ol' city on its ear! There was nothin' those two madcaps wouldn't do or try. Why, ah've seen them doin' the Charleston and the Bourbon Street Rag on top of these very tables many a time. A fair scandal they were. But you couldn't help likin' them. Ol' Armand Duchamps—that'd be Arlette's husband—he was no match for 'em; but ol' Jules Lefau, now, he was a man gave as good as he got. Ah remember we was all surprised when Arlette up and married Duchamps. We all thought it'd be her and Jules, y'see. But Jules took his lumps, Ah guess, and married Pernell after a while. She was a bit quieter, but they was both hell raisers. Ol' Jules was a great one for the ladies. Ah used to play in a fancy bordello over on Canal, and he was there two or three times a week. Marriage sure didn't slow him down none. When Pernell died, he was tomcattin' around all over the city, and if he hadn't gone and broke his neck, he'd have been married again at the next Mardi Gras.''

This was news to Penny. ''How did he break his neck?''

''Fell down the stairs at the old Lefau place. Drunk, Ah guess. But he left a lot of sad ladies behind him.''

''How about their children?'' Penny asked. ''Know anything about them?''

Sweet Daddy looked puzzled. ''Ah remember they both had some—not that it slowed 'em down much! Can you put names to them?''

''There were two boys, Pierre and Gaston Duchamps—Arlette's sons—and then Celeste and Jules Lefau—Pernell's children.''

He thought hard as the ''Bolivar Blues'' throbbed in the

background. "Can't say I recollect anything about 'em, but Gaston—didn't something happen to him?"

"Yes, he committed suicide at the Comus Ball fifty years ago."

"Ah, yes, that was it. Bit of a gay blade—took after his ma, but without her stamina."

"What happened to Arlette?" Penny asked, seeing he had nothing further to add.

Mean Gene's quintet had gone into Monk's arrangement of "Just a Gigolo," and Sweet Daddy gave Penny a wry smile and jerked his head toward the platform. "She outlived 'em all, but she went thataway. It was all downhill after Pernell and Jules went, and Duchamps not too long after 'em. One man after another she had, each one younger than the last, till she died. Ah think it was in the late fifties sometime. Reg'lar old hag by then—lived in an apartment over on Dauphine; family didn't want no part of her." He sighed and looked reflectively at his empty whiskey glass.

"How about a refill?" Penny said quickly, and he nodded an enthusiastic agreement.

"You ever hear talk about a dancing lady at the Lefau place?" she asked when the drinks came.

He shrugged. "Well, Ah guess you could call Pernell a dancing lady—she sure was always at it—but not out there, no."

"How about either of them going to voodoo dances, or, for that matter, *anyone* going to voodoo dances?"

He looked disapproving. "Ah'm a jazzman. Ah never had any truck with that kind of bad stuff. Ain't nothin' like that goin' on nowadays." The unaccustomed whiskey had loosened the old man's tongue, and he rambled on about the old jazz groups and the 'old' New Orleans, which to him was more meaningful and real than the New Orleans of the Superdome and the towering skyscrapers. Penny listened in fascination even though it added nothing to her immediate interests. "Ah gave up playin' in the early sixties," he confided. "Wasn't that Ah lost mah lip; it was mah feet. Rheumatism somethin' cruel. Couldn't stand, and you can't blow good settin' down all the time."

Another set finished, and Mean Gene and several of the Knights joined them. It served to remind Sweet Daddy of his purpose. He got up painfully. "Ah thanks you for the drinks, and Ah'll see if Ah can find someone who played that Comus for you. It's been nice talkin' to you."

"The pleasure was all mine," Penny assured him, a little light-headed herself from all the smoke and from the boiler-makers she had downed. She listened muzzily to the backchat of the Knights as, out of the corner of her eye, she followed the slow, painful peregrinations of Sweet Daddy from table to table. She saw him confer at length with a bald-headed man of equal antiquity to himself, and finally both started to shuffle back to her.

"Ah found him," Sweet Daddy announced with pride. "This here's Leroy—played the alto sax. He remembers that ball."

As the Knights returned to the stand, another round of boilermakers came, and Leroy gave Penny a loose-lipped, slightly vacant grin. "Seven o'clock to midnight—six dollars," he announced.

"Dat's when he played at the ball," Sweet Daddy interpreted. "And dat pay was good back then."

Penny had the sinking feeling that Leroy's marbles might have shifted a little, but she persevered. "Why don't you just tell me what you remember about the ball in your own way, Leroy?"

"Oh, OK." He sipped his drink and looked bemusedly at her, as if not knowing where to begin.

"Do you remember the king and queen?" she prompted.

"Oh, yes, de queen was dat de Lesseps girl." He grinned and winked knowingly at Sweet Daddy. "You knows the one. Mah! She was sure pretty that night, all in that shimmery gold. Musta been pushin' forty, but she looked like a kid. Her daughter was there—a princess—and they was as like as two peas. Every man dere was in love with her that night 'cept ol' Jules. They were plenty mad at each other. You could tell, 'cause they didn't even look at each other during all the ceremonial business; and when dey opened the ball and we was playin' Carnival song, 'If Ever I Cease to Love,' she was as rigid as a poker an' a-starin' over his shoulder like she was seein' a ghost."

"Do you remember anything about a young man who committed suicide that night—Gaston Duchamps?"

Leroy's face fell, and he shook his head. "All Ah know is, just around quittin' time, midnight, there was a powerful lot of screamin' goin' on somewheres. Ah didn't see her after that, but ol' Jules was there lookin' like a thundercloud. We heard tell after that someone was dead, but that's all." And that was all, for in spite of Sweet Daddy's prodding and Penny's prompting, it was as far as Leroy could go.

The concert ended in a hubbub of applause shortly after, to Penny's relief, for she was beginning to feel a little ill. The clear night air outside the hall hit her like a sledgehammer, and she was only dimly aware of Mean Gene beside her as he drove her back to the Bayou and guided her tottering steps into the hotel. Abandoning any idea of catching up on Toby's news, she fell into bed and was instantly asleep, her dreams a confused kaleidoscope of gold-clad figures that whirled around a playing fountain, pursued by a dark form rattling a voodoo *asson*, while in the background the frail figure of Sweet Daddy Coglan played a silver trumpet.

She awoke with pounding temples to the phone shrilling in her ear. With a groan she managed to get it off its hook and croaked, "Who is it?"

"It's Jules Lefau, Dr. Spring. I'm downstairs. I wonder if I might come up and see you. It's important."

"*Now?* I'm not even up yet," she said crossly.

"*Please!*" His voice was resonant with urgency.

"Oh, all right," she grumbled. "Give me fifteen minutes to get some clothes on."

She staggered around, swallowing Bufferin, ordering coffee, and soaking herself in the shower. Jules Lefau arrived at the same time as the coffee, and she waved him to the room's single stiff armchair while she quickly gulped two steaming cupfuls. Beginning to feel vaguely human again, she was aware that she must be cutting a pretty sorry figure. Pulling herself together, she looked at Jules and was shocked by the change in him. He was in a black suit of mourning, and his face, though without expression, seemed to have shrunk so that the delicate bonework of his skull was clearly delineated under the pale skin. About him hung an aura of almost unbearable tension. That and the look in his eyes so startled Penny that she helped herself to a third cup of coffee before she could bring herself to speak. "Well, Mr. Lefau, what can I do for you?"

"A lot, I hope." His voice was exhausted. "I have just come from burying my wife. Now that the funeral is over, I have come to ask—no, to beg—that you come back briefly to the plantation and then accompany us to the Royal Street house until the Comus Ball is over."

"You are going *on* with it!" she exploded.

He gave a helpless gesture. "I have no choice, absolutely none, at this juncture. It is a living nightmare but one that somehow I must live through. I need you and Sir Tobias, whom I have been unable to locate." This was news to Penny, but she kept quiet as he went on. "When this tragedy happened, I initially thought I could best serve the interests of my family by stonewalling, by leaving the police running around in circles trying to solve an unsolvable crime. I see now from the terrible effect this is having on my younger children that I was wrong. I am not a stupid man, and I know the police are suspicious of me and my 'alibi.' I was prepared to let that happen rather than face other possibilities, but now I realize that will not be enough. I shall have to be cleared—not so much for myself as for my children. Dr. Spring, I need you to do that."

"As things stand, the only way to clear you is to find the murderer," Penny said tartly, "and I think you know that that also might hit very close to home."

"I don't *know* anything"—his tone was unutterably weary—"but it is what I have been afraid of, and my fear has in all probability brought about this tragedy."

"Well, before I commit myself—and I should emphasize that I am speaking only for myself and not for Sir Tobias—I think we have a lot of clearing up to do. I think you know a whole lot more about all of this than you have told us, and unless you are quite frank with me, I'm afraid there is not much more I can do. I am wrestling with my own conscience at the moment over something I found in Arlette Gray's house that pointed to you, something the police overlooked, which so far I have not told them about. But I will have to unless you can show me some good reason not to. I should tell you that the police have already learned that Arlette Gray's bills had been paid for the last eight months by Lefau Enterprises.

So I must ask you bluntly, Mr. Lefau, was Arlette Gray your mistress, or were you paying her blackmail?''

Jules seemed to shrink a little more into himself, then sighed and said quietly, "All right. I may as well tell you. Yes. Arlette was my mistress. I was keeping her—there was no blackmail involved. We were extremely fond of each other; I would almost have been prepared to swear she was in love with me. When she was found dead under such incriminating circumstances for Mr. Everett, I thought that whoever had been threatening me had accomplished their double purpose—to hurt me and to hurt him—and that it would end there. That is why, after you arrived, I did not want the investigation to go any further, knowing that it could only bring more hurt."

"But surely it must be clear to you now that Arlette Gray was involved in setting John Everett up?"

"Yes, I suppose it is," Jules said haltingly, "but I don't begin to understand it. As I said, we were extremely fond of each other. There was never any question of her pressuring me for money; she could have had what she wanted, and she knew it."

"Let's leave that for the moment. I have to ask the jackpot question. Did you have any part in the murder of your wife?"

"Would you believe me if I said no?" His tone was grim.

Penny looked at him searchingly. "Yes, I think I would. Although I have made great mistakes about people in my time, in general I'm not bad at summing them up, and while I would give you full credit for being a devious man, I would also say you are a feeling one. I cannot believe you cruel, and this case has the touch of an extremely cruel, unfeeling hand. The horrible nature of both murders and the slaying of your dog is evidence of that. But did you have the least inkling that your wife was a target? Do you have any idea who might be behind both operations?"

"No to both." Jules was suddenly incisive. "Despite anything you might hear, Dr. Spring, I was extremely fond of my wife. We suited each other excellently; we understood and complemented each other. Perhaps to an outsider the Creole way of life seems odd, but it is a society that, in spite of all its drawbacks, has endured and has been successful. I think this booming city of ours is proof of that."

"A city of rather marked inequalities, however," Penny put in dryly.

He brushed that aside. "The fact is that the first time I married, I married for love; I was barely twenty-one. And while my first wife was a fine woman, she never really understood what life here was all about, and this led to dissatisfaction for both of us. After her death, I was mature enough to realize this, and I deliberately sought out a wife in my own sphere. Eleanor could not have been more perfect. We liked and respected each other, and she gave me two beautiful children."

"And she didn't mind your being unfaithful to her?" Penny interjected.

He gave a Gallic gesture. "It is the Creole way. It didn't matter so long as the niceties were observed."

"And the rivalry between your two families? Surely, by your own definition of what matters, *that* must have caused dissension between you?"

This time he was impatient. "All this rivalry business has been greatly exaggerated. François Duchamps tends to be a hysterical, dramatic fellow, and his statements should be looked at in that light. The Duchamps and the Lefaus have have always been engaged in a *primus inter pares* competition, but it has never really been enmity. True, my father was by all accounts a rather ruthless man and left an unhappy heritage behind him, but do you know I never even *heard* of all this business about Gaston and Celeste until after I married Eleanor? Celeste never has talked of it. But I think my father was entirely justified: Celeste was extremely young, only sixteen, and Gaston was evidently a very unstable character."

"What business?" Penny said blankly.

Jules looked at her in surprise. "Oh, I thought you knew. Celeste and Gaston Duchamps wanted to get married; my father forbade it, and Gaston blew his brains out."

"At the Comus Ball fifty years ago, where 'there was a powerful lot of screamin',' " she quoted softly. It was his turn to look blank. "So what happened after that?"

"After the ball? Dr. Spring, I was only six years old. I don't know."

"To *Celeste*."

"Oh! Well, she was very upset, I suppose. My mother

took her away to Europe. They were gone about two years.'' There was a wistful note in his voice. "Celeste stayed on over there, but my mother came back. She had started to sicken with the cancer that killed her. And then, when she was dying, Celeste returned.''

"And the circumstances of your father's death?''

Jules's face tightened. "I was away at school when it happened. My father was a man of violent passions. I think my mother must have been a restraining influence on him.'' This, in the light of what she had heard, Penny thought highly unlikely. "Too many women, too much drink. I believe he was drunk when he fell downstairs and broke his neck.''

"I heard he had been planning to remarry.''

Jules frowned. "There was never anything official.''

"Who was in the house when it happened?''

"Celeste, er, the woman he was going with—an Anglo— Armand and Arlette Duchamps, and their son Pierre and his wife—Eleanor's parents. What are you getting at, Dr. Spring?''

"Nothing,'' she said peaceably, although she was very intrigued by what she had just heard. "Just piling up information. I have no idea at this stage what is relevant and what is not. And after your father's death?''

"Well, then it was just Celeste and I until I got married. Celeste did not much care for my first wife; so she spent a good deal of time traveling after that. Europe had given her a taste for it, seemingly.'' He sounded faintly surprised.

It also surprised Penny, who had thought of Celeste as quietly dreaming her life away at the plantation. "Where did she travel?''

"Oh, all over. You name it, she's been there.''

"And lately?''

"No, not lately. She and Eleanor got along well, and after Juliette was born, Celeste seemed to lose interest in travel. She's very fond of my daughter, you know.'' His face softened.

"And what about this voodoo business?'' Penny shot at him.

He was markedly disconcerted. "Juliette had nothing to do with it; it was just a teen-age phase, that's all,'' he stuttered. "I put my foot down and had it out with Elviny, and that was the end of it.''

This was unexpected but revealing. "How far had Juliette gone?" Penny asked slyly.

"Nowhere, it was just childish dabbling. She *couldn't* be involved in this—this *horror*!" he exploded.

"And was Elviny's mother also in your service?" Penny was striking while the iron was hot.

Again Jules was dumfounded. "Why, no! Elviny came with Eleanor; her mother was a Duchamps servant."

"Really, now, that's very, very interesting." Penny murmured as a new pattern began to form in her mind.

Jules looked at his watch and gave a little groan of despair. "I simply have to go. Please, Dr. Spring, if I send the car, will you return to the house for dinner tonight?"

"I must talk with Sir Tobias first," she said firmly, "but I will call and leave a message. Mr. Lefau, I want to help you, but we must talk some more."

"All right, anything you say." He was edging toward the door. "But I beg you to say yes."

After the door had closed on him, Penny sat staring at it blankly, conscious again of the dull throbbing of her hangover. "Damn! Why didn't I ask him about Henri?" she muttered. "Oh, well, I'll do it tonight, after I've brainwashed Toby into going back." But where the hell *was* Toby?

CHAPTER 14

"You might call it a high-class attempt at shanghaiing," Toby said, sitting down very carefully so as not to jar a silver hair on his aching head. "François Duchamps is a man it is extremely hard to say no to or get away from. After he had wined me all afternoon and then wined me and dined me all evening, he insisted I stay the night at his place; and, to be honest, I was in no shape to do otherwise. A remarkably fine brandy he goes in for."

"Hmmph," Penny snorted, studying the hotel's luncheon menu with a fierce concentration; she was a strong believer in food as the solution for most evils and particularly for a hangover. "So did he succeed in his object? Are you transferring to the enemy camp?"

Toby waited in lugubrious silence as she gave her large order to the waiter and then added that a pot of coffee and some juice would be all he wanted. This out of the way, Penny looked at him with an accusing eye.

"I did not commit myself," he said with dignity.

"That surprises me, since you seem so dead set against Jules Lefau."

"I am *endeavoring* to keep an open mind. Besides," he added, "I find François Duchamps a bit much—a very flamboyant type. I'm not sure I believe half of what he says. Anyway, I think it's time to pool results." They pooled.

They were interrupted by the arrival of the bleary-eyed John Everett, who said peevishly, "Oh, there you are! I've been looking all over for you." He slumped into a chair but recoiled with a look of queasy horror at Penny's piled-up plate.

"You, too?" Penny said after a quick glance. "Welcome to the club. So what dissipations did you get into last night?"

"I took Jean and Mimi out for dinner, and then we went on to some of the Carnival dances," John said with a faint groan. "Such nice girls, but so energetic. I'm too old for this kind of thing."

"I should think so!" Penny was severe. "Besides, what would Millicent say?"

"There were two of them," he said feebly. "And they have been so helpful I thought it was the least I could do."

"Well, I wish you'd keep your mind on the business at hand. While you were out having a high old time, we were both *working*," Penny said, stretching the truth a little. "Now we are trying to decide whether it would best serve your interests to move back to the Lefaus' as Jules has asked us to do."

"I'm all for it—at least it's quiet there," John said with a stifled yawn. "This hotel is too damn noisy. There was a party going on in the room next to mine until six o'clock this morning. I don't know where people find the energy."

"Before we decide, I think we should get a clearer picture of what we are going to be aiming for," Toby rumbled. "In other words, we should state our objectives. It strikes me, Penny, that last night you and I spent a lot of time and effort acquiring the same information, albeit from different angles, and if we go on like that, we're not going to get anywhere."

"You're right, up to a point," she conceded, "but we have made progress. We now have a definite link between the first and second murder: Arlette was Jules's mistress, and Eleanor his wife. Unless you are prepared to grant he is a first-class nut and did it himself—and I don't think you are—we have someone here who *hates* him. I've got lots of angles I want to follow up. Jules can give no reason why Arlette apparently turned against him enough to be an accomplice in the framing of John. There has to be one, and I'm still betting pretty heavily on the voodoo connection and Henri." She carefully suppressed the fact that part of her plan had Haiti in mind, knowing this would not go down well with Toby. "Again on the voodoo angle, I feel there is a link between Eleanor Lefau—victim though she may be—and the voodoo. If we get back to the house, I'll be able to take another crack at Elviny

Brosse, who knows a lot more than she is telling. I don't think it was any accident that Juliette, on Jules's own admission, was fooling around with voodoo. These things are so often passed down in a family, and Elviny Brosse's mother was Eleanor's servant. And it may go further back than that, to the notorious Arlette Duchamps.''

"For my part, this information on Benedict and his possible reason for wanting his stepmother out of the way opens up a whole new range of possibilities,'' Toby said. "And I'm still not satisfied about his wife, either. She's so damned elusive; I've got to find out more. And what's more, my putative employer, François Duchamps, in all his ravings against the Lefaus didn't seem to realize he was giving me great cause for thought. Enmity, after all, is a two-way street, and if you are looking for someone who hates Lefau's guts, well, François certainly has to be considered. Apparently he was dead set against Eleanor's marriage; but his parents were still alive at the time, and *they* were quite happy about it.''

"Yes, the whole setup is so strange,'' Penny interjected. "I mean, with all the scandal that surrounded Gaston's death and all, who do we find in the house when the elder Jules falls to his death? None other than Gaston's parents and his brother. I'm beginning to see murder behind everything. What if Jules Senior was pushed?''

John had been sitting glassy-eyed, listening to this exchange, but he finally got a word in. "But why *now*? After all, what you've been talking about is far in the past. If anything was going to be done about it, why not long ago?''

"The book——'' Penny began tentatively.

"But there is nothing in the book that everyone who is concerned in this doesn't already know about!'' John cried. "It just doesn't make sense!''

Toby nodded somber agreement.

"Well, Henri and Arlette Gray are not part of that past,'' Penny said with determined single-mindedness, "and they fit in here somewhere. So I vote we go back to the inner circle. How about you two?''

The vote was unanimous.

When Henri arrived to collect them in the Mercedes, Penny firmly established herself in the front seat beside him. The food had revived her, and she was determined to get something out of him on the trip to the plantation. It was easier thought about than done. "I hear you are originally from Haiti," she started off. "I spent quite a bit of time there some years ago. What part are you from?"

He shot her a quick glance from beneath his hooded lids before answering, after a pregnant pause, "Port-au-Prince."

"Oh, I know that city very well. You have family still there?"

Another calculated interval. "No."

"Of course, I imagine it has changed a lot since I was there," Penny prattled on with unrelenting cheerfulness. "I believe there have been many improvements and that life is a lot easier than it was in Papa Doc's time. Have you been back recently?"

"No."

"I was thinking of making a trip down there shortly. If you have any friends you would like me to contact, I'd be glad to do so."

"No, there is no one."

Against such blank stonewalling she was getting a little desperate. "Mr. Letau was telling me you had an adventurous time getting out," she said, stretching the truth to suit her purposes. "Through the mountains to the Dominican Republic, wasn't it? I would be most interested to hear about it."

Henri launched into his longest speech. "If you do not mind, madame, I am not used to being talked to while I drive. I find it very difficult to concentrate. I am sure you understand."

Thoroughly put in her place, Penny lapsed into frustrated silence.

There was a dispirited gaggle of reporters and photographers at the gate; there were also two very large security guards on the inside. When Henri operated the little black box, they stepped forward menacingly as the reporters surged around the car, peering anxiously inside as flashbulbs popped. The car slid through to safety, and the guards retreated and reclosed the gates.

"Damn them to hell," Henri said, flinching away from the photographers. "They are like vultures waiting for their next victim." Penny felt it was the most revealing thing he had said.

It was Benedict who greeted them. Apart from the mourning band around the arm of his business suit, he showed no marks of the recent tragedy; indeed, he seemed remarkably cheerful. "Your rooms are as they were," he assured them. "My father asked me to tell you how thankful he is you have returned and how much he appreciates your sympathy and understanding."

"He's not here?" Penny said in disappointment. "I was anxious to talk to him."

"He'll be back later. In the meantime, if there is anything I can do, please tell me."

"I'd like to have a word with Elviny Brosse when it is convenient."

"I'm afraid she isn't here," he said easily. "She was considerably upset by my stepmother's death; so Celeste gave her a few days' leave. We have a substitute cook; would you like to talk to her?" His tone was almost mocking.

"No," Penny snapped. "When will Elviny be back, or is there any way I can get in touch with her?"

"Oh, she is bound to be back before the big day." He smiled apologetically. "But no, I'm afraid I have no idea where she is. You could ask Celeste."

But Celeste, it transpired, was out with Grace Lefau, and so, in total frustration, Penny retired to her room, took some more Bufferin and then a nap. John had already sought his room with the avowed intention of doing likewise. Toby, left to his own devices, repaired to the library, where he dutifully called Beauregard to report on his talk with François Duchamps.

Beauregard's reaction was much the same as John's had been. "I don't see what all this ancient history could possibly have to do with what's happened now," he grumbled. "Just more muddying of the waters, if you ask me. The thing you found out about Benedict is looking far more promising. I've been making some quiet inquiries, and it seems Benedict is out to carve a little kingdom of his own. Quite the high flyer. He has had several little things going on the side that I doubt his father knew about. Rumor has it that he lost heavily on one of the recent ones and borrowed from his Arab friends to make good. Shades of Billygate! But there still isn't a shred of evidence to connect him in any way with the other murder. I thought maybe Arlette was his mistress, but it turns out he' been keeping a little redhead in a posh condo over in the Garden District. But we're still working on that angle."

Feeling guilty, Toby did not comment. He had promised Penny not to reveal anything of what she had found until she gave him the all-clear. "I'll tell him myself," she had said, "as soon as I've got something on Henri; but tell him about Jules now and the police will be on him like a ton of bricks. We can't do that to him, Toby." Reluctantly he had agreed.

He had set the wheels in motion on Benedict, and he could not talk to the absent Grace Lefau; so he decided to go back to the quieter waters of research and settled himself comfortably with the Lefau history in an inglenook of the library. After a while his head nodded, the book falling limply into his lap, and Sir Tobias slept.

He was awakened from his nap by the library door shutting and Celeste's voice saying with breathless excitement, "I just had to have a few words with you in private, my dear, to urge you to go along with things as usual for the next few days, however badly you may feel. For me it is going to be a dream come true; please don't spoil it! Your father will decide tonight, I know it."

"Oh, Aunt Celeste, I *know* this means a lot to you"— Juliette's usually fresh voice was weary—"but to me it is just a nightmare! Surely you can see that. If only Poppa would call it all off."

"He cannot do that, you know he can't. Please, for my sake!"

"Oh, I'll go along with it, as I have with the rest"—the young voice was flat—"but are you sure about this queen business?"

"Who else is there? You are too young and certainly would not want that added burden now. Your time will come, my dear."

There was a derisive snort from the girl. "As if I *care!*"

"And Grace would be impossible—an Anglo, and with her background," her aunt went on serenely.

Toby had half risen in his seat, intending to reveal himself, but sank back again in total distress. To reveal himself now, he felt, would be too embarrassing to all parties, especially him. He sat paralyzed as the voices continued.

"But what about the gowns? Mother's dress will never fit you, and there isn't time for alterations."

"I can wear my mama's. I have always cherished it, and we were the same size." Celeste's silvery laugh tinkled with an almost girlish gaiety. "Just think, I won't even have to wear the life mask!"

"How can you laugh in this place?" Juliette said sullenly.

"Oh, my dear, forgive me! But you cannot imagine what this means to me. Once before my dream almost came true, only to be shattered, and now at last it will be so. I know your father feels as you do, but we must *help* him, Juliette. He has such a heavy burden to bear, and you and I, who truly care, must do what we can to ease it. I only wish he had not invited those people back. I can't think why he felt obligated to do so. Sir Tobias is all right—at least he is a gentleman—but Mr. Everett is so *northern*. And that impossible little busybody of a woman! A really terrible person, hobnobbing with the servants and getting them all upset. I certainly hope your father does not intend inviting her to any of the Comus festivities. She'll be so—so—out of place!"

Toby could hear the girl pacing restlessly and cowered back in his chair. "I've got to go, Aunt Celeste. I promised to pick up Vincent." There was a short silence, then, "Before Elviny left, did she say anything to you?"

"About what?"

"You know."

"What was there to say?"

"I still think it was beastly about Poppa's dog," the young voice cried, and there was the noise of a door slamming.

There was a deep sigh from Celeste and then the sound of the door quietly opening and shutting. "Phew!" Toby let out an explosive sigh of relief and eased his cramped limbs. Straight as a homing pigeon he went to Penny's room to inform her of this revealing exchange, only to be thwarted. The room was empty, the only witness to her presence being the rumpled state of the bed. It reminded him queasily of another, similar empty room, and he strode over to the window to settle himself down. Gazing along the avenue between the magnolias toward the fountain, he saw with relief the object of his search. Penny's dumpy little figure was seated on the edge of the fountain, her head bent, in deep conversation with the black-clad figure of Jules Lefau. An unusual movement in the bushes behind them caught Toby's eye, and he tensed. "Hmm," he murmured, "they seem to have the company of an interested eavesdropper. I hope to God Penny isn't opening her big mouth too wide."

"We've only just begun to clear the ground," Penny was saying firmly, "and I would appreciate some more frank answers. Sir Tobias has raised a very valid point. It is quite obvious to both of us that, before you invited us here, you had done some in-depth research—I mean, you had learned things about us that very few people know. He wondered why, and so do I."

"When Mr. Everett suggested you as a possible solution to our problems, it was only natural that I should make some inquiries before inviting you," Jules Lefau said placatingly, "and I tend to be a rather thorough person."

"To the extent of finding out Yon-Figeac is Toby's favorite claret and that I have a weakness for *marrons glacés*?" she said in disbelief. "I would say *thorough* is hardly the word, Mr. Lefau!"

He smiled faintly at her. "It is really very simple. Sir Tobias is a member of the Wine-tasters Club; one telephone call to them was all it needed. And as to your weakness, I simply called your son, who, I found out, is interning at George Washington Hospital in Washington, and asked him. As I said, I tend to be thorough. And I wish you would call me Jules. I feel we have got way past the formal stage."

Penny was not to be disarmed. "And was part of this thoroughness due to the fact that you suspected those threats were originating from your own household and that, in the event of our discovering this, you wanted to know if you could depend on us to keep our mouths shut and let you deal with it?"

His smiled faded, and his face became masklike. "Something like that."

"I suppose you realize that that is no longer possible," she said quietly.

"I suppose so." His voice was bleak.

"Did you suspect that your own wife may have been behind the threats?"

"As I have said, I did not *know* anything; but, yes, it did occur to me. Eleanor was dead set against the book and was a woman who did not like to be thwarted. I was quite wrong, of course, as the murder has proved."

"Not necessarily," Penny said, and Jules looked at her in surprise. "Jules, who hired Henri?"

His surprise turned to astonishment. "Why, I don't know—either Celeste or Eleanor. You'd have to ask Celeste. I remember it was just after our old majordomo, who had been in the family since my father's time, had passed away. But what has that got to do with anything?"

"I am looking for a link, something that will explain why Arlette Gray could have been got at to the extent of turning against you for no apparent reason. I think Henri may be the key. He was from Haiti, as she was. He entered the country at about the same time she did. He may have had some lever with her that succeeded in making her an accomplice and resulted in her death."

"But what has this got to do with Eleanor?" Jules cried.

"Maybe nothing or maybe everything. The fact is that someone here was—is—deeply into voodoo. One person we know about is Elviny Brosse, a descendant of a voodoo queen and a servant of your wife's as was her mother before her. Suppose, just for the sake of argument, your wife had dabbled in voodoo all along, that she became deeply interested, and that when Henri appeared on the scene from its point of origin, she went deeper into it: that she became a white *mambo* and was starting to indoctrinate her daughter in the common hereditary way." Jules looked at her with shocked eyes. "Suppose, also, that she found out about your liaison with Arlette Gray—and, with all due deference to the Creole way of life, I can only point out that most wives in *any* culture are not very enthusiastic about their husbands' mistresses. Then comes the business of the book, angering her still more, and she begins this steadily building charade, which culminates in the death of Arlette Gray. Maybe this was not intended. Maybe then something went wrong and Eleanor got frightened, and then *she* had to be removed."

"By Henri?" Jules was aghast.

"Why not? He strikes me as a man perfectly capable of it, and also as a man with a lot to hide. This is what I want to find out, and I'm going to need some help. Jules, would you stake me and a companion to a trip to Haiti? I think I could find out what I need in forty-eight hours once I'm there, but I've got to get there.''

"Yes, of course, if you and Sir Tobias think it will help——" he began.

"Oh, no, not Toby—he'd be useless. No, the companion I have in mind is black. He will have to front for me while I'm in Haiti," Penny said hastily, suppressing the fact that she was *persona non grata* there. "If you could arrange for our tickets and expenses, I could leave tomorrow and be back before Tuesday.''

"I can do better than that. We have a company plane; my pilot could fly you down. Where do you want to go—Port-au-Prince?"

"For starters," Penny agreed. "So is that all right? Will you lay it on for tomorrow?" As he nodded, she jumped up. "Then, I must go and contact Mean Gene at once; there's a lot to be done." And she hurried off toward the house, leaving Jules looking after her in bewilderment.

Toby watched Jules slowly get up and follow Penny down the avenue, but, strain as he might, he could see no further movement from the bushes. He turned away from the window and was on his way out when the door opened and there came a little shriek from the figure on the threshold.

"Oh, my, Sir Tobias! How you startled me!" Celeste panted, a slim hand fluttering to her mouth. "I was looking for Dr. Spring."

"So was I," he said, "but she isn't here. Was it about Henri, by any chance?"

"Henri?" She looked at him with dazed eyes.

"I know Dr. Spring was anxious to talk to you about him. She had some questions—who hired him, for instance.''

"My sister-in-law; why?"

"Did she help him escape from Haiti? I gather he was a political refugee of some kind.''

"I've really no idea. You would have to ask my brother, Sir Tobias. Henri has always been excellent in his job and is evidently a man of some education. We have never had occasion to discuss his personal life; it was none of our business," she said tartly. "And, please, this household is already in such an upset, I beg you not to upset him, too!"

Toby ignored her. "Ah, that reminds me!" he boomed on. "Will you let me have Elviny Brosse's address? Benedict said you could tell us how to contact her."

"*Benedict* did?" She sounded outraged. "Oh, really, this is too much! Elviny went off without a word! I've no idea where she is, and I am just furious about it."

CHAPTER 15

Dinner was a far cry from the formal splendor of their first dinner at the Lefau plantation. Again they were grouped around the round table in the breakfast room, but, to Toby's mystification, there was no sign of Penny—who never willingly missed a meal—or of Celeste. Their host, who joined them late looking more haggard then ever, barely picked at the food that was put before him; the two younger children were silent, Vincent red-eyed. Only Grace and Benedict seemed at all normal; in contradistinction to the rest, they were animated and cheerful.

"Did Dr. Spring say where she was going?" Toby inquired of his host.

"Into town on business." Jules did not elaborate.

Toby and John exchanged puzzled glances. Toby indicated the empty chair between him and John. "Will Miss Lefau not be joining us?"

A look passed between Jules and Benedict before the former replied, "My sister is rather upset; she won't be dining with us tonight."

Now what? Toby thought, for when he had parted from Celeste earlier, it had struck him that she was keyed up with some intense inner excitement.

There was a short silence. "The dress fits like a glove," Grace Lefau said to her father-in-law. "You'd think it had been made for me."

Juliette's head came up with a jerk. "What dress?"

"Your grandmother's," Grace said smugly. "Imagine, just my size!"

153

Juliette looked at her father, wide-eyed. "*She's* going to be queen?" she blurted out. "But what about Aunt Celeste?"

"Juliette, please!" Jules said, his voice hoarse with strain. "You must know that the queen has to be the eldest *married* lady in a reigning Comus family. It is only in the most extraordinary circumstances that an unmarried woman fills the role. Your aunt knows this as well as I do. I just can't think what's got into her."

"But it means so *much* to her!" Juliette cried. "It's ridiculous. Why can't you change the damn silly rules for once? Grace doesn't give a shit for all this—she cares even less than I do—and you know it!"

"Juliette, be quiet!" her father rasped.

"No, I *won't* be quiet," she flared. "I think it's damn rotten of you—of all of you. God, how I hate this place!" Flinging down her napkin, she rushed out of the room, bursting into sobs as she went.

Toby was rigid with embarrassment and buried his nose in his wineglass, while John Everett concentrated with fierce attention on his plate. "I apologize for my daughter," Jules said stiffly. "She is under a great strain, as I'm sure you can appreciate." They murmured incoherent understanding. "Vincent," he went on, "if you have finished, you may be excused." The boy jumped up and rushed after his sister. Then his father slumped back in his chair and said, "Gentlemen, I wonder if we could talk in my study after dinner? One thing I have decided is to delay the release of this wretched book." He rubbed his eyes wearily. "I simply cannot take the risk of anything else happening." Toby felt this was shutting the stable door after the horse was gone but forbore to say so and murmured agreement.

The episode with Juliette had thrown Grace back into one of her customary sulks, and the meal ended with a discussion between Benedict and his father about the mechanics of their move to the Royal Street house on the morrow. "Celeste will be staying on out here," Jules said tightly. "I expect she will join us for Mardi Gras. She should have got over her upset and seen reason by then. No news of Elviny, I suppose?" Benedict shook his head. "Well, we'll just have to make do with the substitute cook, and you'll be bringing in your maid, of course. The caretaker's wife will be helping out at Royal

Street, and if you would arrange for three of the dailies here to assume the duties there, that should be enough, with Henri to keep an eye on them. I've detailed two of the office drivers to relieve him of most of his driving duties for the next week.''

"I'll take care of it, Dad; you can depend on me,'' Benedict said.

"I hope so.'' His father looked at him, and Toby was interested to see the blond giant flush.

"If you'll excuse us?'' Benedict said abruptly, and he and the petulant Grace departed, leaving Jules gazing morosely at his guests.

"We may as well take our coffee and brandy in the library,'' he said and led the way.

Toby was having a private little tussle with himself. He felt deeply sympathetic toward the absent Celeste and approved of Juliette's spirited defense of her aunt. What if he were to tell Jules of Grace Lefau's antecedents? Would that alter things, or would it merely give the already overburdened man another secret cross to bear? Reluctantly Toby came to the conclusion that it would only serve to aggravate the tense family situation and alienate Benedict, who currently appeared to be the only person his father could rely on. He decided to say nothing.

When they were settled over their brandy and cigars, Jules said to John, "I really do apologize, Mr. Everett, for this late change of mind. I realize if I hadn't dragged you down to make the arrangements for the official presentation of the book, I would have spared you all the worry and grief you have run into. And now it will have been for nothing. Perhaps after Mardi Gras, if nothing further happens, I will be able to make some sensible decisions, but at the moment they are beyond me.''

"Something further is almost bound to happen, isn't it,'' Toby said sternly, "since we intend to discover the murderer? I have had little opportunity to talk to you directly, Mr. Lefau, but I think I should make my own position clear. Both of us know everything that Dr. Spring knows, but out of deference to her wishes I have not informed Beauregard about the link between you and Arlette Gray, a link that will almost certainly clear John Everett of the last vestiges of suspicion. It will, however, place you in an invidious position. Even so, sooner or later I am going to *have* to tell him."

Jules held up a restraining hand. "As soon as Mardi Gras is over," he said quietly, "I intend to tell him myself. If there had been any danger to Mr. Everett, I would have done it sooner, but, as it is, I am clinging to the faint hope Dr. Spring has held out to me; so, until she has completed her trip and decided this issue one way or another, I would appreciate your continued silence."

"What trip?" Toby said blankly.

"Dr. Spring is going to Haiti tomorrow morning, along with that very large black man. My pilot is flying them down."

"What!" Toby roared. "I absolutely forbid it! Of all the insane, dangerous schemes . . .!"

Jules was looking at him in amazement. "Why shouldn't she go if she feels it is necessary?"

Toby took himself in hand with an effort. "I don't suppose she told you she was *persona non grata* there? That the last time, she was escorted out of the country under military guard, and that if she sneaks back in, she may be thrown in jail or even shot as a spy!"

"No, she didn't," Jules said weakly. "She said that she could find out what she wanted in a short time and get back here by Mardi Gras. Otherwise, it would take too long."

"That does not surprise me in the least. But we cannot let her go, and that's flat!"

"Can't let me go where?" Penny's head appeared around the library door, and she beamed at them all before her gaze fastened on Jules. "It's all fixed," she said cheerfully, coming in and shutting the door. "Mean Gene is dusting off his best Sunday suit and will pick me up here to go to the airport at seven-thirty. Your pilot was very cooperative; with any luck we'll be out by Sunday. John, may Mean Gene borrow your briefcase? He has to look businesslike."

"I forbid it!" Toby roared.

"Oh, don't fuss, Toby! It's all settled. I'll be in and out before anyone realizes I'm there. Thank heaven for inefficient bureaucracies! By the time they get around to seeing I've come back, I'll be gone again."

"But the danger!" he fumed.

"Oh, there'll be no danger. I'll go to ground the minute I arrive. That's why I need Mean Gene; he'll be my front man and my legman. We've thought up a wonderful cover story." She grinned impishly at Jules. "Using the revered name of Lefau Enterprises."

"Well, don't expect *me* to come and bail you out if you get into trouble." Toby was unmollified. "I wash my hands of it."

Jules was looking helplessly from one to the other. "Perhaps, Penny, you shouldn't go. I mean, God forbid that I cause any danger to anyone else."

"Don't worry, nothing ever happens to me," Penny said, blissfully ignoring her past record. "And with Mean Gene along, I'll be fine. I think I've got all the photos I need, although I wish now I had lifted the ones of Arlette's parents from the house. I don't suppose . . . ?" She looked inquiringly at Jules, who shook his head. "Did she ever say anything to you about them?"

"No, never. She never talked about her past at all. I never even knew she was from Haiti." His tone was apologetic.

"It occurred to me that since there were no dates or anything on her mother's photo, there is an outside chance she is alive and still there." Penny was thinking aloud. "It would be a great help if I could make contact with her. Is it too late to have a word with your sister about Henri?"

Jules's lips compressed. "I'm afraid so. My sister is not very well."

"She told me that Mrs. Lefau was the one who hired Henri and that she did not know any of his personal history," Toby volunteered grudgingly. "Said to ask you, as a matter of fact."

Jules shrugged. "As I said, I know nothing. Henri has always been very impersonal. Never said anything about himself or his affairs."

"Yes, I noticed that." Penny's tone was dry. She bounced up again. "Well, I'd better go and throw some things in a bag."

"Have you dined?" Jules was once more the anxious host.

"Mean Gene took me to Jimmy's for a poor-boy hot oyster sandwich—delicious!" Penny exclaimed, "But I'll take a drink with me, if I may."

Toby watched her go with monumental and silent disapproval. Jules appealed to him, "Do you think I should stop her?"

"When Penny has her teeth into something like this, she's impossible," Toby growled. "If you try to stop her, she'll just go and do it anyway. Let her go and get it out of her system. Myself, I think it's useless."

For all his gloomy reservations, Toby insisted on accompanying her to the airport the next day, where they met up with Gene—dressed to the teeth in a sharp suit—and a small coterie of Knights, who appeared equally gloomy and disapproving.

"I can understand Toby being miffed," Penny said to Mean Gene when they seated themselves in the twin-jet eight-passenger plane, "but why are the Knights so mad? Is it because you are missing out on some gigs?"

"No, they think Ah'm crazy getting mixed up with you honkies and your business," Gene said with devastating frankness as he looked around him with a lively curiosity. "They're probably right, too. Will you look at this, now! Ain't it elegant?"

"Yes, the Lefaus certainly do things in a big way," Penny agreed as the jet took off. "This certainly beats hanging around airports."

"How come you're in so bad down where we're going?" Gene asked. "You ain't CIA or anything funny like that, are you?"

"No, nothing like that. It's just that I got rather involved in some rescue operations from Duvalier's thugs the last time I was there. As I told you, I was studying present-day voodoo firsthand when the *Tontons Macoutes* started to bear down on some of the good religious leaders there—they were frightened of them, you see. I helped get some of them out. That's why I'm going to have to be very low-key in talking to any officials. You've got your story straight?"

He grinned at her. "Sure have."

The hot humidity of the tropics reached out and embraced them as they landed under a lowering sky and made their way to customs. The official's eyes widened slightly, taking in Gene's size and girth as he presented their two passports. "The nature of your business here, *m'sieu*?"

"Looking over possible factory sites for mah company, Lefau Enterprises of New Orleans."

The official looked impressed. "What kind of factory?"

"Musical instruments," Gene said with a straight face. "You heard about all the music in mah city, Ah expect, and Ah've heard you have some mighty fine drum makers down here."

The man didn't know whether to be flattered or suspicious. "How long will you be staying?"

"Oh, couple or three days *this* time," Gene said grandly.

"And who is she?" The customs man looked at Penny.

"Mah interpreter and personal assistant. Ah haven't the pleasure of speaking your language," Gene informed him.

"And where will you be staying?"

"That Ah have not as yet decided—perhaps in the city, perhaps not. It depends on what information your minister of commerce has prepared for me." He looked at his watch. "And Ah hope Ah'm not going to be late for mah appointment with him. You can get in touch with me anytime through mah pilot, who'll be staying at the Haiti Hilton."

The customs man hastily stamped their passports and waved their baggage through with an ingratiating smile.

"Seems just like home," Gene said with a grin, indicating the huge murals in the ultramodern terminal, showing giant-sized black men and women laboring hard at various menial tasks. "Tote that barge, lift that bale, down here, too. Wha'd'ya know! Ah thought maybe it'd be different."

"It is," Penny said soberly. "Down here they do it on empty stomachs a lot of the time."

"So what do we do now?"

"Now you go and hire a car—there's a stand over there—and then we go to a post office and do some quick telephoning."

"This Duvalier sure put his name on a heap of things," Gene observed as they drove into the city in their rental car. "Everything from the airport on down." Penny pointed out the huge, blinding-white bulk of the presidential palace as they drove past. "Didn't do too badly by himself, either, by the looks of it," he concluded.

"You'd better believe it! Stop here," Penny charged, and they drew up before the central post office. "Better stay with the car, and don't wander too far off. I'll probably be quite a while." She was gone the better part of an hour, but she returned with an air of quiet satisfaction. "OK. We won't be stopping here tonight, we'll go on up either to Pétionville or Kenscoff in the mountains. It'll be safer, I'm told. But first we'll go to the museum and make a contact there. If you get bored, you can always look at the exhibits—it's a great place."

"Lady, around you life is never boring." He grinned.

They went off to the equally modern and streamlined Musée National and, in a room filled with voodoo paraphernalia, picked up their contact, a worn-looking, elderly man with his left hand missing. The museum was almost empty of visitors; so Penny lost no time in getting out her pictures and showing them. "The names I'm interested in, Pierre, are Jean Gris, Arlette Gris, and Henri Legros—except I think the last is not his right name," Penny said. "Jean Gris was an army man and was shot in 1970, I don't know by whom. I'm particularly interested in knowing if his wife is still alive and still here. We'll be at Hungan Thome's tonight. Can you get a message through to me there?" The man nodded. "Henri Legros says he's from Port-au-Prince," she went on. "Does his photo mean anything to you?" He studied it carefully and shook his head. "That, too, might be a lie, of course," Penny muttered. "The girl Arlette was only seventeen when she left; so she'd have been born around 1954. I'm afraid that's all I have for you to go on. Jean Gris is your best lead. Can you get at the army records?" Again the man nodded. "Good. Then, we'll expect to hear from you later. There's money here to pay for the information if you have to bribe your way in." The man pocketed it and disappeared as silently as he had come.

"Not exactly chatty, was he?" Gene observed.

"That's because the *Tontons Macoutes* broke his jaw and knocked out all his teeth, before they chopped off his hand," Penny said grimly. "He is a living symbol of the good old days of Papa Doc—and he was one of the lucky ones, at that."

"You're having me on!"

"I wish I were," she retorted, "but this is the country where it never does to say too much or to be too careful,

Gene. Remember that. Dictatorships tend to be the same wherever they are found and no matter what the color of their skin is."

The big man shivered. "Let's get out of here," he urged. "Ah feel the need of some fast fresh air. Where to now?"

"We'll make for Kenscoff in the mountains. By the time we set there, Pierre will have got something and phoned in, and I am anxious to talk with Hungan Thome, who is an old friend of mine, particularly about the Sect Rouge."

Though the drive along the twisting road up into the mountains was brilliant with sunshine and the luxuriance of hibiscus, azaleas, and bougainvillea blazing along the roads, Penny and Gene were both silent, busy with their own thoughts. At Kenscoff they bore off onto a small dirt road and finally drew up at the neat white house, its roof red-tiled, nestled in a small clearing.

"Before we go in, I'd better brief you, Gene. I don't know who'll be there; so, for your own protection, keep up the front you gave at the airport. Hungan Thome I know and trust, but there may be others. If you are interested in what goes on here, talk to his daughter if you get a chance. She's a graduate of the national university in Port-au-Prince and speaks good English. They used to live there, but Thome found it wiser to move out here: he's a very big wheel in voodoo, and Duvalier was afraid of him. OK?"

"OK," he mumbled uneasily.

They went in to find Thome seated in regal state on an elaborately carved wooden chair with some half a dozen black men grouped around him. He greeted Penny like a long-lost daughter, and she introduced Gene as "a friend who is a businessman from New Orleans."

The *hungan* gave them both a slightly derisive smile. "You have no cause to fear—all these men here we can trust," he said quietly.

She wasted no time. "Any word from Pierre?"

"I have no phone here, but he called Auguste." Thome inclined his head toward one of the men in the group. "Yes, there is news. Jean Gris was an army officer with a bad reputation for brutality even to his own men. As you know, after Papa Doc died, there was a short period when a lot of old scores were paid off and many of his hatchet men were liquidated. Jean Gris was shot during that period. No one knows by whom. His wife is still alive and has remarried, Pierre says to a man who used to be her lover even before Gris went. She lives in a suburb of Port-au-Prince; I have the address. There is no trace of the other man, Henri Legros.''

"Then, that probably is a false name, but I have some photos of him that might stir some memories." Penny handed him the shots of Henri. Thome looked at them, shook his head, and passed them to the man on his right, who in turn shook his head and passed them on. Penny's spirits began to sink at their blank expressions, until the photos reached the very last man. He took one look at them and surged to his feet with an oath. "I know him! But tell me where he is and he is as good as dead!"

"Who is he?" Thome said quietly.

"They used to call him the Butcher of Les Cayes. He was in charge of the *Tontons Macoutes* there—the whole district. His name is Henri Marron. I have good reason to remember him. He emasculated my younger brother and left him to die in his own blood. For that alone he shall die! We tried for him after Papa Doc went, but he was too quick for us; he got away. Took a jeep with two others and went through the mountains. They found the jeep on this side of the border with the other two—both shot in the back."

"Well, you won't have to bother about bringing him to justice," Penny said. "The United States courts may do it for you. He is probably responsible for two murders in New Orleans. What were his methods—garotting, by any chance?"

"Anything that was as slow and as painful as possible," the man said savagely. "He liked to see people suffer. And he was power-mad. He let no one stand in his way."

"There is another thing," Thome put in in a soft voice, looking at Penny, "something that may be the link you seek. The maiden name of Jean Gris's wife—it was Marron."

"Eureka!" Penny breathed.

CHAPTER 16

"The worst of it is, I'm not sure that we've got anything on him that Beauregard can act on. He may be a sadistic criminal, but the regime here would never want him back to persecute him—after all, it is just a variation of the old theme itself. Unless we can prove he committed either of these recent murders, he can't even be held," Penny confessed to Gene as they drove down the mountain the following morning. "I only hope we can find out something definite from Arlette's mother."

"After all the horrors Ah heard last night, Ah wouldn't mind havin' a go at him myself," Mean Gene growled, savagely changing into low gear. "And to think he'd do it to his own people! Ah just can't get over it."

"The bad part is that if he has started Sect Rouge activities in the New Orleans area, you could have a reign of terror among your people there," Penny went on with her own train of thought.

"Not if Ah can help it! What did that old Mama Tio tell you, again?"

"Well, I got the impression from her that nothing was very organized as yet. It's almost as if he'd been biding his time for some reason. But what? What could he conceivably have in mind?" she worried on. "Power-mad he may be, but if Eleanor Lefau was the white *mumbo*, it means he killed his golden goose. It doesn't make sense. Could we have *two* murderers?"

"Maybe he and ol' Lefau were in cahoots after all. Powerful lot of money and heft in that setup. If he got Jules Lefau in his pocket, he'd have it made."

"I can't believe that. Jules is a strong man, in a quiet sort of way; he'd never sit back and just let it happen. No, it has got to be someone Henri could dominate, someone who is weak or mad or as twisted as he is."

"Don't seem that any of the characters you've told me about fit that bill. Hey, we're in Pétionville; don't we have to turn off somewhere here?"

"Yes, take the road to the right." They drove into a neat residential section with palm-lined streets and located a small white villa gaily decorated with scarlet trelliswork and smothered in a riot of bougainvillea. "Well, this is it." Penny was tense. "I think probably I'd better do this one alone, just in case she calls the police. Why don't you wait around the corner, and if you see any signs of activity, hightail it for the airport."

"No way!" Gene said, uncoiling himself from behind the wheel. "After what Ah heard last night, Ah ain't about to leave your side. If we gets into trouble, we gets into it together."

"Well, OK," Penny said dubiously, "but if I give you the high sign, we get out of there fast. I hope my rusty French is going to be up to this! I saw a curtain move in the window, so somebody has spotted us. Let's go."

She marched with more determination than she felt up to the glass-paned front door and rapped sharply on it. There was a pause, and then it opened a cautious crack. "Who is it? What do you want?" It was a woman's voice.

"Madame Dessus? I must talk with you on an important matter. My name is Penelope Spring, and I come from New Orleans. It is about your daughter and about Henri Marron."

The door opened a little wider to reveal a frightened face. "What did you say? I know no one of that name."

"Oh, come now, madame!" Penny took a gamble. "I know Henri Marron is your brother. Do you want the whole neighborhood to know, or are you going to let us in?"

The woman's face was worried and careworn, with but the faded remnants of the beauty she had passed on to her dead daughter. Her eyes were fearful, and she stepped back, her hands falling limply to her sides. Penny and Gene crowded into the small, red-tiled hallway.

"My companion speaks no French, so you may talk freely,

madame," Penny pressed on. "And talk freely you must, if you know what is good for you. I know you are the widow of Jean Gris, who was shot in 1970 for crimes against the people of Haiti; that your daughter, Arlette, left the country at that time; and that you are the sister of Henri Marron, also wanted for crimes against the people and now a refugee under a false name in America."

"I am not his sister," the woman whispered, "only his stepsister."

Penny waved this aside. "You must know, madame, that any connection with Henri Marron, if made known to certain people, would be dangerous for you. This need not be, if you answer my questions. I do not like to threaten, but this is of such urgency that I cannot afford to be nice. You will answer my questions or I will see to it that it *is* known. You understand?"

The woman nodded dumbly, her eyes wide with fear.

"Now, when did you last hear from your daughter?"

"I have never heard, not since she left. It was the way we both wanted it; better for her, better for me. She wanted to go, I wanted to stay—it was that simple."

"To stay because you wanted to marry your lover?" Penny was merciless.

The woman flinched. "My husband is a good man and a good husband," she said sullenly. "Besides, we have two children."

"So you put your first family behind you, but not your brother. Isn't that right?" Penny continued her guessing game.

"Henri was very good to me," the woman whispered defensively. "This house, my husband's business—all from his money."

"And you have kept in touch with him." It was a statement, not a question.

The woman gnawed at her lower lip and nodded slowly.

"And he knew about Arlette."

"He told me she was living a bad life. She was no good, just like her father." There was venom in her voice.

"But recently Henri had need of her." Penny was watching the woman closely. "Tell me, did he not tell you to write to her? What did he tell you to say?"

The silence lengthened as the woman gazed at Penny in

desperation, trying to gauge her mind and knowledge. "Answer me!" Penny rapped out. "That is, if you are concerned about your present family!"

"All right. Henri did ask me to write. He sent me the address. He told me to say that she should help him in a business matter, a plan he had. I was to beg her to do this, because otherwise he would see that people knew who I was. Not that he would have; it was just to get her to cooperate," she added quickly.

"Did she reply?"

"No. I told you, I have never heard. She does not care."

"When was this?"

"Six weeks ago."

"And have you heard from Henri since then?" The woman shook her head.

"Did you keep the letter?" Another shake. "Well, I think you have done your daughter an injustice," Penny said. "She did care enough to cooperate, and I regret to say it has led to her death. She was murdered, garotted, and a symbol of the voodoo *loa* of death pinned to her breast. Does that mean anything to you, madame?" There was no answer, for the woman's eyes rolled up in her head, and she started to slide to the floor in a dead faint.

"Jesus Christ!" Gene exclaimed, catching her as she toppled. "What the hell have you been saying to her? Now what do we do?"

Penny was already making for the back of the house. "Get some water and revive her," she threw back over her shoulder. "I haven't quite finished with her yet. Take her in and put her down somewhere."

She returned with a pitcher of water to find him standing in a stiffly furnished living room, still holding the unconscious woman in his arms. "You sure play rough," he accused.

"Not half as rough as Henri," Penny returned grimly, splashing water on the woman's face. Her eyes fluttered open, and she started to struggle feebly in Gene's arms. He deposited her with great care on a plush-covered armchair and stepped back. "Obviously, then, you are well aware of Henri's connection with voodoo," Penny continued her interrogation. "You must also be aware that he is a man who lets nothing stand in his way. Either he killed your daughter himself or he had her killed. He would not scruple to do the same to you if you were no longer of any use to him—and, frankly, I do not see of what further use to him you can be; so I urge you to tell me everything he told you about his voodoo activities and what he has in mind. He has to be stopped.''

The woman seemed too dazed with fear for comprehension, her head twisting from side to side like a desperate trapped animal. ''He is a *hungan*. He could kill us all!'' she choked out.

''No, he cannot harm you. I will see to that,'' Penny comforted. ''I have friends here strong in voodoo who will protect you. But what did he say about the white *mambo*? What has he got in mind?''

''I swear by all the saints I do not know,'' came the whispered reply. ''All he said was that his plan was laid and the time was ripe, that soon he would have the power to begin again, to be greater than he was here among our people. He would have all the money he needed and the influence, too.''

''But the white woman, did he name her?''

''No, he said nothing of her, save that she would do as he said because she was in his power and without power herself.''

''That doesn't make sense!'' Penny snapped.

A little color had returned to the woman's sallow face. She shrugged. ''I can't help that. It is what he said.''

''And what of the Sect Rouge?''

Madame Dessus surged to her feet, her face livid with fear. ''I know nothing,'' she cried hysterically, ''nothing! Get out! Leave me alone! I have told you everything I know.''

Penny hesitated for a second, looking at her searchingly. ''All right. I hope for your sake that that is so; otherwise, you will hear from us again.''

The woman started to sob. ''Get out! Get out!''

Penny jerked her head at Gene, who made for the door with the utmost alacrity. Once outside, he asked, ''Did you get what you wanted?''

''Not everything''—Penny glanced back at the house—''but I think most of what she did say was the truth.''

''What now, then?''

''I think we'd better get out of here fast. If she has time to think things over, she might call the authorities. We'll get to a phone and you call the pilot to be waiting and ready at the airport.''

"Suits me," Gene said, putting the car in gear.

The woman crouched at the window watching them with hate-filled eyes. As soon as they moved off, she let out a shuddering sigh; then she made for the phone, her lips clamped in a determined line.

As they sped through the city toward the airport, Penny grinned across at Gene. "Well, sorry you didn't get to see more of Haiti, but you can always say you've been there!"

"Believe me, Ah've seen enough of this place to last me a lifetime," he said with fervor. "Ah won't draw a peaceful breath until we are heading in for the U.S. of A. This place gives me goose bumps on my goose bumps!"

They approached customs with some trepidation, and there was a heart-shaking moment when the customs official, after perusing their passports with minute care, said, "I see you arrived only yesterday. What's the matter? You don't like our country?"

Gene plunged back into his role. "Finished mah business sooner than Ah expected. Mighty fine country you got here. Going back to tell mah boss it's just the place for our investors. Yes, indeed, mighty efficient and go-ahead." The man, with a look of mild astonishment, stamped their passports and waved them through.

"Any trouble?" Penny asked the pilot as they hurried up to the Lefau jet.

"Apart from being gouged for the gas to refill the plane, not a bit. Why, were you expecting some?" he said cheerfully.

"I hope not," Penny said, "but the quicker you can take off, the better we'll be pleased—eh, Gene?"

"You said it," the big man growled. "New Orleans, mah home sweet home, here we come!" But as they circled up over the island, a beautiful emerald against the sparkling sapphire sea, he said wistfully, "Looks peaceful enough from up here, don't it? A terrible pity, a terrible waste."

"That about sums it up," Penny agreed.

After they had gone through the ritual of landing and reentry, Penny bustled into the main New Orleans terminal. "You see if you can whistle up one of the Knights to get us back to town and I'll phone Beauregard. No one will be expecting us back this soon.''

"Gotcha, General!" Gene's good spirits had returned. They made for adjoining phone booths.

Penny had some difficulty getting Beauregard on the phone, and when he came on, he was abrupt, almost hostile. "There's been a break in the case. If you have anything to say, I suggest you come to police headquarters, although I doubt whether anything you have come up with will materially alter things. It was as I suspected all along: Jules Lefau is in this up to his ears.''

Penny's heart plummeted. "What break?"

"We received an anonymous letter. In it was a note written by Arlette Gray to Jules Lefau. He denies ever having received it, but it is not a forgery. Our handwriting expert is certain it is her handwriting. Now it is only a question of digging further and establishing the link. I think we've got him dead to rights.''

"What did the note say?"

"What does that matter?" Beauregard was impatient.

"It might matter a great deal, in light of what *I* have." Penny was equally impatient.

"I can't quote it word for word, but the gist of it was that she was involved in something that could hurt him, for him to be on his guard and to meet her at the usual time.''

Penny's mind was churning with possibilities. "Was it mailed or hand-delivered?"

"No idea. All we've got is the note. What difference does it make? It shows he was involved with her.''

"Well, hold off doing anything drastic until I get into town," Penny pleaded. "I have uncovered important information that can shed a lot more light on this whole affair. Henri Legros, the Lefau majordomo, is really Henri Marron, one of Duvalier's major hatchet men in the old regime and a criminal on the run.''

"So what?"

"So he was also Arlette Gray's uncle," she snapped. "But there's a lot more." And she hung up.

"One thousand hells!" she fumed. "Our anonymous friend has done it again, and I'm betting it's Henri. How long before we get picked up, Gene?"

"Al's on his way," he assured her and listened thought-fully as she filled him in on the latest disaster. "Sure doesn't look good for Lefau. Did you know he was hitched up with the Angel?"

"Yes," she confessed, "I've known that ever since we went to her house that night, but I wasn't about to tell the police, because it's all *wrong*!"

Gene chuckled and shook his head at her. "You sure are somethin' else! What if we'd come up empty down in Haiti?"

"We didn't, did we!" Penny was thinking furiously. "But the way things are breaking, we may have to prod Henri into making a move. I can't think what, at the moment, but it's the only thing that will get Jules off the hook. Have you had enough of this whole thing, Gene? If so, say so, but I could use your help some more."

"Ah wouldn't miss this for the world," he chuckled. "Ah'm game for anything short of murder. Come to think of it, if the murderee is Henri, Ah think Ah'm up to that, too." He waved a meaty arm at Al, who had appeared through the doors of the terminal and was looking bemusedly around.

"We don't want Henri dead; we want him very much alive and talking," she said as they hurried out to the cab.

Having said a fond farewell to Gene and the assembled Knights, Penny was relieved to find Toby hovering outside of Beauregard's office. He was looking very unhappy. "Well, thank God *you're* all right and in one piece," he grumbled. "This is enough of a mess without my having to worry about you, too."

"Don't fuss, Toby, everything's fine," she said automati-cally. "Where's Beauregard?"

"In there with Jules and his lawyer."

"I've *got* to talk to him."

At the sound of her voice, the door opened to reveal the frowning face of Beauregard, and behind him she caught a glimpse of Jules and the cadaverous lawyer who had met them and who was looking more disapproving than ever. "So what's all this about Henri Legros, or Marron, being Arlette's uncle?" Beauregard demanded, coming out and shutting the door. "Not that it makes much difference. Lefau has just admitted that Arlette Gray was his mistress, though he's still denying everything else."

A look of relief came over Toby's face as Penny plunged into her recital. "So you see," she concluded, "with clear evidence that Henri has in mind some major plan involving the Lefaus and that he actively recruited Arlette for this scheme against John, it doesn't make sense to point the finger at Jules Lefau just because she was his mistress. Henri would not have scrupled to murder Arlette once she had carried out her part—he's a murderer many times over. Nor would he have scrupled to murder Eleanor Lefau if she were the white *mambo* who was in his power and who, I suspect, had begun to get cold feet about what he was up to."

"You *suspect!*" Beauregard snarled. "That's all it is—supposition. Where are your facts?"

"Where are yours?" she shot back. "Where is your motive? At least I have come up with a motive, and a very strong one, for the first murder."

Toby cleared his throat. "I must say I'm inclined to agree with Dr. Spring, Captain, just on logical grounds. I can see a man murdering his mistress, I can also see a man murdering his wife, but to murder one's wife *and* one's mistress for no apparent reason does seem completely illogical. Unless *you* can supply a motive?"

Beauregard hesitated. "We'll find it." But there was a hint of uncertainty in his voice. "Maybe Lefau got this Henri to do his dirty work for him. But I agree, he'll have to be questioned. Where is he, Sir Tobias?"

Toby shrugged. "I haven't seen him since we all moved to the Royal Street house yesterday. Mr. Lefau would know."

Beauregard opened the door to his office. "Mr. Lefau, where is Henri?"

Penny poked her head around his broad back to give Jules an encouraging smile and a thumbs-up sign. She was surprised to see that he was looking a lot less haggard than he had for days, and when he answered, it was with a voice devoid of strain. "This morning he was going to take Mr. Everett on some errands connected with the book and was to pick up my son Vincent from school"—he glanced at his watch—"half an hour ago. He should be be back at the house by now. Do you wish me to call?"

"Yes but don't talk to him. If he is there, tell him to stay put. We'll be sending a car around to pick him up."

Jules took up the phone. "Hello? Grace? Is Henri there? . . . Well, get me Vincent, then. . . . Not home? Then, Mr. Everett. . . . Hasn't returned, either?" Penny watched his knuckles slowly whiten as they grasped the phone. "Haven't seen him since when? . . . I see. . . . No, I don't know when I'll be home." He put down the phone and looked at them, his face suddenly pinched. "My daughter-in-law says that none of them have returned. The last she saw of Henri was when he drove off with Mr. Everett. It was just after he had received a phone call. She said he appeared disturbed by it." He looked directly at Penny. "For the love of God, what did you find out about him? Was it you who called?"

CHAPTER 17

"She must have phoned him the minute we left the house, and I was so busy thinking of our own skins that I never even thought to warn her off," Penny said gloomily. "What an idiot I am! I thought she would go to the authorities to try and stop us from getting out." It was some time later, and the picture that had unfolded was all bad. The police had been busy. It had been established that the phone call Henri received around 11:45 A.M. had originated in Haiti. Shortly afterward he had left the house with John Everett and driven away in the white Mercedes, but, according to the security guard, when Henri arrived at the exclusive private school at 12:30 to pick up Vincent Lefau, who was having a half-day holiday because of Carnival, there was no one else in the car. After that Vincent, Henri, and the white Mercedes had disappeared, although an all-points bulletin had been put out on the car. Where John Everett had gone was also a complete mystery, but it had been established that at least one of his errands—a trip to the mayor's office to reschedule the book presentation after Carnival—had been carried out.

Toby had a bright idea and phoned Mimi Gardiner at the library. His hunch proved to be half right. "He was supposed to take Jean and me to lunch"—Mimi's tone was aggrieved—"but he never showed up. Oh, and, Sir Tobias, I've got some interesting information for you——"

"Later," he said hastily. "We're in a bit of a crisis at the moment, and we are trying to locate John. I'll call you back later."

"But——" she began, only to find he had hung up on her.

Beauregard was in the awkward position of having his

173

prime suspect now in the role of the father of a possible kidnap victim. Jules Lefau's lawyer had angrily demanded that his client be allowed to go about his business, but Jules had waved this aside. His face was once more set in haggard lines of despair; his worry reflected to a lesser degree on the faces of the rest assembled in Beauregard's office. "If my son has indeed been kidnapped, there is nothing I will not do to get him back. What is the procedure?"

"Well, if there is evidence that Henri has crossed a state line, we can bring the FBI in at once, but I think there is little chance of his accomplishing that with the state police alerted," said the harassed Beauregard. "If the car is spotted, every precaution will be taken to safeguard your son, Mr. Lefau. But if he has gone to ground, the most likely thing is for him to contact you, in which case perhaps you had better return to your Royal Street house and await developments. Since we have no idea what he's got in mind, there is nothing else to be done."

"If I may say something?" Toby interjected. "It strikes me that whatever Henri is doing must be completely impromptu. There is no way he could have foreseen this morning's phone call or made plans ahead of time. He appears to have been very much of a loner, so there must be a limited number of people, if any, in this city that he would turn to—and, similarly, a limited number of places he could go to. Perhaps, Jules, you know some of his contacts." Jules shook his head. "One we do know—this Martinican reader at the Voodoo Museum," Toby continued. "He could be checked on, and the two places that leap to my mind as possibilities are Arlette Gray's house on St. Ann—as I recall, her keys were not found in her handbag, were they?—and the Lefau plantation. The murders apart, with his true identity uncovered, Henri's object may be to leave the country; so presumably he would need money and transportation. He may merely be holding Vincent to ensure that you provide him with both."

"In which case I would most assuredly provide both. In fact, I shall give orders for my plane to be made ready," Jules said

Penny thought with a sinking heart of the two dead *Tontons Macoutes* who had helped Henri's Haitian escape—he was not a man to leave witnesses around—but she said nothing.

Beauregard was already on the phone ordering the Martinican *hungan* to be brought in for questioning. "We'll see him first and then get on to St. Ann Street," he said tersely. "It's grasping at straws, but what the hell. . . ."

But the obviously frightened Martinican, still clad in his long green robe, could tell them nothing useful. "I haven't seen him in several weeks," he stammered. "I know nothing of his business. We only talked of voodoo; he was a *hungan*, too."

"And did you talk of the Sect Rouge?" Penny said.

His deep-set eyes took on a glazed look. "I know nothing of that; it is outside of my knowledge." And that was all he would say. Beauregard handed him over to a couple of detectives for further questioning, drove Jules and his lawyer back to Royal street, and then took Penny and Toby up to the St. Ann Street house.

By now the early winter dusk was falling, and the little house presented a dark face to the dimly lit street. "No one has been here since you were last here. I'm afraid this will be another dead end." Beauregard fitted the key the police had had made into the lock. "I didn't like to say so in front of Mr. Lefau, but if this Henri Marron is as dangerous as you say, he'll probably have got rid of at least one of his hostages already. He would not want to be that encumbered."

Penny said nothing as they crowded into the silent house and Beauregard turned on the lights. The living room was as neat and devoid of life as when she had last seen it. "You see—nothing." The policeman was morose. "Still, we may as well look at the rest. I'll check the kitchen and outside—I remember there's a shed in the garden behind—you check the rest."

Penny made for the bedroom, with Toby following on her heels, but that showed the same neat emptiness. She was just about to leave when she stopped dead in her tracks, causing Toby to bump into her. She whirled around. "Wait a minute! I left the closet door open!" She rushed over to the closet and flung open the door. The clothes that had been so neatly hung were lying in a heaped pile on the floor. She dived into the pile like a cat after a mouse. Her hand encountered cold flesh and recoiled. "Oh, God!" she groaned. "Help me, Toby; there's someone under all this!"

They flung off the remainder of the clothes to reveal the gagged and tightly bound figure of John Everett, scrunched up against the back of the closet. There was no visible mark of violence on him, but his eyes were fast shut. Toby felt for a pulse. "He's alive," he announced. "Go get Beauregard, and I'll get these ropes off him."

Penny rushed out, shouting for the police captain as she made for the phone to call for an ambulance. By the time she succeeded in summoning one and returned to the bedroom, the two men had freed John and deposited him on the water bed and were chafing his blanched hands and feet where the marks of the cruel ropes showed a livid bluish red.

"He was tied in such a way that when he regained consciousness and struggled, he would have strangled himself." Beauregard was grim. "A real sweet guy, this Henri Marron. I don't give much for young Lefau's chances."

"Sounds just like him, though. Do you think John is going to be all right?" she appealed to Toby.

"I should think so. His pulse is strong. He's had a bad crack on the head; he may have a fracture," he diagnosed as the wail of an ambulance increased in volume outside.

The young doctor who arrived with the ambulance said exactly the same thing as John was loaded into the vehicle and whisked off to the Touro Medical Center. Penny and Toby followed anxiously behind in the police car, with Beauregard collecting reports over his police radio. The captain flicked off the switch and turned to them, shaking his head. "Nothing. The parish police have been out to the Lefau mansion, but there's been no sign of Marron there: no sign of the car and, so far as they know, no sign of anything missing from his rooms over the garage. There's been no contact at the Royal Street house, either, though Mr. Lefau reports one uncompleted phone call. The phone rang, he went to answer it, but there was no one on the line. Unless Mr. Everett can tell us something . . ." He sighed and shrugged.

They waited in miserable silence as the doctors in emergency worked over John. One finally emerged through the swing doors and looked over at Beauregard. "Nothing serious," he announced. "No fracture or anything. Must have a hard head, because he took one hell of a wallop. Should be coming around any minute."

"May I question him?"

"For a few minutes. He's going to be damned uncomfortable. Whoever tied him up really did a job on him." The doctor wandered off, shaking his head sadly.

But when, to their vast relief, John's eyes did flutter open, his first words did nothing for their hopes. "What the hell happened?" he muttered, his eyes focusing on Penny. "Where am I?"

"You're going to be all right, John. Can you tell us anything of what happened?"

It transpired that he could tell them very little. After he had left the mayor's office, Henri had asked him if he minded making a small detour because he had an errand to run for Mr. Lefau. John had said he didn't mind, and they had driven to a Lefau warehouse on the waterfront. "It was as quiet as a grave, looked almost deserted," John said feebly. "Henri went in by a side door and came back out with a paper bag full of something. Put it beside him on the front seat. Then he drove back into the Quarter, up toward Rampart, I think. He stopped the car there and just sat, not saying anything, and I was looking out the window trying to figure out where we were, when—whammo!—and that's all I remember." He winced and groaned softly. "He must have hit me with a sledgehammer, by the feel of it. God, how my head hurts! What the hell is going on, anyway?"

"Well, it's like this," Toby began. "It looks as if we've got a nasty kidnapping on our hands."

"Nothing for you to worry about, though, John," Penny comforted, glaring warningly at Toby. "You get some rest, and we'll be back in the morning to tell you all about it."

Toby retreated into outraged silence.

"Can you tell us where the warehouse is?" Beauregard asked, looking significantly at his companions.

"No, but it had a number on it. It said 'Lefau Five.' Does that help?"

"Yes, thank you, Mr. Everett. That'll be fine." Beauregard was heading for the door. "You rest up now."

"Want me to phone for Millicent?" Penny asked before she followed the police captain out.

"God forbid!" John groaned and closed his eyes.

Beauregard was already on the phone by the time Penny

rejoined him. "Your warehouse number five, Mr. Lefau, where is it?" he was saying. "I see. Well, we've found Mr. Everett, and now we'll be checking on this warehouse. It's just possible that's where Marron is holed up. . . . No. You stay where you are in case he contacts you. . . . Yes, Mr. Everett is all right; so there's no need for alarm about your son." He hung up. "Like hell there isn't," he said savagely to it.

He wheeled and raced back to the police car, Toby and Penny right behind him, and snapped a whole series of orders into the radio. "No sirens, and wait half a block away until I get there." He drew a deep breath as he set the car in motion. "Well, here's hoping. Lefau says it's a warehouse scheduled for demolition and not used anymore. Some rebuilding scheme of Benedict's." Toby's eyebrows rose a notch, and he looked at Penny. "He could hide the car there easily enough. He had no means of knowing John Everett would live long enough to tell anyone of that trip. That is one lucky man back there in the hospital, though he may not feel that way at the moment. I hope the kid is just as lucky. Henri must have driven Everett to the St. Ann Street house and then knocked him on the head as soon as he had a clear shot at the house and carried him inside. A quick thinker, Henri Marron."

"I don't want to throw cold water on any of this," Toby said, "but, granted he was making plans as he went along, couldn't the trip to the warehouse merely have been to pick up something he knew was there and needed?"

"Such as?"

"Such as the ropes," Toby said quietly. "I noticed when I was getting Mr. Everett free of them that they were of high-quality nylon, much stronger than you'd find in a normal household—the ropes he could have had in that paper bag."

"Well, I only hope you are wrong," Beauregard snapped, "or we'll be at another dead end."

Unfortunately, Toby was a true prophet. After they had made the approach to the warehouse with infinite caution and had slipped like shadows through the only open door, it was to find nothing but echoing emptiness. "Looks as if you were right, damn it!" the policeman said, indicating a pile of cartons by the door filled with odds and ends of packing material and rope. "It was only a pit stop after all; so we're back to square one."

"There is still the plantation," Toby returned. "It's a big place and still the most likely one, for my money. The parish police have ruled out only the obvious, but there are some other outbuildings on the estate where he could have gone to ground, and there would be plenty of cover among the trees to hide the car."

"It will be no use blundering around out there in the dark tonight. We'll wait for first light and get a helicopter up to see if they can spot the car. It will also give Marron plenty of time to cool down and contact Lefau, *if* that is what he has in mind."

Beauregard dropped Penny and Toby off before the Lefau mansion on Royal, but after he had driven off, Toby still stood on the pavement. "I don't feel like facing them tonight," he said firmly. "How about going to dinner at Brennan's? It's a nice place; you'll like it."

"Suits me. I'm ravenous," Penny said. "With all the excitement there's been, I've only just remembered I didn't have any lunch."

They strolled down the street to the restaurant, their own gloom in marked contrast to the air of frantic gaiety that prevailed among the crowds in the Quarter. Some were already costumed and masked, and there were impromptu dancing and small bands of musicians on almost every corner as they weaved in and out among the throngs of Carnival-goers. "With all this going on, I would never have believed I could feel as miserable as I do," Penny said. "I can't remember when I have felt more down or more helpless in my whole life. To think of that poor kid somewhere out there . . ." She didn't finish.

"It's no good dwelling on it," Toby advised as they pushed their way into the calmer waters of the restaurant. "Beauregard's doing everything he can. A good man that; considering how crazy this town is at the moment, he's done a great job. Do you know that while I was waiting at the police station, there were three rape reports, four assault and batteries, and I lost count of how many robberies and picked pockets reported. I wonder the police don't go completely insane if this goes on every year."

They dawdled over their dinner, putting off for as long as possible the return to the stricken house. "What's it like?" Penny asked idly.

"The house? From what I've seen of it, a miniature version of the House of the Dancing Lady—the French motif throughout again, some lovely chandeliers, and balconies of that nice ironwork. Jules was telling me that the Lefaus didn't desert the Quarter after the Civil War as so many of the old families did. They've been here ever since some banker Lefau built it in the 1750s. He used to have his counting house on the ground floor." Toby could see that his historical tidbits were not even penetrating Penny's worried absorption. "Look," he went on, "it is no use tormenting yourself about this. Even if you had foreseen that she'd warn Henri, you couldn't have stopped her, and you may have got yourself in a whole heap of trouble down there. In a way, it may all be for the best: whatever he had in mind is finished; he's on the run."

"He's on the run with a perfectly innocent child in his clutches! And, knowing his track record, *that* certainly is no cause for cheer."

"If he's going to save his own skin, he'll need Vincent alive to bargain with. My guess is that he'll hold Lefau up for a large sum of money and a trip to South America. The police are used to setting up deals like this over here; they'll see to it that he gets nothing if they don't get the child," Toby comforted.

"I hope you're right, but he's taking his own sweet time about putting on the squeeze," she fretted. "Why hasn't he called?"

"He probably has by this time." But when they eventually returned to the house, it was to find it void of any signs of life. Toby tapped on the library door and peeked in. Jules Lefau, clad in a long lounging robe, sat hunched over the telephone, an almost empty brandy decanter by his side. He looked up at them bleakly. "Nothing," he said in a flat voice. "Nothing at all."

"Why don't you go to bed and get some rest?" Penny said. "We'll stand by the phone, if you like."

"No," he muttered. "No. I must know. I'll wait."

The dawn brought a call, not the expected one from Henri, but from a excited Beauregard. "The helicopter has spotted something white among the trees at your plantation, Mr. Lefau. They think it's the car. They're setting down on your lawn and going in on foot. I'm sending a car for you all now."

"I'll take my own and meet you there," Jules shouted and rushed up to thunder on Penny's and Toby's doors. Disheveled and still half-asleep, they piled into his Lamborghini sports car and zoomed through the awakening city.

In record time they screeched to a halt beside the two police cars drawn up alongside the garage of the mansion. Beauregard, his dark eyes snapping, strode toward them. "Now we're getting somewhere! It's the Mercedes, all right. No one in it, and the engine's stone-cold. Looks as if it's been there all night. Now, about these buildings, Mr. Lefau?"

"I have a plan of the estate inside——" Jules began.

"If I may make a suggestion," Toby interrupted, "that little padlocked shack I told you about, by the scene of that voodoo bonfire—it's very isolated and well concealed, but I think I can find it again. Do you know it, Jules?"

Jules looked a little bewildered. "There are several, and it has been years since I went into any of them."

"We have to begin somewhere"—Beauregard was impatient—"so we might as well follow along with Sir Tobias. We are going to have to approach each one with care, in any case." He signaled to two troopers, both armed with rifles. "You stay here, Dr. Spring."

"I'm damned if I will," she said indignantly. "Where Toby goes, I go." And her tall partner nodded firm assent.

Beauregard didn't bother to argue but signaled Toby to lead the way. They rapidly came upon the circle of the bonfire, and Toby, after a moment's hesitation, plunged on. When they neared the thicket in which the shack was embedded, he held up a warning hand and silently pointed. Beauregard got out his bullhorn. "Henri Marron! If you are in there, come out with your hands up. There is no way you can get out, but if you let your hostage go, we'll deal. Mr. Everett is safe."

There was dead silence; nothing moved, nothing stirred. Signalling the troopers to cover him, Beauregard edged cautiously up to the shack. "It's padlocked," he called out, disappointment in his voice. "Looks as if it hasn't been opened. Still, bring a crowbar; we might as well check inside."

They all crowded around in silence as the lock gave way with a sharp crack and the wooden door swung open with a creak. A smell of incense came to meet them, and they entered the dimly lit shack. A row of drums stood along one wall. On top of one of them were several *assons* and *ogans*; beyond them was an empty chicken coop.

"Voodoo headquarters, all right." Penny led out a slight sigh and looked around. A pile of sacks in one corner twitched as she looked. "Over there!" she stuttered.

Jules Lefau was past her like a flash and was pushing aside the sacks. Underneath lay the bound and gagged figure of his son. The boy's eyes were open wide with terror. His father clutched him to his chest with an incoherent cry, tearing ineffectually at his bonds, as Beauregard squatted down beside him and sliced them apart, an expression of vast relief on his face. His freed arms laced tightly about his father's neck, Vincent croaked, "Poppa, Poppa—I thought I was going to die. Henri has gone mad!"

"It's all right, it's all right," his father soothed, cradling him like a baby, tears of release spilling down his cheeks. "All is well now. It's all over."

Penny and Toby looked at each in the gloom. "All over?" she muttered. "But where the devil is Henri? And what's he up to?"

CHAPTER 18

When Vincent Lefau had calmed down enough to tell his story, it only added to the general mystification. He had been taken to the main house, where a police paramedic had looked him over, given him a sedative shot, and pronounced him whole. With its shutters closed and the chandeliers blazing, the house had taken on a ghostly, otherworldly air, which was enhanced for Penny by the sudden appearance of Celeste at the head of the twin stairway. She stood silent and pale, her light eyes fixed, looking down at them all, until Jules ran up the stairway to her. There was a rapid, low-voiced exchange, and then Celeste glided away in the same ghostlike fashion. Something about her appearance there troubled Penny, but she could not put her finger on it.

Vincent had been bound with none of the savagery that had been used on John Everett, and his story confirmed the impression that Henri had almost gone out of his way not to terrify the boy. "After he picked me up from school, we drove out here," Vincent related. "He told me Juliette was preparing a surprise for you for the Carnival and wanted my help on it. We went out to that shack, but Juliette wasn't there, and then he became all strange and excited. He told me that if I did as he said, I wouldn't be hurt, and then he began to tie me up. I got frightened and struggled, and then he hit me. He said he had to go away and that you, Poppa, had to help him and that I'd have to stay with him until you did. After that he would let me go."

"Did he say how your father had to help him?" Beauregard asked.

"He was muttering a lot in French, and I was so scared I

183

didn't get all he said to me, but there was something about the plane. He said he was going to call my father and then he'd come back and untie me, but he covered me up with those stinking old sacks and went away. He didn't come back.'' Vincent's voice trembled. "I was afraid he'd just left me to die.''

"When was this?" Beauregard said hastily, hoping to avert another tear storm. The boy gulped back his tears. "I don't know—I didn't have a watch—but by the time he left, it was starting to get dark.''

"What time did the phone call that wasn't completed come through, Mr. Lefau?" Beauregard asked, frowning.

"It was almost quarter to five. The phone rang only twice, and just as I picked it up I heard the connection cut.''

"Must have changed his mind," the captain muttered. "Why? What could have happened?" But it was not a question that was to be easily answered.

No one at the mansion admitted to having heard or seen anything of Henri. The garage apartment was gone over again, with no results; the grounds were thoroughly searched but yielded nothing; the House of the Dancing Lady was searched from attic to cellar—again nothing. "How about testing the voodoo things in the shack for fingerprints?" Penny suggested. "That may tell us who else was in on his operations." But Beauregard had already thought of that, and his fingerprint man had come up empty: none of the objects carried identifiable prints.

"Frankly, I don't give a damn what's happened to him," the resilient Jules stated with a relieved smile. "I have my son back, for which I owe you all my undying thanks, and that is really all that matters to me. Now I'm going to take Vincent home and make sure that none of my children move an inch without the strongest security guards available until this business is finally settled.''

"Where is your daughter, Juliette?" Beauregard asked casually.

"She's been at Royal Street with Benedict ever since all this began, and he has strict instructions not to let her out of his sight.''

Jules bore off his son in triumph to the Lamborghini, leaving Toby and Penny to be brought back by Beauregard.

They drove in relieved silence, which was broken by Penny. "That's it!" she exclaimed suddenly. "That's what was worrying me. How did she get there?"

"Who? Where?" Toby came out of his doze with a start.

"Celeste. She just appeared at the top of those stairs. She didn't come through the big doors from the other house."

"Maybe she was there to start with."

"Wandering about Jules's house in a bathrobe? No, she must have come in from her side. But that means there must be another entrance on the second floor. I never noticed one," Penny fretted. "I must ask Jules."

"Why? What does it matter now?"

"Probably it doesn't, but I'll ask him all the same."

With the homecoming of Vincent, it was as if the cloud of darkness that had been hovering over the Lefaus had lifted. The recent tragedies apparently banished from mind, the gaiety of Carnival seemed to have infected the household. Everyone wore a smiling face, and a cheerful Benedict cornered Penny soon after she got back to the house. "How would you like to come along and look at the Comus floats, Dr. Spring? I've got to go and see that the final touches are in place, and I thought you might like to see them in their pristine glory."

Penny had just completed a call to the hospital, where the doctor had assured her John was coming along fine and would probably be fit enough to be released later that day; in consequence she, too, was feeling cheerful. "I'd love to. Can Toby come, too?"

"Of course."

But on hunting around for him, it was only to find that, after a phone call, he had departed for the public library and a rendezvous with Mimi Gardiner. "Oh, well," Penny sniffed. "That's his tough luck."

"Tell me more about the general order of things on Mardi Gras. I really know very little about it, never having seen one," she charged Benedict as they drove toward another Lefau warehouse complex, where the floats were being assembled.

"Well, it starts off at seven in the morning, when Zulu's king arrives by water: the Zulu parade starts everything off. The next high point is Rex, our only unmasked monarch, whose procession starts from its den at ten in the morning—

although there are other processions in between. There are more than sixty krewes now, you know.'' His tone was disapproving, and for a second he looked exactly like his father. ''Momus and Bacchus follow after Rex, and then the culmination of it all is Comus, which starts at approximately seven in the evening and gets through about nine, when the King of Comus toasts his queen on the balcony of the Municipal Auditorium, after which they proceed inside to the Comus Ball. At midnight Rex and his queen come on a state visit, and with this meeting Carnival officially ends, though naturally the crowds go on celebrating long after that.''

They had drawn up outside one of the warehouses and were walking slowly past the long line of floats over which people were swarming like so many ants. Purple, green, and gold, the colors of Carnival, alternated as the dominant color themes. ''It's a very elaborate business, usually,'' Benedict went on. ''Luckily, we are only *re*-creating this year. We had all the plans and books of designs, costumes, and so forth, from the parade of fifty years ago; so it has been easier than the other times.''

''Other times?'' Penny echoed in surprise. ''You mean your father has been Comus king before?''

''Why, yes! This is a small krewe—only about two hundred and fifty members, and some of the members find the high cost of Carnival no longer supportable. So people who can afford it—such as François Duchamps and my father—tend to be kings more often than in the past. Dad was king about six years ago, and once just after he married Eleanor, and twice when my own mother was alive.''

Then, why, Penny thought, her puzzlement returning, had the trouble started *now*? Henri had been here six years ago. What was so special about *this* Carnival? Was it the book, after all? But, if so, *what* in the book? Her unease, which had temporarily been banished, returned.

''Every procession has to have a theme,'' Benedict rambled on. ''The theme of this one was and is 'The Fairy Courts of Chilvary of Oberon and Titania.' My grandfather was Oberon, my grandmother Titania.''

''And who was the changeling child they were at war over?'' Penny quipped and was astonished to see Benedict's face freeze and his look of sudden suspicion. She had evidently hit a very raw nerve, but she could not conceive of what it signified.

"This is the float on which my father and his court will ride," Benedict said quickly, indicating an enormous glittering mountain of white and gold that soared to an incredible height above them. "It doesn't look like much now, but it has thousands of tiny lights concealed all over it. When lit, it really is a spectacle."

"It's quite fantastic!" Penny gasped. "Your father is going to ride on that throne right at the top? Is it safe?"

His cheerfulness had returned. "He'll be a lot safer than the rest of us," he chuckled. "At least he'll be sitting down. The rest of his court have to stand up on that mountain. Fortunately, those built-in shields have struts that we can hold on to."

"You're in the procession, too, then?"

"Oh, yes. I'm a duke this year, complete with gold armor. Luckily, it's plastic! Vincent is a page."

"And Juliette and Grace?"

"Juliette is crown princess, and Grace is the Comus queen." Again a strange expression flitted across Benedict's large face and was gone. "But the women take no part in the actual procession. For one thing, it is far too dangerous nowadays. The police have cracked down a lot in recent years, ever since Al Hirt, the famous trumpeter, almost got killed by a brick hurled from the crowd one year. But one can never guard against the stray loony in any big crowd."

"Your father certainly is vulnerable so high up there," Penny murmured, craning her neck.

"It was built that high deliberately so that the float can be maneuvered right up against the balcony at the Municipal Auditorium and he can toast his queen face-to-face. It's the high point of everything."

"Could any guards ride with you?"

Benedict looked positively shocked. "Oh, no. Only the Court of Comus. This year there won't be many of us; we're not a very prolific family: just three dukes—one being a remote cousin of my father's—and the page."

"Who is the other duke?" Penny asked promptly.

"François."

"François Duchamps?" Her voice rose to a squeak of astonishment.

"Yes. After all, he *was* the intended queen's brother; so he is 'of the blood,' as we say."

"But after all those things he said about your father!"

"Oh, well, that was just François, very hotheaded. He rarely means anything by it," Benedict explained calmly. "My father is always a duke in the Duchamps processions. There aren't many of them, either, you see."

Penny was so amazed that she was silent.

"See those bags on either side of the throne?" Benedict went on. "Those are filled up with the choicer favors that are thrown to the crowd. We all have some to throw, of course, but these are really worth having—jade and pearls, as it was before, but with the price they are today, those alone set my father back six thousand dollars." For the first time his tone was disapproving.

"Will we be able to watch your procession from the Royal Street house?" Penny got her voice back.

"Oh, no, not anymore. The processions have been banned from the Quarter since 1972: the dangers from the crowds and the fire hazard in those narrow streets have become too great. Actually, it's a blessing. We can make the floats wider, and so they're a lot more stable than they used to be. Your best vantage point will be the Lefau building on St. Charles; it's near the beginning of the procession. We follow the same route as Rex does now: down St. Charles to Canal Street, up that, then down Basin Street to Rampart, where the whole thing winds up at the auditorium. If you watch at the Lefau building, it will give you time to make your way to see the climax at the auditorium—though I'm not sure I'd advise it." He looked down at her small form. "The crowds are unbelievable, and you wouldn't see much. Besides, you'll be all dressed up for the ball."

"Oh, yes," she said doubtfully, "that. It seems a bit odd to get dressed up in a formal just to look down from a balcony."

"Rules are rules," Benedict said cheerfully. "Now, if you had been born a Creole, Dr. Spring, you could have been down on that ballroom floor as a krewe member in your own right."

*   *   *

The same phrase was being echoed across town. Toby and Mimi were back in the Howard Johnson's across from the library, which Toby was beginning to consider a second home. "I feel deeply sorry for her," he was saying, "but rules are rules, I suppose."

A slight frown marred Mimi's fair brow. "What rules?"

"The rule that the Queen of Comus has to be a married lady."

"That's not right. I mean, Comus doesn't have a rule like that. Momus does, but not Comus." She was definite.

"But I heard Jules Lefau himself say so!"

"I don't care. There is *no* such rule. In fact, there have been quite a few unmarried Queens of Comus. It is the king's prerogative to choose who shall be queen. Mr. Lefau may have a reason for not wanting his sister to be queen, but I can assure you the one he gave isn't it."

"You are certain of that?" Toby was puzzled.

"Absolutely. I was a history major at Tulane, and I did a special project once on the krewes."

He shook his head in perplexity. "Strange! I really don't begin to understand these people. Well, what was all this exciting news you had for me? I'm sorry to have cut you off so abruptly yesterday, but, as I explained, it was rather a crisis."

"Yes. I'm glad it all turned out well, but in the light of that, all this stuff I've been gathering probably won't be of much use."

"There are still a lot of things that haven't been explained," Toby urged. "Go ahead!"

"I was going over some of the wills and found a couple of odd things. Arlette Duchamps, for instance, left twenty-five thousand dollars to her 'devoted attendant, Robert Harmon.' I checked, and he apparently was a male nurse who looked after her in her last days. He was also Grace Lefau's father!"

"But I thought she was from a Baton Rouge family."

"So she was, but it was her *mother's* family that was mainly based there. Her father moved up there later and set up in business, but he was married right here, and Grace lived here as a small child. Evidently it was not the only money that Harmon had had from Arlette, either, because after her death Pierre Duchamps put in a petition disputing the bequest, claiming, 'undue influence and previous endowment' on Harmon's part and 'diminished responsibility' on his mother's account. But the petition was suddenly dropped and the will probated as is.''

"So compared to the Lefaus, Grace Harmon was very much 'below the salt,' '' Toby reflected. "I wonder how she and Benedict ever got together?''

"I think I know that.'' Mimi was leafing through her notes. "Yes, here it is. Benedict was in Tulane—a business major. Grace was two years ahead of him in the same school. Her father did pretty well in his business, apparently, and she was an only child. I don't know anything about the circumstances of the marriage, of course, other than it was sudden and took place the year after she graduated.''

Toby was getting a little restive. "You said there was something else?''

"Yes, Pernell's will. The de Lesseps weren't in the same league as the Duchamps and the Lefaus, but they had money, too. She left all hers to Celeste, with nary a mention of her son or her husband. She must really have been a early version of an ardent feminist. Anyway, Celeste was a rich woman even before she inherited her portion from her father's estate.''

"Jules was only a small boy when his mother died,'' Toby pointed out, "and presumably, as his father's heir, would not have needed any of his mother's estate.''

"Yes, except that Creoles tend to get quite flowery in their wills, and boys especially are usually made a fuss of. You know—'I leave my beloved son my undying love, knowing that he is otherwise provided for'—that sort of thing. But nary a word in Pernell's. I just thought it a bit odd.'' She gave a wistful sigh. "But, then again, now that all this business about the sinister butler has come out, it's all beside the point, isn't it? Unless there is anything else you'd like me to check on?''

"No, but you really have done some splendid research. You certainly would be an asset to any serious scholar.'' Toby felt awkward. "I hope you will allow Mr. Everett and me to take you and your friend out to dinner tonight, on this eve of Mardi Gras.''

Mimi colored prettily. "That would be very nice, thank

you. I'll ask Joan and let you know, shall I? Will John be all right by then?"

"Oh, yes. No concussion or anything like that, and I know he won't want to miss any more of the festivities, now that our troubles seem to be over," Toby said, cheering up. "The police can handle this affair from now on. A bit strange the way Henri just dropped from sight, but then, if he had two murder charges to face, he probably decided a clean pair of heels was more important than money or whatever else he had in mind. And with all the hurly-burly of Carnival, I doubt whether the police will ever catch up with him. Just as well, I suppose . . ."

They looked at each other in silence for a long moment. "I wonder," Mimi said softly. "I wonder if it *is* all over. I've got such a strange feeling. . . ."

CHAPTER 19

"Strange she should say that," Penny observed when Toby was relating the conversation later. "I've got much the same feeling myself—a sense of incompleteness. There are still things going on around here that I don't understand. For one thing, Jules may have chosen Grace as his queen, but he's obviously as mad as hell at her. He ignores her completely, doesn't even so much as look at her. And now you tell me there was no real reason Celeste could not have been queen, as she longed to be! I do think it is all extremely odd."

"Well, it's probably some sort of intrafamily fight, and none of our business, thank Heaven!" Toby intoned piously. "Frankly, I'll be glad when Mardi Gras is over and we can get back to Oxford. John is off the hook and out of danger, which was our main concern, after all. I think we've rattled quite enough family skeletons without unearthing any more. Let 'em stay in their closets. And I grant there are loose ends in the case against Henri, but I for one am not anxious to tidy them up. He's gone, and that's that."

"Yes, but *is* he? What if he's lurking around to have a final go at Jules? On top of that fake mountain, Jules will be worse off than a sitting duck. I wish they could safeguard him in some way."

"If Henri had been after Jules's blood, he could have got him long before this. If he were after anyone's, it would far more likely be yours," Toby observed. "You blew the whistle on him and brought his long-term schemes to naught, whatever they were. I shall be keeping an eagle eye on you tomorrow, you can be sure of that."

"Then, you'll have to be up bright and early. I'll be off at six-thirty," she said with a twinkle.

"Six-thirty! What on earth for?" He was horrified.

"I want to see the Zulu king arrive. I've promised Mean Gene to watch the Zulu parade, and that starts at seven. It sounds like the most fun of the lot. I'll probably take a nap after the Rex procession in the afternoon to recharge my batteries for the evening. But if you and John are taking your scholarly girlfriends out tonight, you're not going to be in any shape to rise at the crack of dawn."

"Hmmph! Well, watch yourself, that's all I ask," Toby said rather lamely. "I'd like to get through at least one case where we both come out of it with a whole skin. I've got to pick up John from the hospital now. Want to come along?"

"No, I want to have a word with Jules, and then I'm going to have a little get-together with the enigmatic Grace. She's turned all amiable and '*grande dame*' with me. When I gushed over the house, she said she'd be delighted to show me through it—and I'm going to let her. Maybe I can open her up a bit."

"Rather you than me. So what are we doing about tomorrow?"

"If we don't see each other before," Penny suggested, "how about rendezvousing at the Lefau building about ten-thirty to see the Rex procession? Oh, you aren't going to wear that ghastly antique monkey suit to the ball, are you?"

"Of course not!" he said, very much on his dignity. "I've my ordinary formalwear with me. I'll wear that."

"Then, why did you bring that other monstrosity along?" she persisted. "It looks as if it had been made for your father around World War I."

"It was. John said we might have to go to some fancy-dress affairs; so I brought it along to go as an 'old English gentleman.' Luckily, we haven't had to—a relief for which I am duly thankful. How grown people can get so worked up about a carnival is quite beyond me. Do you know, I saw a chap walking down Bourbon today dressed like Superman. In front, that is—behind he was stark-naked except for a pair of BVDs!"

Penny chuckled. "Just wait until tomorrow night! You haven't seen anything yet."

She sought out her host, who was just on his way out. Although the strain had gone from his face, Jules was looking apprehensive, and she soon learned why. "If you've got some questions, why don't you ride with me out to the plantation? To tell you the truth, I could use some support." He gave her a nervous smile. "I want to make my peace with Celeste and see if I can persuade her to come back with us. I'm sure she'll come to the ball, but I don't want her taking off with any bad blood between us."

"Taking off?"

"Yes. She informs me that as soon as Carnival is over, she is going for a long sea voyage—the Caribbean and South America. It is probably just as well; all this business has been very upsetting for her."

"It's too bad she couldn't have achieved her wish to be queen," Penny said bluntly.

Jules's face tightened and darkened. "Sometimes one has to do strange things to protect one's nearest and dearest, but I would rather be misunderstood than risk her being hurt by life any more than she has been. She is upset enough by Eleanor's death and with Juliette going away."

He was full of surprises. "Where's Juliette off to, then?"

"I've decided to let her go to New York to college. I know her mother was set against such a thing, but rather than risk alienating her from the family forever, I think it is best that she go and get this out of her system. I don't suppose it will last long once she's there." He sounded optimistic. "And when she does come back, with just the three of us at home, it will be easier. She has never got along too well with Grace."

"Are they leaving too?" It was beginning to sound like a major break-up of the Lefau family.

"Yes, I have suggested to Benedict that it is high time he set up his own ménage, particularly since his business interests are becoming so distinct from mine." There was a hint of bitterness in his voice. "He is negotiating for a house in the Garden District. I think that will suit us all better."

Curiouser and curiouser, Penny thought. "So it will just be you and Vincent at home for a while?"

Jules's face lightened again. "Yes, and probably high time, too. I have never given him the amount of attention I should have; it is time we get to know one another. With Benedict being so much older and so tied up with me in the business, and with Juliette demanding so much attention, well, Vincent has been rather neglected. I intend to remedy that.''

Penny looked at the determined set of his finely molded jaw and believed him. So son number one had blotted his copybook, and son number two was about to be groomed as the new heir apparent: a very interesting situation in the offing.

"So what were those questions you had for me?" Jules asked.

"It was nothing very important, but the other day when we brought Vincent in, Celeste appeared from *up*stairs. I just wondered how she got there."

"She probably heard the noise and came in the quick way—through our suite. There's a door in our bathroom that leads into her part of the house. It was put in during my mother's last illness so that Celeste could keep an eye on her. Why?"

"I just wondered, that's all," Penny answered vaguely, not wishing to point out that it was another possible avenue for Eleanor's killer to have used.

"Was there anything else?" They had reached the deserted gates of the mansion and were sweeping up the empty driveway.

"Only that I wondered if you can't be protected in some way while you are on the float. It worries me that you'll be in such a vulnerable position. Can you wear a bulletproof vest and perhaps have a security guard standing behind your throne, just to keep an eye on the crowd?"

He threw back his head and laughed, but it was a mirthless laugh. "You think someone is still after my blood? Well, they are welcome to their best shot. It would be almost a relief—and quite a dramatic way of going out, don't you think?"

"Jules, that's not like you!" she protested. "And it *is* a possibility, with Henri still not accounted for. Won't you even consider some precautions?"

He drew up with a jerk in front of the shuttered house. "That damned costume is heavy and hot enough as it is. I shudder to think what it would be like with a bulletproof vest under it! So the answer is no. But thank you for caring." He sat staring straight ahead of him. "I have lost a great deal recently that was very dear to me. Perhaps I will get over it in time, perhaps I won't, but the shock and the grief are very much with me; so you must forgive me if I sound fatalistic, but that is precisely how I feel.''

Penny was genuinely distressed. "I wish we could have been of more help to you."

He gave her a faint smile. "Oh, you have. Believe me, you have.''

Jules let them into the echoing hall and through the great double doors to the twin house. He led the way up the left-hand staircase, Penny following and looking about her with interest. The accent here was very different from that of the main house; here the dominant theme in both decoration and furniture was the Art Nouveau movement of the early part of the century: Tiffany shades, Lalique crystal, bead curtains, and tassels everywhere. The old black woman suddenly appeared in a doorway and looked at Jules with disapproval. "Ask my sister if she will give me a few minutes, Nana, will you?" he said formally. She nodded silently and withdrew.

"Interesting decor," Penny remarked, sensing how tense he was.

He cleared his throat nervously. "Yes, these things used to be in the main house. They were all my mother's. Celeste had them moved in here after my first wife redecorated. Strange how most of this stuff is back in fashion. It's worth a small fortune." He gave a little start as a door farther up the hallway opened and the servant beckoned.

Penny and Jules went into a little boudoir furnished in the same theme, the only exception being an exquisite little rosewood Victorian writing desk by the long window. Celeste was seated at it, collected, but her pretty, faded features grim. "I have bad news for you, Jules," she stated as they came in. "No doubt you have come to ask for the necklace. I am afraid it is gone. Henri did not leave empty-handed. Come, I will show you. I did not discover this myself until this morning." She led them into a small room opening off the boudoir, where an oil painting huge askew on one wall. She drew it aside to reveal a small, old-fashioned wall safe, which gaped open and empty.

"Have you called the police?''

"No." Celeste was perfectly calm. "Nor do I intend to until after Mardi Gras. I refuse to have them tramping uselessly about my house. There has been enough of such upset."

"But that's absurd!" Jules protested. "All your jewels!"

"Not all. There were but a few oddments in there apart from the necklace, which, as you know, I like to keep near me. The rest are in the bank. And I fail to see what is absurd. The police are after Henri anyway. Either they will catch him or they won't. If they catch him, they will recover the necklace, which is all I care about and which he will have a hard time selling—it is too well known."

"It's a diamond necklace," Jules said in a hasty explanation to Penny, "given by my father to my mother for the Carnival and worn by all the Lefau queens since then. At least let me notify the police of the loss," he appealed to his sister.

"*No!*" She was adamant. "I must remind you, Jules, that the necklace is my property and that it is none of your business. I'll tell them in my own good time, but I'm afraid Grace will have to go without it." There was a certain satisfaction in her voice.

"There is still the paste replica," he reminded her. "She can wear that."

"Excellent! If you don't tell her, she won't know the difference." Her tone was sarcastic. Penny looked at her and at the safe, which showed no sign of being broken into, and began to have her own thoughts on the matter. But for once she kept them to herself.

"Actually, I did not come for the necklace but to ask you in the interests of the family to come back with me for Carnival," Jules said quietly.

The pale-gray eyes looked at him without expression. "I had every intention of joining you, but I will be along later. I have some packing still to do. Juliette will be picking me up when I have finished. Now, if you will excuse me? I still have a lot to do." It was a firm dismissal.

Jules stared to go, then hesitated and blurted out, "Celeste, please believe me, I did not do this to hurt you. I had reasons, very good reasons, for acting as I have done. You must try to understand this and forgive me."

"Oh, I am quite sure you had your reasons." The cold

eyes clamped on his, and Penny felt a little icy trickle down her spine. She thought as they gazed at each other that she caught a glimpse of the abyss that lay between them, where the shadows lay coiled and black.

"Yes, it really is a most attractive house," Grace bubbled, "but I shan't be sorry to have a place of my very own at last."

It was later, and Penny was in the middle of her grand tour with the totally transformed and ebullient new *doyenne*. "You are moving?" she inquired innocently.

"Oh, yes! Benedict is buying a really *marvelous* house in the Garden District, a very select area. The Quarter has become so tatty, I think, with all the tourists and everything," Grace said grandly. "And after tomorrow night—well, it will be a whole new era beginning! Now they will seek me out. They'll accept me quick enough now!"

"Who?" Penny continued her role of dumb innocent.

"Why, everyone who matters in New Orleans society! I am out of the shadows and into the limelight." Grace poured them two hefty slugs of sherry from a cut-glass decanter and held hers up as if to toast this bright new future. "I speak no ill of the dead, Dr. Spring, but, actually, it has been very difficult for me. My mother-in-law was so *hostile* to both Benedict and me, and the others took their lead from her. Being an Anglo, too, surely you understand." Penny murmured something unintelligible, but Grace was too wrapped up in her own thoughts to notice. "Really, the way most of these Creoles go on, you'd think they were the only people in the world who mattered or who had ever done anything." Her full lips pursed out in a grimace of distaste. "And yet underneath all this civilized veneer they are *rotten*, believe me! My father was a very successful man, but did that matter to them? Not a bit. I wasn't *one* of them." For an instant her inner venom showed, but she collected herself and said with a laugh, "Anyway, I'm not above playing their little games, even if I do think this preoccupation with the past is so much nonsense. I can hardly wait to see François Duchamps's face when he has to pay homage and dance with me at the ball tomorrow. And I intend to dance and dance and dance!" She made a little pirouette of joy. "How I love to dance!"

"So, by all accounts, did the queen you will be representing," Penny said drily.

"Oh, the precious Pernell!" Grace snorted. "All the balderdash Celeste talks about her sainted mother! What a shocker she was—just like Eleanor's grandmother. The stories I could tell about them if I wanted to!"

"Yes, your father was connected with Arlette Duchamps in some way, wasn't he?" Penny said in a silky voice and was rewarded by a sudden suspicious stare from the dark eyes.

Grace sobered. "He befriended and advised Arlette in her old age. Her own family treated her terribly, you know. Shall we go on with the tour?" Suddenly she was in a hurry to be gone.

"New Orleans is such a great place for ghosts. Is this place haunted?" Penny asked as they crossed the courtyard to the *garçonnière*.

"Not that I know of, though Eleanor loved the place so I wouldn't be surprised if *she* came back," Grace said as she let them into her living room, which was a strange and ill-assorted mixture of period and modern decor. "She used to stay here sometimes all by herself." She gave a little shudder and headed for a modern bar set against the wall. "More than I'd like to do, I must say. This house can be very spooky when there's no one around."

"Well, there was always the caretaker and his wife, I suppose." Penny was becoming a little bored.

"Yes, but they live beneath us, out here. She used to stay in the main house all by herself, said she liked it that way. Often after the Carnival Balls she would have Henri bring her back here and let the rest go back to the plantation. Jules would get so mad! Like on the night you arrived, for instance."

Something clicked in Penny's memory. "The night we arrived?" she echoed sharply. "Eleanor stayed here?"

"Yes. As I said, Jules was furious because we had guests."

"Are you certain she was here?"

Grace looked at her in astonishment. "Of course I'm certain. I picked her up here the next day to go for a fitting." She waved a hand at the bottles on the bar. "A drink?"

"No, thank you," Penny said hurriedly. "Do you know if Sir Tobias is around?"

Grace seemed perplexed by the sudden change. "I think he

and Mr. Everett went out together a while ago; they said they'd be out for dinner.''

"Well, thank you very much for the tour. I have held you up long enough; I'm sure you've got a lot to do for tomorrow. I'll look forward to seeing you then in all your finery.'' Penny was abrupt. "I should see about some things myself. Good night.'' She bustled out onto the balcony and then down into the courtyard, where she stopped and looked up, her thoughts in a whirl, her heart pounding with new discovery. A watery moon shone fitfully down between scudding clouds, and a low wind rustled the bushes in the courtyard and soughed in the creaking shutters. "If Eleanor was *here* the night we arrived, she couldn't have been the dancing lady I saw,'' she mumbled to herself. "And if *she* wasn't the dancing lady, who was?''

CHAPTER 20

The worry had stayed with Penny all night. Could she have been wrong about Eleanor? On the face of it, it did not seem possible. Eleanor had hired Henri; she had been close to him. Elviny Brosse had been Eleanor's servant; she would have had cause to resent Arlette. And Eleanor's own husband had suspected she might be behind the anonymous letters. Furthermore, there had been no sign of voodoo activity since her death. It all fitted, and yet she could not have been the dancing lady. Who else, then? Possibly Juliette, who had been dabbling in voodoo? Determined to have a heart-to-heart talk with her about it, Penny had searched for but had not found her; and, on taking her problem to Jules, she had discovered that Juliette was not even under the parental roof.

"She is spending the night with a friend, another princess-to-be. She is still very upset about tonight; so I thought it better, in the interests of family peace, to arrange it this way," he said apologetically. "If it's important, you can call her."

"No, it can wait," Penny said. "It was just a loose end I was checking on."

It remained in the back of her mind as she hurried to the levee to watch the Zulu king come ashore in all his barbaric splendor of ostrich plumes and colobus-skin mantle and take his place in the Zulu procession. It stayed with her as the early-morning crowd roared its approval of the scantily clad nubile young Negro dancers, clasping snakes over their heads or rattles and tom-toms in their hands as the ancient calinda of the voodoo dances throbbed by. When the float with Mean Gene and the Knights of St. Pierre passed by, their sheer exuberance banished the worry for a while. Gene was truly overpowering as Baron Samedi in a tall top hat with long streamers of black crepe, a white skeleton painted on his black morning suit, making him seem a true sepulchral giant of death. The Knights were all dressed as skeletons, and the float was decorated with voodoo symbols. Penny caught a glimpse of Sweet Daddy Coglan seated on another float, a silver trumpet to his lips and an expression of bliss on his wrinkled face as the thin, silvery notes rose pure into the morning air. But, at the same time, she found herself searching the faces of the crowd for Henri. . . .

The procession passed her by, and she headed through the packed, hectic crowds toward St. Charles Avenue and the Lefau building. It took her a long time, so that when she arrived, it was to find Toby and John already there, both of them bleary-eyed from their night on the town. As Penny helped herself to the lavish buffet luncheon that had been laid out for the krewe members, the two men trailed silently after her, watching with queasy horror her piled plate, while she confided her problem to them.

She had half hoped that Toby would brush it aside as a detail of no importance, but he did no such thing. He was as perplexed as she but came up with another suggestion. "It could have been Elviny, I suppose."

And John confounded both of them by adding, a little peevishly, "I never did think Eleanor Lefau was a very likely candidate for this mysterious white *mambo* of yours; she just wasn't the type."

"Where could Elviny have got to?" Penny appealed to Toby. "Has Beauregard found any trace of her?" He shook his head. "Mind you, with all the rest he has had on him, I don't think he has looked too hard. If we could only find her, maybe we could get a lead on Henri. To disappear as he has, he must have had help from someone, and as a *hungan* he probably could demand her cooperation—from fear if from nothing else."

"Well, one thing's for sure," Toby said gloomily, looking down from the balcony at the milling crowds beneath. "There is nothing to be done about it now. And tomorrow we leave— praise be! We can pass this on to Beauregard before we go and leave the rest to him. I think I see the first float coming.

Why don't you just put it out of your mind, eat your lunch, and enjoy?''

The theme of Rex was New Orleans in the twenty-first century, led off by a scarlet-and-silver band clad in tight-fitting space suits. As the floats with their science-fiction and super-modern themes rolled by, the crowd went wild with delight. Rex, the only unmasked king in Mardi Gras, beamed down on his subjects, distributing his largesse from a space capsule perched precariously on top of a replica of the International Trade Mart, his portly figure and rufous face making him seem a space-age version of Santa Claus. The cheers followed along after him like a gigantic undulating wave as he passed.

"What next?" John asked with a huge yawn.

"Bacchus, I think.'' Toby looked at his program, elaborately embossed with the insignia of the Comus krewe.''

"Well, I think I'm off to Royal Street for a nap," Penny said, catching John's yawns.

"Great idea," John agreed. "I'll come with you. How about you, Toby?"

"Oh, I think I'll stay for a couple more.'' Toby was secretly getting into the swing of things but hated to admit it. "How are you going to get back here?''

"Mean Gene is going to pick me up at Royal Street about six-thirty to be here by seven," Penny explained. "In full dress, he thinks I'll need some help getting through the crowd in one piece. I've arranged with Jules for him to come up and watch with me and then steer me back to the Municipal Auditorium for the finale.''

Toby's eyebrows shot up. "That's a bit of a break in tradition, isn't it? I thought this was just for the krewe and Lefau employees.''

Penny grinned. "In a sense Mean Gene *is* a Lefau employee. Jules is terribly grateful to him for his Haitian trip, so grateful, in fact, that he's going to try and save Jerusalem Hall for them. The Knights are now one hundred percent Lefau backers.''

"Your bright idea, I suppose," Toby grunted.

"A pretty good one, I thought," she riposted. "Then, if I don't see you back at the house, I'll meet you here again, OK?"

*   *   *

Penny was more tired than she had admitted to herself. When she awoke, dusk had already fallen. To her annoyance, her watch had stopped, and her traveling clock nestled unwound in her bag. "Damn!" she exploded. "It would be just like me to be late!" Poking her head out into the corridor to seek the necessary information, she saw the back of a fair-haired, slim figure clad in a shimmering gold-and-white gown at the end of the corridor. "Grace!" she called. "What time is it? My watch has stopped." The figure hesitated, then turned slowly, and Penny saw that it was Celeste. "Oh, I'm sorry. I didn't make out who it was in this dim light. Am I dreadfully late? I'm afraid I've been asleep. Where is everyone?"

Celeste's voice was flat and cold. "It is a little after five-thirty. The men have already left. We shall be leaving shortly for the auditorium. You had best hurry."

"Yes, thanks," Penny muttered and popped back in. "*That* certainly was a clanger," she told herself as she bustled into the shower. "But from the back those two could be twins. Oh, dear!" She struggled into an evening gown of emerald-green velvet, which gave her the look of a plump leprechaun. She tried to make her hair look halfway presentable, then slid with a slight groan into high-heeled evening pumps and dithered over whether to wear her slightly moth-eaten evening wrap or her all-purpose raincoat. She peered out the window to check on the weather and saw that a light rain had started, so settled rather thankfully on the raincoat. Similiarly, she discarded her small evening bag in favor of her usual capacious shoulder bag. "I can hide them under the seat at the auditorium," she comforted herself. "No one will notice." Hurrying into the silent corridor, she tapped on Toby's door. When she elicited no response, she checked her watch again, saw it was six-thirty, and hustled down into the hallway, where she stood backed up against the door of the downstairs cloakroom, peering through the sidelights of the great front door, watching for the tall figure of Mean Gene.

The house was as quiet as a grave as she moved restlessly from foot to foot, aware that her feet in the unaccustomed high heels were already beginning to throb. "Oh, damn! This will never do. If I'm going to do any walking, I'll have to wear my flats." She bustled upstairs, changed, put the pumps into her handbag, and rustled down again, vaguely aware that the hem of her dress was wet. "How on earth . . .?" she grumbled, but the bell pealed and there was the sepulchral figure of Baron Samedi looming on the doorstep.

"My, don't you look smart!" Mean Gene boomed diplomatically as she opened the door. "All set? We'll have to hustle if we're going to make it by seven." They hustled.

Toby, who looked spendid in evening dress, and John, who looked exactly like a plump penguin, were already ensconced on the balcony, drinking champagne and peering expectantly toward the faint cheering on their right, which signaled the beginning of the Comus procession. Toby handed Penny a glass of champagne, which she gulped down thankfully, and looked her over with a critical eye. "Umm, not bad," he observed, "but you've got a stain on the hem."

"Yes, it's wet out. Did you bring your raincoat?" He nodded as the first purple float trundled past.

It seemed to Penny as the procession unfolded that the reaction of the crowd was far more muted than it had been in the morning. Whether it was the rain or sheer exhaustion from too much spectacle and excitement, there was a certain forced and automatic air about the cheers that greeted each float, bearing its load of fairies and characters culled with equal impartiality from Shakespeare's *Midsummer Night's Dream* and Malory's *King Arthur*.

Gene, who was watching with a critical eye, delivered a devastating summation. "It's pretty enough," he said, "but it's too old-fashioned. It ain't grabbin' 'em like it should." He was right. Although the floats were pretty and tasteful, there was an air of irrelevance about them; they were like expensive toys from a vanished past that had lost their meaning.

As the glittering white-and-gold mountain slowly came into view, the cheers swelled in enthusiasm, but as it edged by, Penny felt a queer little thrill, almost akin to horror, as the erect figure on the glittering throne turned his face toward the balcony and the sardonic, heavy features of the long-dead Jules stared blindly up at them: it was like looking at a phantom made flesh. She let out a little gasp, and Toby looked at her quickly. "You all right?"

"Yes, but those life masks are almost too good, aren't they?" she said weakly and gave a little shiver.

The tall figure of Benedict and the handsome profile of François Duchamps in their glittering armor, and Vincent in a gold tabard, kneeling by his father's feet, all faded into insignificance beside that grinning, sardonic face on the high throne. The king raised his arm in slow salutation as the float passed the Lefau building and was gone. The crowd began to surge in behind it.

"Well, that's it. You want to try for the auditorium now?" Gene asked.

"I suppose so," Penny said dubiously. "You coming along, Toby? John?"

Toby tossed back the last of his champagne with a slight sigh. "Do I have a choice?"

They got down to the street to find an altercation going on in front of the building. Cyril the clarinet was struggling in the arms of two husky security guards. "Ah tell you, Ah gotta get a message to someone in there," he was yelling.

"Hey, Cy! Ah'm here," Gene boomed. "What's up?"

Cy stopped struggling and panted, "Not you—the doctor lady. Mama Tio wants to see you. Urgent. Somethin' to do with Elviny Brosse. Says to hurry 'cause there's death around you!"

They exchanged alarmed glances as the security guards dropped Cy on the pavement. "Ah'll go first. We gotta go north to get above Rampart and away from the crowds," Gene rapped out. "You others stay around here." And he launched into the crowd.

Considerably the worse for wear, and panting heavily, they arrived before Mama Tio's ramshackle house, where all the lights were blazing and from which came the sound of chanting. They plunged on in, to be met by a sea of black faces and an overpowering wave of spicy incense. The crowd parted silently as the hunched figure of Mama Tio beckoned with a gnarled finger to Penny. She scurried over to the carved chair on which the ancient *mambo* sat enthroned. "Elviny is in the back room. She wants to talk to you— hurry! There is little time," the old woman croaked and indicated a door.

Penny shot through it like a lightning bolt. In the dimness, Elviny Brosse was sitting on a straight chair, her face buried in her hands. As Penny erupted through the door, she looked up, and Penny was shocked at how her ravaged face had aged. "I can't go on," Elviny whispered. "You've got to stop her. She's mad, quite mad. I don't care what happens to me anymore. She must not kill again. She must not kill Mr. Jules. Oh, my poor dead lady!"

"Who?" squeaked Penny. "And why?"

"The *mambo*—Celeste," came the almost inaudible whisper. "She thinks she's Pernell. She wants revenge."

"Oh, my God! What is she going to do?"

"Poison. The toast—the toast will be poisoned. She had to be queen," Elviny whispered. "Go! Stop her! Even if she kills me for it."

"But she isn't queen!" Penny cried. "Grace is."

Elviny peered uncertainly at her in the dim light. "Are you sure?" There was a faint hope in her voice. "But she will manage it somehow. Go, please go!"

Penny rushed out frantically toward the three men, looking in their respective ways so utterly incongruous in the crowded, brightly lit outer room. "Big trouble. We've got to move fast! John, you try and find Beauregard. Toby, Gene, you've got to get me to the Municipal Auditorium before Jules makes it there. We've been all wrong. Celeste is out to get him. Elviny says by poison. We've got to stop her before they get to the royal toast." They all made for the door in a rush.

"Wait!" came the sudden command from Moma Tio. "My eyes are dim, but my smell sense is yet keen. You"—she pointed at Penny—"there is fresh-spilled blood on you. I smell it—fresh human blood!"

"What on earth . . .?" Penny began, then remembered her inexplicably wet hem. "Oh, God! Toby, you'd better get over to the house and see if anything is amiss there. Maybe in the front hall." John made for the door, Toby on his heels. "Gene!" Penny cried to the spectral figure. "You've *got* to get me to that auditorium!"

"Even if Ah have to carry you," he roared and, seizing her by the hand, towed her out into the night.

Throwing dignity to the winds, Toby loped across Rampart and down the almost empty length of St. Ann. Faint cheers from his right reached him, marking the slow march of the Comus procession, as he turned the corner into Royal. He sprinted the short distance to the Lefau house and pealed frantically at the bell, praying that there would be someone, anyone, to let him in. After an agonizing interval the door opened a crack, revealing the caretaker's wife, holding a small baby in her arms. Toby rushed past her into the hall and looked desperately around. From beneath the cloakroom door ran a small, telltale dark trickle. Steeling himself, he opened the door. Distorted features grinned up at him from a seminaked body. He clutched at the doorjamb for support as realization swept over him. "Oh, dear God, no! Not her!" he groaned and turned blindly away. "I must get to the auditorium. At all costs, I must get there in time."

"Where the hell are we going?" Penny yelled as Gene pulled her along. "The auditorium is the other way!"

"And we gotta get to the other side of Rampart and as close as we can to it by the side streets to have even a *hope* of getting through that crowd," he roared, tugging her down Ursuline and then along Burgundy. As they approached Dumaine, she saw what he meant, for the crowd was surging up it like soldier ants on the march. He stopped momentarily and parted the tails on his suit of mourning. "From here on, you clamp onto mah belt under this cummerbund and stay behind me. Don't let go for a second or the crowd'll sweep you away."

Penny nodded and clamped on, and the oddly matched pair plunged into the surge. It was an inch-by-inch battle, and as they won their way back to Rampart, she saw with a sense of doom that the glittering mountain was already in sight and heading toward the large balcony that projected from the auditorium. It was bathed in the harsh glare of floodlights, and she was thankful to see that it was currently empty.

"Any hope of you gettin' inside?" Gene panted as he elbowed and shoved his way through.

"No, I don't think so. Only krewe members allowed in until eight-thirty. After that they let the balcony invitations in. But if you can get me to the door, we'll give it a try. Or, if we can get to the float, I'll warn Benedict and he can get to his father."

Even as Penny spoke, a new roar went up from the crowd, and she saw the long French windows onto the balcony opening. Gold-and-white-clad figures, carrying large bouquets, were slowly emerging and ranging themselves along the back of the balcony: the royal court of Titania was making its first appearance. "It's no use. Forget the inside. Even if I gained entrance, they'd never let me up on the balcony in time. You've got to get me within yelling distance of the float."

He was too involved in pushing and shoving to answer, but they started to angle out toward the police barrier along the street. "Ah'm gonna try and get a cop to help," he panted. "When Ah gets there, you do the talking."

Peering around his back, Penny was trying to make out what was going on on the balcony. She saw Juliette's chestnut head appear, and then a red-headed girl's. There was still no sign of Celeste, but an extra-loud roar went up from the crowd as the slim figure of the Queen of Comus emerged, the great collar of diamonds winking at her throat. The life mask of the long-dead Pernell Lefau looked down upon her subjects, and the queen bowed her crowned head in graceful acknowledgment.

Penny and Gene had reached the crash barrier and a helmeted policeman. "Officer," Penny gasped out, "this is an emergency. Please, help us get to the Comus float. We've been alerted to an assassination attempt on the king."

The officer looked at Gene's towering figure and then her dumpy one with a smirk. "Nice try, lady, but *no one* gets across this barrier."

Penny plunged into her handbag and produced her engraved invitation. "I'm not kidding," she shrilled. "Look, I'm a guest of Mr. Lefau's—a friend of Captain Beauregard. You must have heard of the Lefau murder! Now *his* life is in danger. For God's sake, hurry, man, or it may be too late!"

The white mountain was almost at the balcony. The king was on his feet, bowing to his queen. There was still no sign of Celeste, but a page had appeared on the balcony bearing a tray on which reposed two large golden goblets. *"Please!"* Penny begged. "It's a matter of life and death. If you don't want another murder committed under your very eyes, let us through!"

The cop looked uncertainly at her. "Well, OK," he conceded, "but if this is a trick, I'm warning you, you're in a heap of trouble!"

Gene vaulted over the barrier and lifted Penny across, and, with the policeman in front of them, they sprinted the few feet to the float. "Lift me up!" Penny yelled. Seizing her around the waist, Gene hoisted her with incredible strength high in the air. "Jules!" she screamed at the top of her voice. "Don't drink that toast! Poison! Benedict, Vincent! Get to your father. Don't let him drink. It's Dr. Spring. Stop him!"

The next few seconds were like the slow unfolding of a silent film. The king stood atop his mountain, his hand outstretched toward the queen, who was slowly reaching out her own, holding the golden goblet. His gauntleted fingers clasped it, withdrew it from her grasp, and raised it high in the air as the crowd roared and she turned to pick up the other. No one seemed to be paying the slightest attention to the little green-clad figure screaming her head off in the arms of the black giant. The lips of the king moved, and the goblet slowly came toward them. The queen's lips moved in answer, and suddenly Penny saw Juliette's dark head jerk forward in attention and was aware that her frantic gestures had caught the girl's eye at last. Then the whole scene became animated. Benedict suddenly looked toward Penny and caught her screamed words. She could see him glance upward, startled, to see the goblet almost at his father's lips. His mighty bellow joined with hers. "Don't drink, Father! Poison!"

On the balcony, Juliette had flung herself violently upon the queen, and there was a tussle going on that startled the crowd into silence, so that a thin screaming could be heard. "He must die for what he did to her. He must die!"

The life mask ripped under Juliette's frantic fingers and peeled away to reveal Celeste's face, distorted with hate. Transfixed, Jules Lefau stood rigid; then his arm slowly began to move again as he tipped the goblet up. "Benedict!" Penny screamed. "He's going to drink it! Use your lance— knock it down!" But it was Juliette who tore free from the clutching hands of the madwoman on the balcony in time to dash the goblet from her father's lips.

CHAPTER 21

New Orleans, and especially the krewe of Comus, would not forget this particular Carnival for a very long time. For the first time in its long history, the Comus Ball was held without its royal court and with the knowledge that its two real queens had been murdered, its fake queen had been removed, raving mad, in a straitjacket, and its king saved from the cyanide-laced champagne of the royal toast by the crown princess, who had apparently rescued him from public suicide. The city seethed with rumor and surmise; no one knew what it was all about. The only certain thing seemed to be that nothing would be quite the same ever again.

Trying to piece together what it *had* been all about was now the weary task of the principal actors in the drama. Their star witness, Elviny Brosse, freed from her fear, was talking and talking and talking. . . .

As she talked on and on, a frightening picture emerged of the secret life that had gone on at the House of the Dancing Lady, a picture that chilled the blood with its creeping madness revolving around the insane desires and fantasies of two unbalanced and disparate people.

"It began when Pernell Lefau was dying and with that old journal," Elviny confessed, for the journal of Desiree Lefau had been found secreted in Celeste's rosewood desk and had confirmed Toby's surmise that this Lefau lady had been involved in the voodoo activities of her time. "Celeste was as madly devoted to her mother as she madly hated her father, who she was convinced had deliberately destroyed her happiness. When her mother died, she built up this fantasy and began to plan revenge. She started to study voodoo; many of her travels were for this end. When I came to the plantation with my poor dead lady, Celeste was very excited when she found out who I was, and she asked me to teach her. I told her all I knew, but already she was beyond me in most of it. We held the rituals—all the house servants were involved. We did no harm, we meant no harm, and we did not know what was in her mind. But then came Henri. . . . You tell me she said it was Mrs. Lefau who found him. This is not so. Celeste had met him in Haiti; she helped him escape. It was she who brought him here. And he was a wicked, wicked man."

"Do you know where he is?" the stupefied Beauregard interrupted.

"I don't know. Mama Tio says he is dead. I think Celeste may have killed him, too. If you search the plantation, you may find him. But you may not; she was very, very clever at the end." Elviny's voice had dropped to a whisper.

"We'll get the parish police on that right away. Go on!" Beauregard commanded.

"Well, Henri had his own schemes. Celeste was delighted with him because he told her so much, but he went to work on her—feeding her hates and subtly, oh, so subtly, gaining control over her. He was waiting for his chance and for the right moment. He had to be very careful, because she was clever, too, and as cunning as he was."

"But what did he have in mind?" Beauregard was getting impatient.

"To get her so much in his power that he'd have control of her money, and to contrive that she, and she alone, remained at the plantation, so he could use it as a sort of headquarters. That's what I think, but I don't know for sure. Henri never confided in us, not about anything. I don't know how he was going to clear everyone out of here, but he must have had some scheme—I just don't know."

"So, after waiting for so long, why did he start to make his move now?" Toby broke in with equal impatience. "Was it something to do with Arlette Gray—or with Grace Lefau?" He still was sickened by that nightmare moment when he had gazed down at the distorted face of the Comus queen, who had been first garrotted by her own paste necklace and then her throat cut from ear to ear by her mad replacement, in ghastly reenactment of Eleanor Lefau's death. Nor did he like to recall his futile battle through the pressing crowds to get to the auditorium, which he had only reached at the moment when the frantic Celeste had burst free of her captors and had tried to hurl herself, clawing and screaming, at her brother's throat.

Elviny shook her head. "No, it goes back further than that." She glanced over at the stone-faced Jules. "To just after last Carnival when she knew you were going to be king again and intended re-creating the Titania pageant. She's been getting steadily worse ever since. Part of the time she was Celeste; the rest of the time she was Pernell and convinced she had to be queen to right the wrong done to her daughter. Henri saw she was getting worse and must have believed he could not afford to wait any longer. But I didn't know he meant any harm to you, Mr. Jules, honest, I never did. I think it was the book that did it. She said you wrote that Gaston was a thief and that you were every bit as bad as your father, who had spread that lie. She said Gaston had died for love of her and that her father had killed him as surely as if he'd shot him himself. Henri heard how she ranted on about it, and that gave him all these other ideas."

"He sent the anonymous letters?"

She nodded slowly. "He told her he'd see to it that nothing about her dead lover ever came out—that as a *hungan* he would stop it."

"So he killed Arlette Gray?"

"Something went wrong then. He didn't mean to kill her; he just wanted to make a scandal for that publisher man to scare off Mr. Jules. He knew how dead set Mr. Jules was against scandal and publicity of any kind, and figured if he could show him he was capable of carrying out his threats, Mr. Jules would back off and not put the book out. Arlette Gray must have threatened him in some way so that he had to kill her to shut her up."

"But he killed Mrs. Lefau as well!"

They were surprised when she shook her head vigorously. "No. That's when *everything* started to go wrong." Again she seemed to be talking to Jules. "The business of the dog. It was to make her sick, he said, so that Celeste would be queen in her stead at the last minute. But Celeste was beyond reason by then; she made sure of it—she killed her. And I think Henri knew then that his schemes were done for, that she was beyond his control.''

''And you let it happen!'' Jules's ice-cold voice cut in.

''Oh, Mr. Jules, I was so afraid! I ran away because I thought they'd kill me, too.'' She buried her face in her hands and started to sob.

''But you knew she was going to kill Mr. Lefau, too,'' Beauregard persisted.

''No!'' Elviny looked up, tears streaming down her ravaged face. ''I only heard that when I sneaked back to the house for some of my things and found Nana in such a state. Oh, Mr. Jules, why didn't you let her be queen? It was the final straw. She was convinced that you were no longer you but your father come back to spite her again. Nana heard her talking to herself; she was going to let nothing stand in her way this time.''

Jules got up abruptly and strode out of the office, slamming the door violently out after him. Penny, with a warning look at Toby, slipped out after him, to find him slumped on a bench outside, staring blindly into space. ''All right, Jules, I can quite see you've had enough of it in there,'' she said quietly. ''I'm sure what Elviny is telling the police will satisfy them, but I'm not so easily satisfied. There are two questions I want answered, and I want them answered now!'' Her voice was hoarse and rough from all the shouting she had done the previous evening but held such determination that his blank eyes slowly focused on her. ''You heard me and you heard Benedict last night, and yet you were still going to drink that poisoned cup. Why? And I want the real reason you refused to let Celeste be queen. Did you know she was mad; did you know all this?''

He sat staring at her, and when he did speak, he appeared not to have heard her. ''In this time of Carnival I have lost two women I loved most dearly, I have learned my son has betrayed me, I have learned——'' He broke off and started again. ''Celeste was the only mother I ever really knew; she is very, very dear to me. When I realized who it was last night, when I realized what she was trying to do to me, when I thought I knew the ultimate secret that had tipped her over the abyss and who had revealed it''—he choked—''I just didn't want to go on; that's all. I could not bear any more cruelty. There is just so much that a man can stand.''

''Just as well, then, that your daughter has more sense than you have,'' Penny said brutally, ''or we'd have another use-less death on our hands. But what ultimate secret are you babbling about?''

He looked up at her with haggard eyes. ''The real reason my father could not allow her marriage to Gaston Duchamps. The reason that was revealed that Carnival night so long ago, which caused Gaston to go into an antechamber and blow his brains out.''

''What was it?'' Penny cried out in a frenzy of impatience.

''They were brother and sister.'' Jules's voice was a stran-gled whisper. ''My father was Gaston's father, a fact that not even *he* knew until that night, when Arlette Duchamps—that *stupid*, loose woman—realized she could not keep silent any longer. Gaston—the result of a little 'fling' she and my father had had at another Carnival twenty years before. The secret that, after the suicide, was kept between my parents and Arlette for the sake of the two families.''

''And which was passed on to you.''

To her surprise Jules shook his head. ''I was completely unaware of it until a few days ago. I thought the facts were as I had written them in the book.'' He passed a shaking hand over his eyes and sighed. ''Since you've heard this much, you may as well hear the rest, because it will answer all your questions. My parents died with the secret sealed between them, but Arlette Duchamps lived on to an unpleasant dotage—and in that dotage she talked to her male nurse, Robert Harmon. I don't know whether all the money she lavished on him was a result of that indiscreet revelation, but the story evidently made a tasty tidbit for the Harmon family circle.'' Again he paused, his face working with emotion.

''After Eleanor's death, it had been my firm intention to let Celeste be queen, knowing how much it meant to her. Before telling her, I informed Grace of my decision as a courtesy. She told me to think again, that she was tired of the role she had been playing and that she wasn't going to wait any longer. If she were queen, she would keep quiet; otherwise she would tell Celeste what I have just told you. I could not face that or what it might do to her. So''—he shrugged listlessly—"I gave in. I couldn't think of what else to do. I had been worried about Celeste for some time, but I had no idea she was already so far removed from reality. And because of my decision, that poor vain girl is dead and my sister hopelessly mad."

"You can't blame yourself. You heard Elviny in there; it's *not* your fault," Penny said brusquely. "Anyone would have done the same."

"It was my responsibility," he said and buried his face in his hands.

"And now it is *over*. This terrible thing is *over* and done with. And you have the rest of your family to think of—Juliette and Vincent, who love you and need you desperately, and Benedict, to whom you may have done an injustice. If Grace blackmailed you, do you think she'd have been above doing the same to him? I suggest you have a very open talk with your son. It strikes me that everyone has gone around hugging secrets to their bosoms in the interests of family honor that would far better have been aired long since. What is badly needed is more togetherness and less tradition."

He looked up at her with the faint suggestion of a smile. "What a sensible woman you are, and how tiresome you must find us Creoles! It occurs to me that I have been acting and sounding very much like François Duchamps. You must see me as a weak, self-pitying fool."

"I sce you as nothing of the sort," Penny answered gruffly. "I see a deprived little boy who, in spite of rotten parents, grew into a sensitive, caring man. I see a man who loves and is loved by his children, a rich, powerful man who can do a lot of good in the world now that this nightmare is behind him, a man to whom suicide or exile should be the most ridiculous of solutions."

"How you do read my mind! So you don't think I should fold up my tent and gently slip away?"

"I most certainly do not! 'There have always been Lefaus in New Orleans,' " she quoted him. "And I sincerely hope there always will be. Besides," she added with a grin, "I have a vested interest in your staying. You have to save Jerusalem Hall for Sweet Daddy and his cronies, remember?"

His smile broadened, and he shook his head at her. "You really are an impossible woman! No wonder Sir Tobias is so devoted to you. Not only do you pull me back from the brink, but now you are planning my future for me. I wonder how he survives it.''

"You get used to it after a while,'' she assured him.

The door opened, and Beauregard emerged from his office. "Ah, there you are, Mr. Lefau. I was afraid you'd gone off. I've just had a medical report on your sister. Our people say that her mental condition precludes any possibility of her being brought to trial. She will have to be permanently committed to a mental institution, but, under the circumstances, *where* can be a matter of discussion between us.''

"I'll be right with you.'' Jules's voice was firm and decisive again. He got up and looked at Penny. "You're not leaving now?''

"No, we can't get out tonight after all. We are planning to go first thing tomorrow morning.''

"Good. Then, I'll see you back at the house tonight.'' His charming smile sunned her, and he was gone, passing Toby in the doorway.

"So what have I missed?'' Penny demanded.

"They've unearthed Henri—stabbed in the back. She must have got him when he was putting through that phone call to Jules. For wholesale slaughter, this case beats all,'' Toby said gloomily. "Otherwise it was just a question of dotting the i's and crossing the t's. Elviny said Celeste had had some idea of grooming Juliette to follow in her footsteps but that when Jules got wind of Juliette's voodoo dabbling and put his foot down to Elviny, Celeste changed her mind. She really was fond of the girl. You were right about the necklace: there was no robbery. Celeste just intended to wear it herself, as she did. And as for Arlette Gray, it seems she was talked into the original scheme by Henri as just a plain blackmailing scam on a visiting businessman, but, not being any fool, she found the connection between John and Jules, tried to warn Jules, and got liquidated for her pains. What's your news? I see you cheered our host up.''

She told him. "Umm. Nasty little bit of work, that Grace,'' Toby said. "Not much more of a loss than Henri. I'm glad now that I did what I did.''

"What did you do?''

"Oh, Benedict was doing a breast-beating to me earlier

about this deal with the Arabs. Anxious to make amends. I suggested he talk everything over with Jean Rivers at the Historical Commission; he seems to like attractive blondes.''

"Why, you cunning old devil! You are getting as bad as I am," Penny said with admiration.

"Well, you never know," he murmured obscurely.

"So we're free to go? John, as well?"

"First thing tomorrow, and we can get out of Boston tomorrow evening. Praise be!"

"What are they going to do about Elviny? I suppose technically she is an accessory to all this."

"I suspect they aren't going to do a thing. She had nothing to do with the actual killings. She has cleared up the mystery by her testimony, and so I think everything will be quietly swept under the rug. Lefau wouldn't stand to see her railroaded, nor for most of this to come out, and, with his influence, no one is likely to buck him. What *are* you doing?"

"Seeing if I have enough money left to buy Mama Tio another pound of snuff. If anyone deserves it, she does. Without her, we'd never have got to first base on this thing."

With a sigh, Toby reached for his wallet. "Here! Be my guest!"

Penny was a little disappointed as they assembled to make their farewells the next morning to find no sign of their host. Benedict, who was looking remarkably relieved for a recently bereaved husband, was doing the honors instead. "My father had to go and make some arrangements about Celeste, but he asked me to tell you he'd try to make it out to the airport. Are you sure we can't send you out in one of the cars?"

"No, that's all right. It's taken care of," Penny said. "Mean Gene insisted we go with him."

The giant arrived, looking more like a pirate than ever in a purple shirt and bright-green pants. As he loaded the bags into the cab, he kept chuckling delightedly to himself. The reason for his mirth became apparent when an old flatbed truck pulled up in front of the cab. It had evidently been part of the Zulu parade and was still gaudily decorated. On it the Knights of St. Pierre were all assembled, complete with their instruments. "What on earth is that!" Toby asked in quiet horror.

"You're going out in style," Mean Gene informed him, "with a real New Orleans send-off. We're going to play you out of town."

"Good God!" Toby hastily crawled into the cab and tried to disappear into the upholstrey.

"If you're driving us, who's playing trumpet?" Penny asked Gene as she scrambled in between Toby and John.

"Look!" Mean Gene commanded and waved his hand.

The Knights obediently parted to show Sweet Daddy seated on a chair, with a beatific smile on his wrinkled face. He raised his silver trumpet to his lips as they slid into motion, and the slow, sweet notes came to them through the open window. *"For all we know, we may never meet again. . . ."*

Their exit became something of a triumphal procession as they sped through the awakening city. People waved, cars honked, and there were scattered cheers. "It's more than we deserve," Penny remarked, clearing her throat rather hard. "We didn't exactly cover ourselves with glory in all this, did we? We somehow managed to get hold of all the vital facts, but we never did put them together in time to do any good."

"I find this to be just punishment," Toby said in a stifled voice. "But I may point out that we *did* achieve our primary object: John has come out of this smelling like a rose. But do me a favor, John, and don't put out any more vanity publications for rich men with secrets! Or, if you do, *don't* call on us!"

"Believe me, I'm cured," John assured him. Unlike Toby, he was thoroughly enjoying their unusual send-off. "I thought detecting was an exciting business, but never again! If anything like this ever comes up, I'll hand it over to the police and run for the nearest cover!"

The airport became a hurly-burly of fond farewells, and as they made their way out onto the tarmac, the Knights regrouped on the observation deck of the terminal and began blasting away at a final version of "For All We Know." The silvery notes followed them up the stairs, where they turned to see that the Knights had been joined by the slim, elegant figure of Jules Lefau, who raised an arm in final salute. *". . . we may never meet again. . . . Tomorrow may never come, for all we know. . . ."* The notes faded and died as they took their seats, with Penny in the window seat.

"Boy, am I glad to be getting out of here! Will I ever be glad to get back to Boston!" John said with relief. "I'll even be glad to get back to Millicent. She'll be meeting us, by the way."

He received a savage elbow in the ribs from Toby, who jerked his head silently toward Penny. John looked over to see tears streaming down her small face as she gazed fixedly out to where the Knights were waving frantic farewells. But her eyes were focused on the still figure who grasped the railing in much the same position as they had first seen him at the ill-fated House of the Dancing Lady and who was gazing with equal intensity at the plane. "What's the matter? Is there anything we can do?" John whispered in dismay to Toby.

Toby shook his head. "No, let her cry it out. Worried about him, that's all. She'll be all right once I get her on the plane to London tonight. I can manage her." He heaved a complacent sigh. "After all, I'm used to it."

Other Books from the Foul Play Press

Margot Arnold

The mysterious adventures of British archaeologist Sir Toby Glendower, and American anthropologist Penelope Spring, will take you to the near and far corners of the globe.

> *The Cape Cod Caper.* 192 pages $4.95
> *Death of A Voodoo Doll.* 220 pages $4.95
> *Exit Actors, Dying.* 176 pages $4.95
> *Zadok's Treasure.* 192 pages $4.95
>
> ... and more to come.

Phoebe Atwood Taylor

Enjoy the adventures of the Cape Cod Sherlock, Asey Mayo, and his north-of-Boston counterpart, Shakespeare look-alike Leonidas Witherall. Written in the 1930s and 1940s, they are as popular today as when they first appeared.

Asey Mayo Cape Cod Mysteries

> *The Annulet of Gilt.* 288 pages $5.95
> *Banbury Bog.* 176 pages $4.95
> *The Cape Cod Mystery.* 192 pages $4.95
> *The Criminal C.O.D..* 288 pages $5.95
> *The Crimson Patch.* 240 pages $4.95
> *The Deadly Sunshade.* 297 pages $5.95
> *The Mystery of the Cape Cod Players.* 272 pages $5.95
> *The Mystery of the Cape Cod Tavern.* 283 pages $5.95
> *Out of Order.* 280 pages $5.95
> *The Perennial Boarder.* 288 pages $5.95
> *Sandbar Sinister.* 296 pages $5.95
> *Spring Harrowing.* 288 pages $5.95

Leonidas Witherall Mysteries

> *Beginning with a Bash.* 284 pages $5.95
> *File For Record.* 287 pages $5.95
> *Hollow Chest.* 284 pages $5.95
> *The Left Leg.* 275 pages $5.95
>
> ... and more to come!

Available from booksellers in the United States and Canada or by mail from the publisher, The Countryman Press, PO Box 175, Woodstock Vermont 05091-0175. If ordering by mail, please add $2.50/order for shipping and handling. Thank you.

Prices and availability subject to change. 4/1989.